RETURN OF THE SISTAH SAMURAI

a Champloo Novel

RETURN OF THE SISTAH SAMURAI

a Champloo Novel

TATIANA OBEY

WANDERLORE PUBLISHING LLC

www.tatianaobey.com

Cover illustration by Félix Ortiz

Wanderlore Publishing LLC
10228 E Northwest Hwy, #339
Dallas, TX 75238

v 2.0

ISBN: 978-1-967908-99-8 (trade pbk.)
ISBN: 979-8-9856649-9-7 (e-book)
ISBN: 978-1-967908-98-1 (hardcover)

PLEASE NOTE CONTENT AND TRIGGER WARNINGS
violence, misogyny, pregnancy, attempted suicide, and ritual suicide

to all my girls who like to fight

This book is not appropriate for men that are too insecure,
too easily triggered, or possess egos that are too fragile.
Rated M for mature men.

VISUAL GLOSSARY

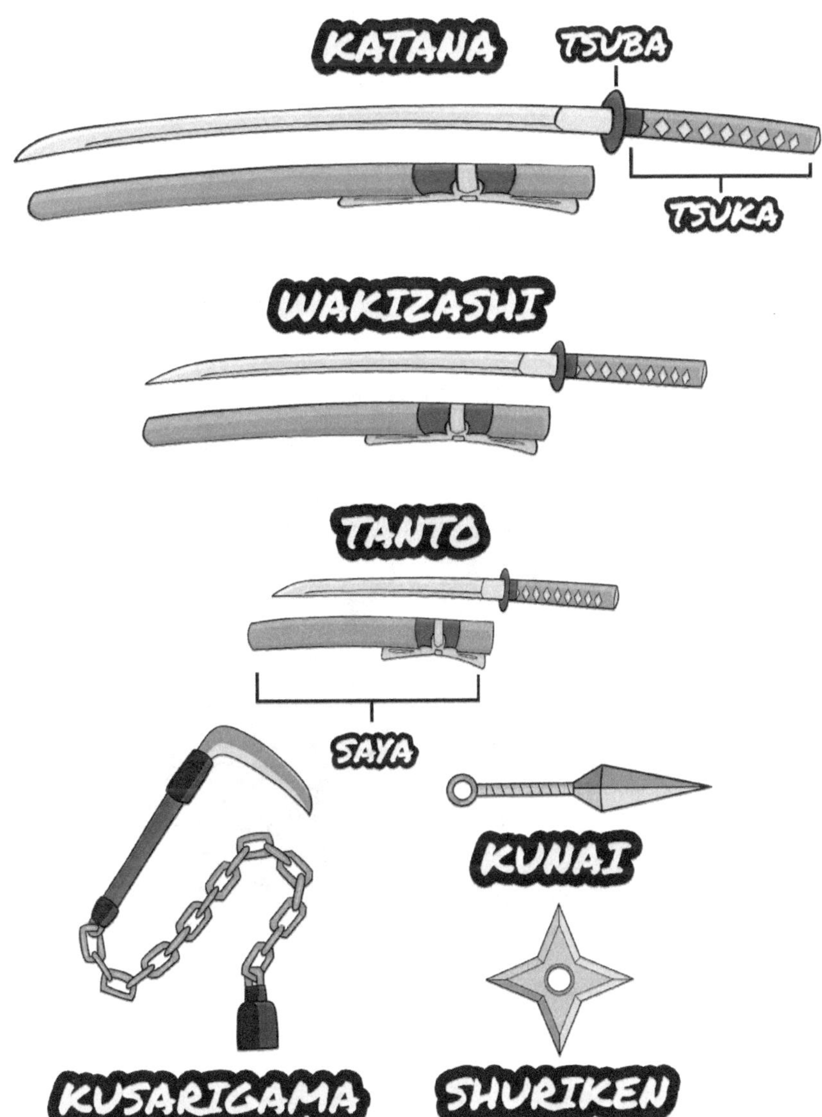

Return of the
Sistah Samurai
mix #2

SCAN ME

THE PLAYLIST

SISTAH SAMURAI VOL. 1!

13. BLACKBIIRD—BEYONCE

14. SAILORMOON—2.0
LAYA & BABY TATE

15. WONDERWOMAN
LION BABE

16. OTAKU HOT GIRL
MEGAN THEE STALLION

17. FAMILY AFFAIR
MARY J BLIGE

18. SURVIVOR (REMIX)
DESTINY'S CHILD & DA
BRAT

19. LIKE A GIRL—LIZZO

20. NO SCRUB
TLC

20. TWERK
CITY GRILS

21. INSECURE—JAZMINE SULLIVAN

22. WHAT I CHOOSE
TAYLOR HALL

23. OWN YOUR OWN
YAZMIN LACEY

24. VENOM—LITTLE SIMZ

25. HISS—MEGAN THEE STALLION

BONUS SONGS: FEEL
GOT TO B

SISTAH SAMURAI VOL. 2

1. HOT BUTTER SUMMERTIME—FLYANA BOSS

2. WAIT A MINUTE!
WILLOW

3. WHATCHU KNO ABOUT ME
GLORILLA

4. ANXIETY
DOECHII

5. MISS SHINEY
KAIIT

6. BLACKGIRLMAGIC
MAYYADDA

7. BOOTY BRAIDS
NILLA ALLIN

9. WHO'S GOT
THE BOOM
SOPHIA ERIS

8. PROTECTOR
BEYONCE

10. ZOOM
LEIKELI47

11. TYRONE—ERYKAH BADU

12. FAFO—THOT SQUAD

FEELING GOOD

The seasons stay changing.

It was about time I retired my old, faded kimono. The fabric had acquired a collection of stitched scars and mottled bruises, and aged stains that painted the faded black like liver spots. It had served me faithfully during winter and much of early spring, becoming comfortable like the presence of an old trustworthy friend. But some friends came in seasons, and as I've gotten older, I've begun to recognize when it was time for them to go their own way.

I discarded the dense cloth of shadow and exchanged it for an airy one of light. The white hemp weighed less than the tough winter cotton. In the polished bronze mirror, loose cherry blossoms wrapped around my mounds like endless hills.

I looked so different from the last time my reflection had my attention. My granny always warned how baby weight changed you, and how the years grinded you down—made you more brittle and slower and heavier, with weight harder to keep off. But all her portents and warnings I used to fear, echoed like guidance and preparation now. I didn't recognize it then, but granny had been teaching me what to do and how to handle myself when the time came. She taught me how to treat age like any other ailment—nothing that couldn't be fixed up by one of her natural remedies.

Her Black-Don't-Crack Recipe was as follows:

A pinch of sunshine, a dollop of affirmation, a cup of confidence (season to taste), and a dash of pride until the ancestors tell you to stop. Boil with love until the concoction overflows. Then put your foot in it. Take it every morning until the insecurities clear up and the doubting pains ease, and you're back to loving your beautiful, perfect self.

I patted down a grey strand of hair sticking out from the afro. There, at the corner of my lips, was an unfamiliar smile that might start sticking if I wasn't too careful. But I didn't wipe it off. After all, it was matching the rest of me.

I slid open the bedroom door.

The twins, Alex and Ari, sat at the table eating their breakfast: dirty rice stuffed omelet, with a side of spicy miso soup. Usually, I skipped breakfast and hustled out of the door as fast as I could, with the hopes that an early start meant getting home sooner. But for whatever reason, despite all logic, it never worked out that way. This time, I tried something new.

I sat down at the table.

My six-year-old twins, used to kisses on the forehead before my leaving out of the door, quieted at the sudden change in routine. They stared at me as if I was a ghost haunting my own house, one who had finally decided to make a ruckus for attention. In many ways, my morning presence felt ethereal, as if a harried wind could blow me right out of the house. But I had rooted myself to the floor now, and I refused to be moved.

My husband smiled at the sight of me. He didn't acknowledge the decision. He simply slid me an omelet, sat at my side, and engaged the girls in conversation.

I smiled at how grains of rice stuck to Ari's cheeks, and the way Alex panicked every time her food threatened to touch (oh, how the world would come to an end if her rice and eggs weren't served on opposite sides of the plate). A dangling thread from the sleeve of her yukata caught my attention, a sleeve barely long enough to cover her wrist. Somehow you could blink, and children were already growing out of their clothes.

"I'll pick up new fabric from the village today," I said. "It's about time you two had new yukatas."

The twins exploded with excitement, chattering about what colors and sort of patterns they wanted to wear. For once, their excitement didn't scrape across my being like chipped nails on wood. Was it because I had the chance to rest yesterday? While I felt guilty for taking time to myself, I couldn't help but notice that something was different about this morning. I had more energy. I had more patience. I had more mental space to embrace change and absorb the details of the day, instead of those details bouncing right off of me into a black void of what I had chalked up to memory loss and getting old.

It wasn't until that moment I realized how numb I had become to the world, how I had wrapped myself in a protective cloak so that nothing, not even the things I wanted to get through, could penetrate that thick mist of burnout and exhaustion.

Now that it was possible, I resolved to take more days off. I would be more present. I would be more available. I would be there for my girls who were growing up so big and so fast on me.

The door behind me slid open. Sistah Simone dragged herself out of the room with a yawn that could catch flies. It moved through her whole body, inflating her chest, squeezing her eyes closed, and releasing through the arms. She had taken her braids out the other day, and her natural curls framed her face like a ginkgo leaf. With her haori tied above her belly button, she stepped out of the room with slits in her hakama, showing off well-oiled legs with each step.

She looked at us around the table. "I got time for breakfast?"

"No," I said. Sunrise was stretching into the room, as big and expansive as Sistah Simone's yawn had been. We couldn't afford to linger any longer. Not only that, but I had woken her up an hour ago. It wasn't my fault she had turned over and decided to keep chasing sleep. "It's time to go."

Sistah Simone pouted, sticking that bottom lip so far out someone could grab it and use it against her. I had half a mind to use it to drag her out the door, but she quickly brightened when my husband offered her a bamboo bento box. He said, "No worries. I already prepared this just in case."

She opened the lid to reveal cat-shaped rice sleeping on a bed of soft lettuce leaves, and star-shaped carrots decorating their dreams. She gasped and clutched it to her chest in delight. "No one has ever made me a bento before. You are the best brother-in-law a girl could ever ask for!"

She tucked it protectively under one arm, and then tackled the girls, who laughed and shrieked at the sudden attack. "I'll see you two later, yeah?"

"See you, auntie!"

She gave the girls a wink before tossing off her house shoes, sliding on her sandals, and leaving out of the front door. The light of sunrise consumed her like a greedy, hungry lover.

As routine, I kissed my husband goodbye. But this morning continued to prove unlike any other. There was a heat to the kiss that had my hand clenching the sleeve of his ocean patterned yukata. The press of his grip on my waist licked at my awareness like a hungry fire. His scent was of the red pine trees that grew around the house, and the camellia oil rubbed into his closely shaved beard. He smelled like home, tempting me to stay.

"Ewww!" the girls chorused behind us, jolting me back to reality.

We pulled away from one another, and a boyish smile stretched across my husband's face, which had my heart doing flips like salmon swimming upriver. Time seemed to pause as I stared into the umber of his eyes. Sometimes, I wish we had the time to get lost in each other, that he could ruin all my plans and delay me indefinitely. But even when we were younger, our relationship had always been stolen moments and brief encounters. Then, came the twins. Had there ever been enough time for us?

"Pink looks good on you," he said, with a smile I wanted snatch away with a kiss.

"It always has," I acknowledged. I belted my swords and turned for the door with the fading heat of him against my chest.

"Wait, you're forgetting something."

He pressed the thin wired glasses into my hand. I didn't need the glasses. I didn't know why he kept trying to force them on me. Besides, if I brought them, I'd accidentally crack them fighting a demon or something. I didn't need them. So, I left them behind, on top of my house shoes.

I plucked my shades from the crest of my yukata and fitted them over my eyes. Then, I walked into the sun.

Sistah Simone was leaning against the rock pillar of the gate post, picking at the bento box with the tips of her painted nails as she waited. I didn't think I'd ever get used to the sight of her, like some rare bird you spotted once a season. Mentally, I had stopped calling her 'Little Sis,' not wanting to get too attached and bracing myself for when she moved on. She looked up, as if her presence was no big deal, as if she had always been in my life just smirking over my shoulder.

We fell into step with one another as we started down the mountain path.

The morning air was cool, but I had no doubt it would get warmer further down the trail. The cherry blossom trees that wreathed the mountain were finally beginning to shed, and pink rain drizzled atop our heads with every gust of wind that shook the boughs. The other day, the petals had felt like a nuisance, but now they adorned my hair like cherished accessories.

The difference a day could make.

"You remember that one time we had a training exercise in the mountains and that one Sistah slipped right off the trail?" Sistah Simone laughed at the memory—laughing, talking, eating, and walking all at the same time. I'd have spilled something all over my clothes by now.

Normally, I would've been annoyed by any sort of reminiscence, but for once, it was nice to hold space for those we've lost. For just a fleeting moment, we reincarnated the dead with our stories.

"We found her a couple of hours later, hanging from a tree by her obi," I said, remembering.

One sentence of contribution, and Sistah Simone was chatting on her own. With well-placed, 'hmms' and 'hmmhmms,' she held a whole conversation with herself for hours. The way she chatted reminded me of morning birds—constant, without pause, and a hint of musicality to it.

After so many years without seeing each other, I had expected awkward silences and the unwelcome pressure to hold my side of the conversation. We'd participated on joint missions before, but she graduated a few years after me and there were other Sistahs I was closer to. But perhaps the years have chipped at the parts that hadn't fit so well. Now, it just clicked.

It was surprisingly easy.

Maybe too easy.

After she had emptied her bento and grown tired of hearing her own voice, she activated the music player she carried on her hip.

The music player was a demon drop, items unnatural to this world that slain demons have left behind. I didn't much care for them, and the Sistah Samurai had a policy of disposing of them whenever they were found, but that was years ago, and now they've become so much a part of society that sometimes it was hard to remember what didn't belong.

With factory ink and a braided talisman, she kept the music player powered as we walked. Before, I would have balked at such irresponsible use of ink, but there was something about music that added more color to the world. It added a layer of magic to your surroundings, and pulled notes from the air like ink pulled power from the soul. I had forgotten how much music used to move me.

"Quiet," I commanded.

The crooning ended abruptly as she deactivated the talisman. In the ensuing silence, she placed her hand on her katana, her nails a hushed tap as they curled around the hilt.

I cocked my head, listening.

There.

I swiveled on my heels and cut through the giant maw that shot towards us out of the trees. On contact with my blade, the attacker scattered into a whirlwind of paper.

The storm of white reformed behind me. I turned to counter, but at the hint of heat, I leapt backwards. Sistah Simone blasted the demon with a brilliant plume of fire that exploded from the talisman she had kissed to her lips. The demon of paper howled. Its edges crackled and curled as it burned. Succumbing to smoldering embers, the tattered remains released a glitter of golden souls.

"That was easy." She smirked. The bright light of her fire talisman faded, already out of ink from the force and power of the attack.

"Watch out!" I shouted.

A second demon charged out of the forest. She rolled to avoid the charge, sweeping up leaves in her curly hair. She landed near enough for me to pull her up by her arm. Without thought, we aligned ourselves in a two-person formation and faced this second demon.

It looked a lot like the first one—a hunched creature on all fours, scales made of paper, and strange glyphs that striped its hide like lines of poetry. But instead of one elongated head, this demon had two heads that glared at us with a challenge. I'd never faced this demon before, but I've seen its like drawn in the pages of the clan's bestiary.

I told Sistah Simone, "It's the Sequel Demon."

"The fuck is that?"

"It's supposed to be harder and tougher than its predecessor."

"Yeah, well, we'll see." She charged forward and sliced at the demon so fast, her katana created a whirlwind of steel. But the attacks were ineffective as the demon burst into a cloud of paper before every assault.

The demon's second head aimed for her back, and I lunged forward to cut off the attack. Against my blade, it devolved harmlessly into square sheets of bark paper. I could see the fibers in the parchment as they floated past my face. Some of the pieces sliced through my sleeves, stinging like paper cuts. I tried slashing through its sagging middle, cutting through unnecessary plot lines, but it remained a huge beast of ideas that seemed too large to wrangle.

Sistah Simone's fire talisman had defeated the first version, but I only had one fire talisman in the fold of my obi. I would need to end it with one attack.

The swarming paper reformed over our heads, a large shadow of expectation and pressure hovering over us like storm clouds. The paper that had made up one of the heads transformed into dainty fluttering wings that somehow held the massive beast aloft.

"*It flies,*" Sistah Simone groaned. She spat a curl out of her mouth, which had stuck to her shiny lip gloss.

The demon roared, spitting sharp paper in our direction, to cut at us with criticism. I sliced the demon's words with my katana until a pile of discarded drafts collected at my feet.

"I have an idea," both I and Sistah Simone said at the same time.

She challenged. "It'll take two talismans."

I smirked. "Mine will take one."

"Overachiever," she teased. "Alrighty then, what do you need me to do?"

"All I need is a boost."

I ran towards her. Catching my meaning, she cupped her hands together and planted her feet as if we were two naughty girls trying to peek over the onsen wall. I stepped into her hands and with a heave, she threw me into the air. I reached and grabbed a hold of the demon's neck. I pulled my weight up and over the body of the demon and straddled it. At this height, the sun wrapped golden arms around the treetops, a luminous muse of possibility and endless inspiration.

There was resistance for only a moment before the demon folded and scattered apart in showers of paper.

I tucked as I fell, rolling along my shoulder as I hit the ground. The momentum carried me back up to my feet, but I fell back down to one knee, where that familiar twinge in my left hip reprimanded me for my daring. Sistah Simone raced towards me and helped to steady my balance as I lifted myself to my feet.

"What was the point of that?" she asked.

Catching my breath, I pointed with my chin. She spotted where I had pasted a talisman onto one of the papers that formed the demon, and its collarbone was now stamped with the kanji for FIRE.

I grinned. Some demons needed editing. But some others—you've got no choice but to kill your darlings.

I activated the talisman, and the entirety of the demon went up in flames. Bright tongues of fire licked the air and ash peppered the road. The freed souls became as bright as morning light.

Beside me, Sistah Simone popped, locked, and dropped it in celebration of our victory. I shook my head at how she always found some reason to dance. But I didn't stop her. We all honored our Sistahs in different ways.

"Do you need a healing talisman?" she asked after all that dancing. "I can make one out of the factory ink I have. It's not as good as the inksmith's ink, but it's good enough to heal some cuts and bruises."

"Save it." I shrugged off the pain. It was always the left hip or the right knee. No point in wasting good ink when it would always hurt one way or the other. "Come on. We're behind time."

We descended the mountain. We crossed the valley. We waded through the water. We strolled through the bamboo forest, and walked underneath wreathes of crane. This time, when entering through the village gate of Chigakure, my shadow was my own.

"You missed a day," the inksmith grumpily said when he saw me. He'd never admit it, but I could see his worry despite the fact Sistah Simone had picked up my ink yesterday on my behalf.

"I took the day off," I told him.

I had napped underneath the cherry blossom tree. I had taken a long indulgent bath. I did the girls' hair, twisting their coils in my fingers and creating mazes out of their scalps, like how my mother had once done for me.

"Hn," the inksmith responded. I prepared to cut my forearm. Sistah Simone followed suit, but then the inksmith warned, "No matter the amount of material you give, I can only produce one vial of ink a day for you. I'm already at my limit with other orders and it's as fast as I can go."

Sistah Simone's steel paused over her arm. *"What? That's it?!"*

If it was possible for the inksmith to produce more than a vial a day, I'd have bled my whole arm out by now. But I couldn't force the ink to boil or cool any faster, nor could I help him invest in better and larger equipment like that of the big ink factories. His was a slow, deliberate, and precise art. Quality could not be sacrificed for speed.

"It's alright," I told her. I hadn't expected all my problems to go away just because she had popped into my life out of the blue. Sometimes, progress was one step at a time. So, I cut my arm. I dabbed off the sweat on my forehead and I cried into the sun. Then, I exchanged my blood, sweat, and tears for a single vial of ink.

I nudged her with my shoulder in an attempt to dislodge the clear frustration and disappointment from her face. She followed me despondently as we turned back toward the road.

"Wait, aren't you going to check it?" the inksmith called after me.

Had I forgotten to do that? I considered it for a moment, but then realized I could save all that time for other things. I nodded my head, respectfully.

Strolling away from the inksmith's stunned expression, we continued through the village.

"One vial," she said in frustration. "There's two of us, but one vial. I might as well go to the factory and barter for more ink. It might not be the best, but at least it's something."

If she wanted to use inferior ink, that was her choice. I wasn't going to stop her. But she'll learn quickly that the ink produced at the factory in this town was watered down good-for-nothing crap.

"I'm going to go eat," I decided.

"Of course you are. *I'm* gonna swing by the factory. We can't live off of one vial of ink forever. I'm serious about making a life here, and I'm tired of the rounin life."

The fact she was planning on staying caught me by surprise. We hadn't talked about her plans, and I half-expected to wake up one spring morning to find that she had fluttered away. Nor could I bring myself to ask her to stay just because my life was a little easier with her in it. I had already braced myself for her departure.

Before I could respond, she disappeared into the crowd. Not about to go chasing after her, I made my way to my favorite restaurant. The ramen chef greeted me, and I nodded in turn. I sat down at my table and placed my swords, Fuck-Around and Find-Out, along the bench. I created my standard set of offensive talismans and left enough ink remaining for the protection talismans around the house. The music of the shamisen swelled when the food arrived.

For once, I ate my lunch in peace.

I finished early to have some time to purchase fabrics for the twins' yukatas. I was drawn to the bright and colorful fabrics of one of the market stalls. The vendor looked real surprised when she saw me. Her expression dripped with curiosity, but she was a resident of the village long enough not to ask any questions.

"This one has been popular with the little girls of the village," the vendor said carefully, as she offered one of the fabrics for me to inspect. I frowned at the weird looking animal painted in a repetitive pattern. What was that? And why was it wearing human clothes and a bow on its right ear?

"I designed it myself," the vendor said. "I heard about it from the Street Prophet—a little girl who looks like a cat. It's cute, ain't it?"

Maybe I needed my glasses after all, because I wasn't sure we were looking at the same thing. I pulled the fabric closer to me and peered at it with scrutiny.

"Are you sure it isn't a cat dressed like a little girl?" I asked, unconvinced. Either way, it was disgustingly cute.

Perfect for the twins.

Before I could hand over any ink to pay for the purchase, the vendor asked, "Sistah Samurai, I purchased this protection talisman. Could you check it for me?"

Sometimes, instead of direct payment, people requested my services in exchange for goods. I studied the talisman that she handed over and frowned at the wobbly calligraphy and the places where the ink was too thin. Even my daughters could have done a better job. It was laughable at best.

"I wouldn't use this at all," I warned her. "Never buy a talisman from this person again."

"Would you mind, Sistah Samurai?" the vendor asked, and offered the ink she had collected for the day.

I nodded and used her materials to create a stronger talisman. With good ink, a protection talisman could last for twenty-four hours. But this one, made from factory ink, would last only twelve. But something was better than nothing, and at least this one would work better than her last one.

"Thank you for your protection," she said, gratefully. She added an extra roll of fabric to my purchase and wrapped them in a neat package for me to carry. I tucked them under my arm and walked toward the northern village gate.

When I arrived, the gate guard handed me a letter, which informed me that Sistah Simone had decided to get her hair done. Since it would take hours for the braider to finish, she decided she would stay overnight in the village. No doubt she would also visit with that geisha she fancied.

As I returned home, the sky leaked saturation, heralding the arrival of spring showers. I hadn't thought about bringing an umbrella, but it seemed, it was time to start carrying one around. Thankfully, the rain held on my journey home, nor did I encounter any more demons.

Good, because I was still feeling twinges of pain from the fight earlier that morning. On average, I encountered about two demons a day, but that number sometimes fluctuated depending on their migration.

My husband and the girls were outside pulling up weeds when I approached the house. The twins swarmed me with hugs and immediately demanded to see what was inside the package I carried under my arm.

"Wash your hands first," I told them. While they raced to complete the task, I activated the protection talismans around the house.

When they returned, the twins lost their damned minds at the sight of the anthropomorphic cat on the fabric. Thankfully, the vendor had given me an extra roll so they wouldn't have to fight over it. They each clutched a fabric roll in their arms and refused to let go of it even while they ate dinner. Because of the added excitement, it took longer to get the twins to bed, but their eyes snapped close real fast with the promise that Hubby would start cutting the pattern for them tomorrow.

After a bath, I found my husband sitting on the deck, drinking a warm cup of green tea lemonade as it began to rain. I joined him and together, we watched the rain hum.

It didn't feel right sometimes—him isolated on this mountain, but it was a decision he had made knowing that he could risk the entire family if he was ever recognized by the local warlords or his family's political opponents. This was his land, but it had been usurped when his father died in the capital alongside the other regional daimyos when the demons overran Edolanta.

"Are we okay?" I asked.

I honestly didn't know. We barely had time to check in with each other. Often, I would be so tired when I came home. I would eat dinner, take a bath, and go straight to sleep. Our lives were so drastically different from the illicit courtship that had started our relationship—full of passion and spring hope.

Anxiousness raised goosebumps along my skin when he took a moment to respond. My heart raced, sprinting faster than the sound of the rain tapping against the roof. He placed his hand over mine, tying our fingers together in a gesture that calmed me more than the tea.

He admitted, "I miss you."

It was the first time he said it out loud, a soft implication that our current situation wasn't enough. But until now, I didn't know how to give him more within the strict bounds of the day-to-day reality that we lived.

He pressed my palm against his cheek and leaned into the warmth. His handsomeness always stole my breath away. He was far too handsome for a samurai who used to be a retainer to his father. He deserved soft silks, luxurious dinners, and soft pillowed courtesans who could pour tea with finesse. Instead, all he got was callused hands that only knew how to hold a katana. I served him with my entire being like a samurai to a daimyo.

But did that make me a good wife?

He glanced at me over my palm, and I could feel him studying all of my uncertainties and insecurities. I used to be so confident years ago.

"I miss you, but I understand," he told me. He kissed his gratefulness into my palm.

Overwhelmed by the sudden need to have him closer, I

hooked my leg over his lap. But I had forgotten about that damned hip. I huffed when he caught me about the waist as my weight unceremoniously dropped against him.

"Oh, I didn't mean—" I began apologizing for the very awkward and unsexy-like move, "believe it or not, I jumped from the back of a demon today."

When I looked up, I found him studying me, all fond and with amusement. I forgot what I was saying, and the throbbing pain of my hip faded into the background. I cupped my hands along his jaw and told him softly, "I've missed you too."

I didn't feel as tired at the end of the day as I usually was, and I needed this reconnection. I had met him in my thirties, comfortable and established enough in the ranks of the Sistah Samurai to ever think anyone could possibly sweep me off of my feet. How wrong was I, and how utterly unprepared I was against the tsunami of emotions that overtook what should have been my duty. But that was an old guilt, and like that old, faded kimono, it was time to let it go.

Passionate emotions filled me up again like rain clouds, full to bursting with a spring rain that could nourish paddies and fields. I nodded, consenting, and he didn't hesitate.

He welcomed my mouth as his hands untied the knots of my hakama, and I felt alive again. The material of the juban was so thin, I could feel every deliberate motion of his hand as he stripped me out of it, like whispers of old trysts against my skin. I didn't know why I'd been so afraid to touch him before now, perhaps scared to discover that we had lost something that couldn't be regained. Our courtship might have been full of passion and summer heat, but that night I learned that our love was as patient and enduring as garden stones.

The cherry blossoms had fallen, but it had been a good spring.

KAYLA

AGE: 22

FAV FOOD:

BROWN SUGAR MOCHI

INTERESTS:

FASHION DESIGN

CRAFTS

HANGING W/FRIENDS

WILLPOWER: ★★

VISUALIZATION: ★★★⯪

KANJI PROFICIENCY: ★★★

WEAPON PROFICIENCY: ★

CHAPTER 1

HOT BUTTER SUMMERTIME

KAYLA

"You're sure we're going the right way?" I complained. "We've been walking foreeeeeever."

It was only the beginning of summer, but let me tell you, I was NOT made for the heat. The baby hairs I so carefully laid in swooping circles to my forehead had sprung free thanks to all of the sweat and humidity. My feet were growing pinched and sore in my custom platform shoes. Maybe they weren't the best walking shoes, but they looked sooo cute, and I wanted to look my best if we ever did get to where we were going. First impressions were so important, you know?

"Let me check," Imani paused as she pulled out the map. I stood on my tiptoes to peek at the lines on the rolled parchment, but I was annoyingly too short to see over her forearm. She thankfully lowered the map so that I could look, but I was quickly reminded of the reason why she was in charge of directions. Those intimidating lines looked like nothing more than vibes and suggestions to me. Why couldn't a nice friendly arrow appear out of thin air that could just point us to our goal?

Giving up, I slumped to the ground. The hot road toasted my thighs, and my layered pansy skirt bloomed around me.

I drooped with exhaustion, such a helpless wilting flower in this heat. My feet hurt, and my stomach was keenly aware that we were running low on supplies. I slumped my heavy backpack off my shoulders, which I had made from string and a fabric patterned with the cutest plump bumble bees. The loose arrows in the backpack rattled as I swung it around into my lap, where half of Teddy-san's upper body hung out of the opening. I hugged Teddy-san in my arms and rested my chin on his yellow fluff. His soft fur did make me feel a little better, exactly the emotional support that I needed.

Wait. What was that?

I blinked and leaned under the glare of the sun to spot a tall, shadowed sentinel. I gasped in excitement, hopped to my feet, and shifted Teddy-san back onto my back. I ran toward the signpost guarding the middle of the crossroad.

Halfway there I was reminded why running was the *worst*. My platform shoes felt like stones on my feet, and I petered to a stop, bending over to prop myself against my knees.

Imani glided past me on her fancy rolling shoes along the dirt road, sending a gust of wind against the back of my thighs. She swiveled around and fluttered backwards down the road, and I stuck my tongue out after her. Her shoes were a demon drop that she had found years ago. I tried wearing them once but making them go was much harder than she made it look. She swept by lazily, like wispy summer clouds. The wind dislodged a sunflower she had pinned into her loc bun and it floated towards me like a yellow butterfly. It landed against my chest and stuck itself into the lace of my collar.

My shoulders slumped when I reached the sign and found that whatever had been written on it had long since faded, weathered down by the seasons. I almost let my disappointment overwhelm me, until I noticed a stone couple squatting beside the signpost. An offering of fresh flowers lay at their feet, freshly picked, and not even wilted yet.

Someone had been here before us.

"Look, Imani-chan," I said, pointing for emphasis. This

was the first sign of people that we have seen in days. A set of footprints led northeast, towards the mountain.

"This way, then!" I declared.

With renewed optimism, I pulled the sunflower caught on my clothes and offered it before the small couple in gratitude. Maybe it was the wrong road, but hopefully it would lead us to people who could give us directions to where we were trying to go.

When we first set off on this adventure, I knew it wouldn't be easy to trek halfway across the island, but as long as I had Imani at my side, I knew that we could do anything—even if that anything was doing the impossible task of finding the last Sistah Samurai.

Before us, abandoned rice paddies stretched as far as the eye could see, bursting with tall swaying grass in the summer sun. The grass was so tall, it could swallow me. Not to say that I was *short*, but some of the grass could even reach Imani's shoulder. I paused in relief when a cooling breeze ruffled my skirts, trembled my purple afro puffs, and dried some of the sweat stuck to my skin.

Then, the road shook and rumbled like an earthquake.

Imani's legs rolled out from under her, and she landed hard on her backside. All of the pains and the inconveniences of the heat fled in my panic as I raced to help her. I reached for her arm, but honestly, it didn't feel very stable up here either, so I dropped down beside her. We held each other as the ground continued to shake.

When the quaking stopped, I peeked my eyes open to find that a gate had appeared in the distance, a dark staining chasm on the bright yellow road. The temperature had also dropped, and every goosebump was a pinprick of sewing needles along my skin. And yet, despite the blast of cold, the air wavered and warped like a really hot summer day. *And* I had to pee. It was such a small detail compared to the rest, but when you've just witnessed the opening and closing of a multiversal bubble, sometimes your brain gets stuck on the reality you could make sense of. The overwhelming pressure in my bladder felt more manageable than the gate that had erected itself in our path, and the decrepit elongated figure that was guarding it.

"A demon," I whispered. Even though Imani and I didn't have the chance to graduate from the Salon, the Sistah Samurai's training academy, I still remembered the lessons I learned during that time. "I think it's the Gatekeeper demon."

But did I remember how to defeat it? Absolutely not.

The demon's chalky face stared with a blankness that bore through us, as if we didn't exist. Unmoving, its masculine and desiccated frame guarded the front of the gate like a terrifying wraith, a grotesque statue of bone meant to scare and intimidate all those who dared to approach.

Imani and I glanced at one another, knowing that we only had one talisman left. With a nod, we shot off into the grass in a mad dash to get around it. Imani had to clomp awkwardly in her skates, like a baby foal, which meant I was keeping up with her for once. When we thought we had reached the end of the demon's gate, I yelped, startled as it shifted. In a blur, the demon and the front of the gate had moved before us— keeping us from going any further. We raced back toward the road, and again, it moved and barred our path.

This wasn't a demon we could run away from.

"We're going to have to fight," I said, reluctantly. Fear trembled down my arm as I reached into the stitched pocket for the last talisman.

After the destruction of the Salon, Imani and I had traveled for a few years until we found a quiet town and settled. I opened my tailor shop, Imani helped me with deliveries, and we were happy. But it didn't last. Demons overran that town too. Too often, we've had to start over just for it all to be destroyed, but I refuse to let that vicious cycle win. I refuse to let constant failure define my twenty-two years of life. It was why I needed to find the last Sistah Samurai, to finish my training, so I wouldn't be afraid to dream again.

Imani and I looked at each other and nodded. She pulled

the naginata from her back, and I placed a talisman onto the curved shard of the polearm.

"I've got you," I told her.

Digging her heels into the road, Imani raced toward the demon on her rolling shoes, and the cute dragonflies I had stitched onto her back pockets grew smaller with her speed.

Suddenly, her shoes clamped down, biting into the dirt road as she skidded to a stop with a gasp. She yanked at an oval demon drop she carried on her hip. "My egg! It hatched!"

"*Imani-chan!*" I shouted. She was lucky the demon wasn't actively attacking her. So far, it had only moved when someone tried to get past the gate.

I raised my bow and arrow. I stretched the string taut, cutting a line into my cheek as I aimed past Imani. The demon's vest was decorated with all sorts of trinkets and accessories I had never seen before. There was an item in particular that caught my eye, a pink crescent moon wand that was pinned next to a white and green radar and an ominous black book strapped to its chest. Beneath the armor of items, it wore a layered skirt comprised entirely of cards. Honestly, it looked rather stylish.

"Okay! I'm ready!" Imani shouted.

I activated the talisman on her naginata and the weapon roared with fire. She lunged at the demon, but its shoulder caved in to avoid her blade. Gross. Imani swiped the naginata towards its torso, but the demon's back bent into stairs around it. It kicked out, heavy wooden getas that struck Imani in the chest and sent her flying to the ground. On instinct, she brought up her polearm to defend against a follow-up attack, but the demon didn't move.

Instead, it smiled with a mouth full of narrow fangs. It asked us, "Oh, yeah? What's your three favorite anime?"

What? What was an 'anime?' Was this some sort of riddle that we had to solve in order to get past? To give time for Imani to recover, I answered, randomly shouting my three favorite foods, "Fried fish onigiri, matcha vanilla ice cream, and brown sugar mochi!"

The gatekeeper grew twice as tall as it glared at me and raged. "You know nothing! You do not belong here!"

Whoa. Intense reaction, much? I tried different answers, but every response elicited more anger. At first, I wondered if this was some sort of trick or riddle, but then I began to realize that no matter how I answered, it would never be enough for the gatekeeper. It would always twist my words as an excuse to bar me entry. I couldn't run, but no amount of talking was going to defeat this thing either.

"I BELONG!" I yelled in my platform shoes, bouncy layered skirt, and purple afro puffs that defied gravity. It laughed at me, and I raised another arrow defiantly. It stood there judging me, underestimating me, looking *down* on me.

I may be tiny, but I was mighty as fuck.

I shot the arrow, and the demon swatted it away with the gnarled tree limb of its arm.

"YOU DON'T BELONG!" it bellowed. It was so loud the boom of its voice gusted up air, tousling the bow at my back and sending my skirts fluttering around me. But I was not intimidated. Demons have taken everything from me for too long. They've taken away my joy, my livelihood, and my dreams.

But no more.

I grabbed another arrow and let it fly. The demon roared in laughter when it pinged harmlessly against its armor, striking the wand and separating it from the main body. It grew ever taller. But it was so busy laughing at me and mocking me and trying to intimidate me, that it didn't see what was happening behind its back.

"Try and stop us!" I declared.

Imani rolled straight past the demon. She jumped forward with a flying kick and her rolling shoes slammed into the iron bars, crashing open the gate.

She made it through.

The demon screamed. It grew so tall, as if someone had reached down from the clouds to stretch the demon until it burst. Clouds of bright yellow souls lit up the sky. A sudden sunrise in the middle of the day.

I raced to where Imani had fallen in the field of tall grass. I tackled her in relief, and she grinned at me. The grass stained her yellow overalls, and her bun of locs had come undone.

"Look what I managed to grab," she said, smiling.

She showed me the card she had yanked off the demon's skirt. It depicted some sort of white dragon with angry blue eyes. Between you and me, it looked kind of ugly, honestly. But Imani loved collecting those demon cards. I liked the cute ones, but Imani cherished every weird looking card that she happened to find.

Even though it wasn't for me, that didn't mean I couldn't cheer her on. "It looks great, Imani-chan! I can't believe you found another one for your collection."

She nodded, pleased. While she admired her new card, I ventured over to where the demon had disappeared. Its presence had left a black scar that cut through both sides of the road and into the grass. Sometimes, people planted sunflowers over such scars, as they were known to absorb toxicity from the soil.

I reached down and picked up the pink wand that had fallen off the demon. It had a half-moon at the top and a crystal in the middle. Now, *this*, was cute. I tucked it into my bag next to Teddy-san and told him to take care of it for me.

"I'm out of arrows. Is there any more ink left in the talisman?" I asked Imani.

She checked on the talisman still clutching onto the blade of her naginata. The ink had faded, but it wasn't completely gone yet.

"A little," she told me as she picked herself up and brushed the grass from her wide pants.

That was our last talisman. I really hoped that eventually, maybe soon, fingers-crossed, we would find the village of Chigakure and the last Sistah Samurai that protected it.

Oh, I really hope she likes me!

Together, Imani and I returned to the road. We chose the mountain path, walking in the footsteps of those who came before, guiding our way.

AGE: 23

FAV FOOD:

SOUP CURRY

INTERESTS:

ROLLER SKATING

CARD COLLECTING

NATURE

IMANI

WILLPOWER: ★★

VISUALIZATION:

KANJI PROFICIENCY: ★★

WEAPON PROFICIENCY: ★★★

CHAPTER 2

WAIT A MINUTE!
IMANI

The road grumbled as I shifted my weight forward and applied the brakes of my rolling shoes. I stood in awe at the sight of the village ahead, which had burst from the trees as sudden as an unexpected pothole. The eaves of the wooden gates curved, doors flung open, beckoning like the warmth of a cozy ryokan. Across the top, a wooden plank read, "Chigakure."

With a sweep of my leg, I raced back to where Kayla had been trailing behind. I hopped over a stone, swiveled around a divot in the ground, and widened my legs into a spin, happy that we had finally found the village that we were looking for. As I glided along in my rolling shoes, my body flowed with a confidence and a smoothness that made me feel as if I was soaring. I leaned my weight on one leg as I swiveled around, throwing out my arms, falling back against a pillow of wind.

Kayla carried Teddy-san in her arms as she walked, conversing with him like the dolls I was only allowed to play with when I was little, when I longed to be outside climbing trees and catching bugs with my brothers. My dad didn't like girls acting like boys. I've spent most of my life fighting his voice in my head, but when I put on my rolling shoes it all just… faded away. And I was just easy breezy me.

"Imani-chan, what is it?" Kayla asked. I twirled around her in excitement, crouched down to my haunches. I kicked out my foot as I rode the momentum around her.

"There's a village up ahead," I told her. "We found it."

She squealed and set off at a run with the furry feet of Teddy-san swishing from side to side. I easily caught up and followed her all the way to the massive wooden gates. A guard lounging underneath its shade straightened as we approached.

He looked at me first, as most did since I was taller. A nervous anxiety struck me. Despite my previous excitement, my words stuck to my teeth. I didn't know why it was so easy when it was just Kayla and I alone, but with other people, words always felt trapped in my throat. A pressure I couldn't describe bore down on my shoulders, like the weight one felt near a dimensional bubble, as if I'd fold into a marble and have my entire being suctioned away. I deflected my eyes, hoping he would pretend that I wasn't there.

"Hi! I'm Kayla!" she enthused, and my shoulders dropped in relief when she seized the guard's attention. "This is Chigakure, right?! We heard that there is a Sistah Samurai protecting this village here. Is that true? Can you introduce us? What does she look like? What does she wear? Is she *amazing????*"

The guard stepped back, hitting against the inside of the gate, overwhelmed by her exuberance and her barrage of questions.

"You're looking for the Sistah Samurai?" someone asked.

I had been watching this newcomer out of the corner of my eye. He was lounging against the wooden wall and had inched closer and closer at Kayla's every question. He looked to be about our age. He was certainly taller than Kayla, but shorter than me.

"As the best tour guide of Chigakure, I would be happy to introduce you to the Sistah Samurai. But right now, it's too early in the morning. They haven't arrived yet. But while you wait, would you like the official tour? I'll give you a discount, of course," the boy said, with undeniable charisma dripping from his grin.

I opened my mouth to caution Kayla from accepting his proposal, but even she eyed him with a squinty face of doubt. She crossed her arms. "No thanks, we're not interested."

He studied both of us, and in realization, adopted a more dramatic feminine air, modulating his voice to make it obvious he was a safe space. He flicked out his hand toward us, and only now did I notice the black paint on his fingernails. "Empress, your dress is so cute!"

Kayla brightened and was won over. She twisted to show off the swish of her skirts. The massive bow at the back bounced like a bunny at the compliment. "Thanks! I made it myself!"

"I made this too!" he said, showing off his yukata. It was cut in a masculine style but decorated with red peonies that matched the hanafuda earring he wore in his left ear.

"It looks fabulous!" she exclaimed as she took the boy by the arm and skipped with him into the village. Looking as if she was the one giving him the tour, she chatted with him as if they had been friends for years.

I moved to follow but noticed how crowded the village was. I would have to take off my rolling shoes. I reached out in a pathetic attempt to tell Kayla to wait, but only managed a meagre croak. But I didn't have to worry. A second later, she paused, looked around, and dragged our tour guide back towards me. She always did a good job of keeping up with me.

"That's right. It's too crowded to wear your shoes. I should probably secure Teddy-san too," she said. She stuck out her tongue and pushed the plush teddy bear into her bag and then tightened the drawstring. "Sorry, buddy."

I leaned against the village wall and pulled off the shoes, revealing my feet, wrapped in Kayla's fabric scraps to prevent blisters.

"What are they?" our tour guide asked.

"She got them from a demon drop a few years ago. Stellar, aren't they?" Kayla asked.

"We have a Street Prophet in town," the tour guide said. "He fell into one of those multiversal bubbles a few years back and can identify some of the demon drops. I could take you to see him."

"That would be so awesome!" she exclaimed.

I finished slipping my feet into my sandals. Like always, the flatness felt odd, as if suddenly, these pair of feet weren't mine. All of my confidence and smooth motions transformed into gangly awkwardness—a monarch butterfly into a cricket. I knotted the strings of the roller shoes and hung them around my neck. Then, I followed flat-footed after Kayla and our tour guide down the road.

Had he introduced his name? If so, I hadn't heard.

True to his role, the tour guide pointed out places of interest and shared funny anecdotes about various buildings, but I struggled to focus on anything he was saying. There were so many people, and I felt anxious as I tried my best not to bump into anyone, or even worse, give anyone cause to say something to me.

"Is this what you do? Give people tours?" Kayla asked curiously.

"Not really," he said, pulling at his neck. "A lot of new visitors are refugees, and the local order of Brotha Monks provides shelter for new arrivals, so most people are looking for directions to the temple. But it's easy to get lost and turned around, so I offer to guide them there. This is the first time someone has taken me up on an actual tour. Oh, here is the souvenir shop. If you're a fan of the Sistah Samurai, you definitely have to check it out."

"A souvenir shop?!" she exclaimed. She disappeared through the divided entryway curtains. I entered behind her and couldn't figure out where to settle my eyes: the various woodblock prints, lacquered floral inros, or the cherry blossom-themed accessories. Kayla *ooh-ed* and *aah-ed* over everything. We didn't have any money to buy souvenirs, but I knew she was studying them to figure out how she could replicate them.

To Kayla, the shop was an endless supply of ideas, but the claustrophobic space and all the shiny things demanding my attention felt too overwhelming. Too much. It was as painful as if someone had littered sharp glass all over the shop. I squeezed myself into the corner of the store, and checked on my small egg-sized companion, another demon drop that I had picked up a couple of weeks ago. My shoulders eased and relaxed as my world zoomed in on my newly hatched monster, drawn in little blocks on the screen.

"Is anything signed?" she asked, her voice now part of the background as I watched my cute little pet bounce on the screen as I fed it a piece of food.

"Well," the tour guide winced. "She doesn't know that this shop exists. She would probably shut it down if she did. She very much keeps to herself and likes her privacy. The village tries to respect that, so we don't bother her much. The other one is much nicer, though. She'll even pose for corner sketches if you ask her."

My attention snapped away from the digital pet as Kayla screamed, "There's another one?!" so loud that the shop owner audibly shushed her. She quickly apologized and whisper-shouted instead, "There's another one?!"

"Yeah, she showed up at the beginning of spring and has been hanging around ever since. She even complimented me on my nails once!"

Kayla turned to me, knowing exactly where I had sequestered myself. "Did you hear that, Imani-chan? Two Sistah Samurai!" She swiveled back around, almost knocking down the wooden charms in her haste. "When can we meet them?"

"They come into town around noon, but let me tell you that you do not, *under any circumstances*, want to interrupt their lunch. We'll try to catch them a little before then, but we still have some time. Come on, let me introduce you to the Street Prophet," he offered.

I unfolded from my nice, cozy corner and followed him and Kayla out of the store into the bright light of the summer sun.

"Why are you so interested in meeting them, anyway?" the tour guide asked.

Kayla motioned to herself, and then further behind her towards me, somehow always including me in the conversation no matter how distant. "We were training to become Sistah Samurai, but never finished. We were hoping the Sistah Samurai here could help us complete our training. We just happened to hear about her a few months ago."

We crossed the street, and for a brief moment, a familiar face stuck out from the crowd. But when I turned to catch a second glimpse, the mirror of my older brother was gone.

No. It couldn't be.

I had a lot of siblings, and I wasn't close to any of them, nor had I seen them since I had run away to begin my training with the Sistah Samurai. Maybe it had been déjà vu, or maybe it had been someone else with a scar through their left eyebrow.

My older brother had gotten that eyebrow scar as punishment for failing to look after me. I had been missing for a whole day, but even though I had been found safe under the crawlspace of the house, my father still wanted to teach him a lesson and had ordered him to choose his own switch. It was that switch that had caught him in the eye.

I hadn't seen the punishment, but I had heard the screams and then the muffled tears, until the toys had consumed me, and I had escaped into my own little world. They say demons come from other dimensions, but I found that we make pockets of our own worlds every day.

I hadn't meant for my older brother to get in trouble, but he had hated me for it ever since. Or at least I thought he did. The day he caught me sneaking out of the house, ready to run away, he didn't stop me. Those black moonstone eyes had seared into my soul, and I thought I would know them if I ever saw them again.

But maybe I was wrong.

Someone knocked into my arm. Fabric scratched against

my skin as someone else did their best to avoid me. Someone else huffed, "Watch out."

I hadn't realized I had stopped in the middle of the street. A pressure overwhelmed my chest. A knot of panic formed in my throat, and—a hand wrapped around my wrist.

"*EXCUSE ME!*" Kayla demanded. She parted the crowd through sheer force of will as she led me through a maze of a thousand eyes. I collapsed in a shadowed alley, between two shops, and took comfort in the walls protecting me from being perceived by everyone else's gazes. My heart pounded in my ears. I counted my breaths as my panic began to recede.

"Is she alright?" the tour guide asked.

"She's not feeling well, but she'll be alright." She turned to me and raised her fists. A distraction from the panic. Automatically, I pounded her fists and flowed into the comfortable rhythm of a hand-clap game.

"Double double this this, double double that that, double this, double that, double double this that!" she sang. After, she asked, "You alright? We can always find somewhere to stay and look for the Sistah Samurai tomorrow."

"No. I want to see the Sistah Samurai. I want to meet the Street Prophet," I said.

"Let's go then."

I pulled the monster egg from my pocket, and I let it consume my attention as I followed after her. Perhaps, my behavior was odd to other people. Going from the verge of a panic attack, and then immediately fine the moment after. But I was convinced all beings were made of multiple universes, and my panic and anxiety were just one of many that I traveled through.

There was a large cypress tree in the middle of the main street. Instead of cutting it down, the village had allowed this small patch of greenery to grow on the corner, where two roads intersected. Underneath the tree, stood a curious man in clothing I had never seen before. He wore a sharp and glossy tailored shirt and pants that looked woven from the black sky of another world. Shaded leaves dappled his face as he regaled a gathered crowd with stories of strange animals and metal palanquins.

Kayla planted her hands on her hips, like many in the back of the crowd trying to determine if his words were true or if he was the most creative storyteller they'd ever met. But I found that most times, there was something other-worldly about storytellers, about their power to summon the unimaginable to our plane of existence and make it real. I was more confident the more this man spoke, in the cadence and rhythm of his tale—that he had been touched by the alien and the strange.

"You're sure he's not making this stuff up?" Kayla asked. The tale ended and the crowd broke out in applause. Some people offered little trinkets in thanks—coins that have been devalued by the demand for ink, small beads, and feathers. The Street Prophet gathered up this motley collection as if it was some great treasure.

He looked up at us, and his gold tooth glinted in the sun. He offered up a brass coin and grinned. "Y'all know how much folks will pay for this if I ever make my way back? Antiques, they call them."

Then, his eyes lit up when he saw the egg in my hand.

"My sister used to have one of those," the Street Prophet said and waved us over. He held out his hand, clean and well-manicured, and I cautiously handed my monster pet over to the prophet to inspect. He traced his thumb over the purple translucent shell with a sense of nostalgia. "It's called a Tamagotchi. Take good care of it. The battery won't last."

He handed it back over and I clutched it to my chest, alarmed. Because it was of demonic origin, I had hoped it would last forever. I was saddened to hear that, like all pets, it was just as mortal.

"Wait, are those roller skates?" he asked even more eagerly, reaching out to lift the shoes so that he could better see the orange wheels. His nearness brought the smell of flavored tobacco smoke that clung to his clothes. "Ah, I remember back when we used to light the roller rinks up. Those were the days."

Confused by the prophet's foreign words and odd accent, Kayla looked to the tour guide for an explanation, but our tour guide shrugged. "He's always like this. Just go with it."

So often, it was easy for people to dismiss what they didn't understand, but I recognized a kinship. This Street Prophet was more than someone who had lost his way and returned. He was a fellow world-walker. It seemed so obvious, and I wondered why the others couldn't see it. When he had touched the skates, a different world had lit up in his eyes and he was there now, among the glittering stars and fractal moon of his roller rink.

I ventured to say, "Roller skates?"

"Yeah. I had been pretty smooth back in the day. I could show you, but these knees aren't what they used to be."

I touched the shoes reverently, from the glossy wheels to the firm yet soft brakes that protruded from the front. Kayla had decorated them for me, drawing some of my favorite things on them as a gift. Dragonflies and stag beetles. Warblers and fly catchers. Fanciful mushrooms sprouting on both heels.

Roller skates. I finally had a word for them.

"What about this?" she asked, eagerly. She thrust forward the pink wand she had picked up from the demon we defeated.

The prophet took it and poked at it with his finger. He shook it and then bit into the handle like a merchant checking for authenticity. He made some dramatic whirling motions with it. Finally, he answered her, "This is the special weapon of a moon princess that shoots heart beams and moon dust."

"Wow," she said, in awe. "How do I make it work?"

The prophet raised his eyebrows, as if that was the funniest thing he had heard all day, and told her, flatly, "You are not a moon princess."

She instantly deflated.

Our tour guide patted the back of her hand, and offered, "At least it's hard enough to whack someone on the head?"

"You know what? You're right," she said, brightly, as she raised it in the air like an unsheathed katana.

"And this?" I asked, offering the card that I had taken from the demon.

The Street Prophet sighed. "Does it look like I know every single card game these kids be playing nowadays?"

I didn't know how to answer that, but he sighed as he looked into my hopeful face. Then, he closed his eyes and swirled his hand over the card. I waited in anticipation, wondering if he could sense the dust of other universes lingering on it. Then, he flipped it over and stated, "It's a Blue-Eyes White Dragon. It's rare, I guess."

"What are the numbers at the bottom?"

"That's the attack and the defense?"

"What are the orange circles for?"

"Uhh, its armor level? Or maybe it's health points? Yeah, the health points. Either way, that's enough. I'm done for the day." He placed a rolled sheet of paper between his lips and lit it with some sort of plated box that sparked fire. I stepped away from the strong smell of it.

Like how Kayla had offered flowers to the roadside kami for our safe travels, I reached into my pocket for one of the old empire's gold coins that I had stolen from my father. The prophet grinned wickedly at the sight of it, and it chimed when I dropped it into the collection plate.

Was he a hustler or a storyteller? A charlatan or a dreamwalker? Perhaps the Street Corner Prophet was all or none of these things, existing in between definitions just like his corner existed in between roads.

Smoke snaked from his person as we walked away.

Our tour guide showed us the market as the last stop on his tour. Kayla's eyes immediately lit up at all of the different fabrics on display. She fluttered toward the closest vendor, touching the silks and hemp to discern their quality even though we didn't have ink to purchase anything. It was nearing lunch, and the market was thinning out in response.

A bunch of teens were crouched over something in the shade between two stalls, and I was tall enough to see that they were playing demon cards. The cards were all different sizes, some blue with a red and white ball on the back, others with a black and orange swirl like the card I held in my hand. There was one distinctive card that was much larger than the others—it was pink, with a winged feline on the front of it. I've never seen a card like it before. Despite the mismatched cards that treasure seekers have risked life and death to retrieve from demons, somehow, someway, someone had made a game out of them.

I wasn't aware of myself when I had walked over, or when I had bent over to observe their game. The boy I leaned over had a card with what looked like a giant metal person. From my position, I couldn't read the name of it, but I longed to have it in my collection.

"Imani? Where did you go?" Kayla asked, distantly. After a while, she was at my shoulder. "There you are! Jaden says we need to go. It's almost lunch and the Sistah Samurai are probably in the village already."

"Do you mind?" One of the boys snapped at Kayla's loud tone of voice. "Can't you see we're concentrating here? Go off and play with your dolls or whatever."

She frowned. Then, she pressed her hand against the speaker's head and leaned over his shoulder. "Oh, you're playing those card games." She looked at me, and without having to say anything, she immediately knew what I wanted. Even though we needed to get going soon, even though we didn't have the money to linger for more than a day, she still prioritized what I wanted—even those wants I couldn't bring myself to say. She told the boys, "Imani was the best player in the village where we came from. You should let her play with you."

The group of boys looked up at us and laughed, not all that dissimilar from my own brothers, who used to laugh and mock me for any strange thing that I yearned to do. My brothers laughed at me when I wanted to join their kickball games. They laughed at me when too much stimulus sent my anxiety crashing. They laughed at me when I declared that one day I would become a Sistah Samurai. I hated that years later, those words had still not come true. But that was why I was here, to finally complete my training, and to prove my family wrong.

But all their attention bowed my head and hunched my shoulders. Unable to handle it, feeling myself beginning to crack like ceramic pottery, I turned on my heels to run away.

"Do you even know what we're playing? We're playing with demon cards that come straight off of demons. What would a girl know anything about that?"

"Whatever, we need to go anyways," Kayla said.

"Look at them crying and running off, *just like a girl.*"

I stomped my feet hard in the dirt. My fists clenched, and then some other being, some other Imani from a different universe, seemed to possess me and swivel me around.

Kayla tugged on my arm, but I couldn't bring myself to walk away. I confronted the arrogant group of boys. I pulled the bamboo scroll I wore across my back, and I held it aloft. It clacked open, each bamboo tile revealing card after card until it dropped all the way down to my feet, filled with all of the demon cards that I've collected over the years.

Their jaws dropped at the sight of my collection.

A savage grin stretched across my face, and one would be forgiven to think that shy, timid Imani had been possessed by a demon in that moment, but it was all me. This was a piece of me too, for perhaps we all carried demons in our own ways.

I said, the words cutting smooth and sharp like my naginata, "Just you watch. You're all about to get your asses kicked. By a *girl.*"

SISTAH SIMONE
AGE: 36
FAV FOOD:
DANCING SQUID SASHIMI
INTERESTS:
FIGHTING
DANCING
MUSIC
WILLPOWER: ★★★★
VISUALIZATION: ★★★★⯪
KANJI PROFICIENCY: ★★★★⯪
WEAPON PROFICIENCY: ★★★★★

CHAPTER 3

WHATCHU KNO ABOUT ME

SISTAH SIMONE

"I'm gonna say it." I leaned onto the inksmith's rinky-dink wooden counter and told him, "You know you need an apprentice, right?"

Big Sis shot me a warning look, and girl, I know, I know, we can't risk pissing off the inksmith, yadda yadda yadda, but I was damned tired of this old song and dance and not a one of us saying anything. Let Big Sis be the nice one, but it was about time someone said the damned truth.

"We need more than one vial a day if we're expecting to survive out here. You need an apprentice."

The unruly cotton ball brows of the inksmith clashed together so hard, I wanted to grab him by his scruff and shave them right off. Even more so when he jutted his chin out stubbornly like a damned tree burl. Then, that old curmudgeon demanded, "If you don't appreciate my hard work, you can give it back then."

"Look here, old—" I started, but Big Sis shoved me until I was hop-scotchin' to the side. *Rude.* She bowed at the waist, all apologetic and shit, trying her hardest to appease the ego of the old man whose stubbornness was going to get us all killed.

"My sincerest apologies," Big Sis said. "We truly do appreciate all of your hard work. My Sistah is still getting her footing here in town—"

"She's been here for two months now," the inksmith grumbled.

Big Sis elbowed me in the side. I acted like I didn't feel it and crossed my arms stubbornly. She whisper-threatened, "Apologize now before I tie you up by your braids."

Most times, Big Sis was the calm one, but I could hear the low-key panic in her voice. At the end of the day, she had a lot more to lose if the inksmith decided to refuse us service.

For her, and for her only, I decided to apologize. No matter that I didn't believe in it. I strongly disliked leaving my fate in the hands of any man. Somehow, they always fucked it up or actively chose their own destruction over wounding their precious fragile little pride.

I gave a dramatic bow, flipping my hair, and the beads clipped the counter. The inksmith looked utterly incensed as he stared at the new chips in the wood. "My bad, old man. I meant no disrespect. I can assure you that you are definitely my favorite crotched old—"

Big Sis snatched the hem of my sleeve and dragged me away. I laughed as I stumbled forward, using the momentum to continue down the road. Our shadows stretched like a slinky before us, with my gold hoops dangling and her 'fro waving in the wind.

It was the beginning of summer—that time when the weather was nice and toasty, before the humidity thickened and threatened to suffocate and drown everyone in their own sweat. Big Sis had taken to wearing a bamboo hat to shade from the worst of the heat, but I relished in it. Summer was my favorite season.

Along the streets, vendors sold yellow watermelon and candied fruit. Children raced through the streets with shaved ice dripping rainbows from their mouths and hands. Older women sat outside their shops, slumped in their chairs, gossiping, while fanning themselves with paper fans. A pair of friends walked past us, sharing a fish-cone ice cream. There was something about the brightness of summer that energized me in a way like no other season.

Big Sis cut her eyes at me. I couldn't see them behind the shades, but I knew she was glarin'. She was a woman of few words, but her face could communicate a hundred of them with just a look. I raised my hands, innocently.

"You need to stop talking off at the mouth," she scolded. "You know his type. The more you push them, the more they double-down despite all sense. From now on, I'll engage with the inksmith."

I did know his type, but I refuse to coddle old stubborn fools. Life would be so much easier if everybody had sense.

"He did have an apprentice once," Bis Sis said, more softly. "His grandson. The inksmith hasn't trained an apprentice since."

"*And?*" I asked, not at all sympathetic to the old man's grief. "Someone's got to bring it up. He can only produce a vial a day for us. Will we have to make this trip down the mountain every day for the rest of our lives? That's not sustainable and you know it. What if something happens? What are you gonna do then? You know damn well you're not gonna purchase any ink from that factory, because you're right, that shit was crap. So, what then? Are you going to move closer?"

"Too dangerous," she huffed.

Moving closer seemed like the easy solution, but the more souls concentrated in one spot, the more likely it was to attract a demon. Living isolated on her mountain was a safety precaution. Village walls failed too often, and there were too many people in a village to protect everyone all at once. Her family was technically safer, farther away, but did she expect for us to keep up with this routine for the rest of our lives?

I also knew that she couldn't risk anyone recognizing her husband (my precious brother-in-law had to be protected at all costs), but still, there had to be other options. I might have been younger than her, and a lower rank, but we were the only two Sistah Samurai left, and someone needed to challenge her. Respectfully.

"What if someone tries to kidnap the inksmith?" I asked. "There are any number of things that could go wrong. Didn't you say that the inksmith has forgotten to activate his protection talisman? Are you truly going to risk everything for one stubborn old man?"

I've quickly learned to recognize the tightening line of her jaw, and that more pushing would be unwelcome. I'll try again after she's had her lunch. Food significantly improved her mood, and it was my opinion she was always a little hangry.

"You're right," she said, suddenly, surprising me. I almost done damn near tripped on my sandals. "But we've got to do this smart. No more blabbing out of your mouth or saying slick shit. I'll do all of the talking."

"Ain't slick if I'm always right," I said, smugly. Big Sis shook her head, but I noted that she didn't disagree. As we turned down the path toward her favorite ramen shop, I wondered what else I could convince her of.

"You don't want to try someplace new?" I asked, half teasing.

I swear, Big Sis was like a wolf protecting her familiar comforts. She never begrudged me if I wanted to go somewhere different on my own, but I've been trying to convince her to try a new restaurant for weeks now. Certainly, eating something new every once in a while wasn't going to hurt her, but she patroned that ramen shop as if she had sworn oaths of loyalty to it.

She didn't bother to answer me.

"Gon' get your ramen, then. I've got a nail appointment, and I'll probably stick around to meet Lisa at the teahouse. See you tomorrow!"

I waved behind me as I turned down the next intersection. I didn't mind skipping lunch every now and then, as I've experienced plenty of missed meals over the years, but I needed a new coat of polish. 'Cause ya girl couldn't go around slaying demons with chipped fingernails.

When I entered the nail salon, the nail technician was waiting for me. She was definitely my favorite as she always had my chair ready, and her hand coordination was smooth like honey butter. The first nail salon had been established in Edolanta by a Street Prophet, who modeled it after a similar business she encountered while traveling through dimensions. Ever since, more have popped up around the country, often frequented and enjoyed by the upper class who never worried about toiling in a rice paddy.

It was pricey, but it was nice to sit down and be pampered every now and then. The technician brought out a steaming bucket, knowing I liked it real hot. Steam fogged the air as I dipped my feet into the scalding water. I sighed as she wrapped warm towels around my calves.

The technician offered several colors of nail polish for me to choose from, an array that ranged from blood reds to midnight blacks, to metallic silvers and honey golds.

"Let's do gold for summertime," I decided.

The technician set up the nail polish on the two wooden trays attached to the chair. I soaked my nails in the mixture of beeswax, egg whites, gelatin, tree gum, and flower dyes. As my fingers soaked, the technician massaged my calves.

Who knew if we would ever find a solution to the ink problem, but you know what? At least my nails were painted, my baby hairs were laid, and my braids were all the way down to my booty. I closed my eyes to relax into the massage when the chair beside mine creaked.

I peeked open an eye and was surprised to find a Brotha Monk had filled the seat next to mine. He gathered his floor-length durag into his lap and his chains clanked together as he did so. He followed the technician's instructions and placed his feet into the hot bucket of water.

When it was clear he was only here for a pedicure, I teased, "Not getting your nails painted?"

"Perhaps next time," the Brotha Monk responded amiably. "Greetings, Sistah Samurai. If you don't mind, there is something I would like to discuss with you."

Why did it not surprise me he wasn't only here for some self-care? I rolled my eyes. I have been doing that quite a bit today. I could hear my mama warning me that if I rolled my eyes too much they would roll right out of my head.

"Yeah? What do you got? Is it about the job I completed a few months ago? Did y'all figure it out?" I asked.

"We are still experimenting, but the tests have been… promising so far. But no, I have come to inquire about a different issue. We've had a few arrivals to the village that have reported unusual activity along the roads, and we fear a warlord is looking to make trouble. We're aware that you have engaged with warlords in the past and thought you might have more information on a warlord that goes by the moniker, 'Warlord Scrub.'"

"Never heard of 'em," I said.

There were so many warlords out there, with their own goals and motivations, that it was hard to keep track of all of them and their fragmented claims to territories. But I did agree that ever since Big Sis and I defeated the Pink Diamond Warlord, things have been suspiciously quiet.

"That's unfortunate. We were hoping you might have more information. Our sources are warning that he is marshaling quite a force. We don't know if Chigakure is his target yet, but perhaps it is time for the Sistah Samurai and Brotha Monks to consider an alliance."

That was an idea. Over the years, the Sistah Samurai and Brotha Monks have never played well together, but I liked the vibes I got from this one. Seemed the type whose mama took the time to knock some sense into him.

"Why not bring it up with Big Sis, then? She's higher rank than me, you know."

"Ah. I would bring it up myself, but I have learned how hard it is to request a moment of her time."

He was definitely implying that I should be the one to discuss it with her, but I needed more than just rumors. It was already hard enough to convince her to kidnap the inksmith and lock him up in her compound. I was working my way up to that one, though.

"What have your sources been saying, exactly?" I asked.

We spent the rest of my nail appointment discussing the leads he was following up on. I usually chatted my way through the appointments with the nail technician, catching up on the local gossip, so I didn't mind.

When the technician finished painting my nails, she carefully weaved a cloth through my toes and gingerly helped me to slip on my sandals. I paid her with the factory ink I had saved up from old jobs, but I was quickly running out. Even knowing I should probably be saving it; I spent it anyways. Couldn't take none of it with you when you're dead. Life was too short, and I've died twice already. The first time, when I lost my family, and the second time, when I lost my adopted one that fateful night in Edolanta.

I said goodbye to the Brotha Monk and I crab-walked out of the shop with my toes and fingers still drying. I considered going to the teahouse to see Lisa as I had originally planned, but with a sigh, I turned toward the ramen shop. Big Sis' lunch hour wasn't over yet, and she should know about the imminent trouble that might be headed our way.

I entered the ramen shop and, of course, found Big Sis sitting at her table, her back to the doorway. I hated sitting with my back to the door. I knew she did too, but that's just how much she needed the light from the window to see and create her talismans. That woman really needed to wear her glasses.

Sometimes, I wondered if Big Sis was so loyal to this place because they knew the rules. They didn't approach her. They didn't ask her for things. They didn't bother her. It was a bubble of peace that she had carved out for herself over the years.

But I wasn't Big Sis. I asked the chef what was new on the menu and dabbed up his son as I made my way to the table. The weird cat guy who played cards in the corner sent me a nod, and I winked flirtatiously towards the shamisen. I was tired of being a stranger. I was tired of parting ways and never seeing the same people ever again. I was tired of living the rounin life. I was ready to put down roots with people I enjoyed and cared about.

When I sat down at the table, Big Sis' ramen bowl was mostly all broth than noodles, and she was determinedly picking at the last of them. She raised a questioning brow, and I immediately explained, "I ran into a Brotha Monk at the nail salon, and he thinks we're going to have problem with a warlord soon. Was talking about a potential alliance."

She slurped up a string of noodles and shrugged. "We've taken on warlords before. What do we need the Brotha Monks for?"

"I don't like surprises," I said, simply. "I'm thinking of doing my own investigation on the days I'm in town. You know, talk to some folks. See what's what. We should know what's coming."

I wasn't a big fan of playing defensive and waiting for folks to come to me. I would rather cut our enemies off at the knees before they ever became a problem.

"If you want," she shrugged.

"I—"

A shrill scream sliced through the restaurant. Several patrons swiveled toward the door where the sun shadowed two young women in harsh sunlight. The scream had been so disruptive, it was as if the Kool-Aid Demon had suddenly come crashing through the walls.

The one making so much noise looked like an adorable baby-cheeked bunny that came hopping into the ramen shop in a short yellow skirt of frills and lace, puffy sleeves, and a teddy bear peeking out of her backpack. From the look on Big Sis' face, I could tell she immediately hated everything about the girl. But all I wanted to do was pinch her cheeks like a well-meaning auntie.

The second young woman wore a yellow jumpsuit and had locs with highlights gathered into a bun atop her hair. An interesting pair of shoes with wheels hung around her neck. The moment people turned to scrutinize her appearance, she deflated and stared uncomfortably at a corner of the floor.

I did spot a young man behind them that looked sort of familiar, but he ran away as fast as he possibly could. The remaining two were one of the strangest, and yet the cutest, pair that I have ever seen.

Then, the purple-haired one skipped further into the restaurant.

"Oops, not on the swords," the girl exclaimed as she avoided Big Sis' right side and aimed for her left. The patrons gasped when she plopped right next to Big Sis, onto her bench. I couldn't help but grin, amused by such unexpected entertainment.

"I can't believe we finally found you! We heard there was a Sistah Samurai protecting this village, but then to learn there were two of you?! We just had to come meet you ourselves!" the young woman exclaimed. In her excitement, she accidentally knocked her knee against the table, jostling Big Sis' noodle bowl and causing the broth to spill onto the table.

I debated whether I should interrupt and save this poor girl. *Nah.*

I was having far too much fun watching the show. Over her puffy sleeved shoulder, the second young woman hovered like an uncertain shadow.

Big Sis mechanically turned her head, and the patrons in other parts of the restaurant leaned back, holding their breath. Her eyes narrowed to kunai points. She hissed, "*Who do you think I am? I ain't one of your little friends.*"

"Oh!" The girl bounced up, snapped her hands to her side, and began bowing profusely. I barely restrained my laugh when one of her barrettes snapped off and fell into the bowl of ramen broth. "I am so sorry, ma'am! I was just so excited! I couldn't help myself! We traveled so far to find you! I'm Kayla and this is Imani! We were apprentices at the Salon when the clan fell, and we came to finish our education and to finally become Sistah Samurai! Student Kayla officially reporting for duty, ma'am, erh, Sistah Sensei… ma'am!"

I couldn't hold it anymore. The laughter burst out of me. Tears watered the corner of my eyes. Big Sis' expression slowly warped into one of disgusted confusion. The words dropped from her lips, "*Excuse me?*"

Okay. Okay. It was time for me to save this situation.

"Truly?" I asked the girls as Big Sis cut me a warning glare, but I wasn't minding her grumpy self. This could be the answer that we've been looking for.

Not long after the fall of Edolanta, the Salon was attacked and destroyed by demons and then claimed by an upstart warlord. It had been vulnerable to attack because many of the teachers had been called to the capital to be honored for their service during the coronation. From what I knew, there had been no survivors. But I certainly knew a little bit about surviving despite the odds. I leaned forward further, sliding my elbows across the table, until I was butt in the air out of my seat. "How do we know you're telling the truth?"

Big Sis frowned and demanded, "Stop entertaining this nonsense."

"We should at least test them. Who are we to turn away Salon-trained young girls looking to continue their education?"

"We don't have time for this."

Sometimes, she be straight up lying. But I forgive her for it. "Chill out. You've got time."

She crossed her arms, unable to refute me, and huffed, "I am not participating in these shenanigans."

It wasn't a 'no,' exactly. So, I slapped my hands against the table, careful not to smudge the fresh paint of my fingernails, and grinned. "Both of you against little old me. At the park."

"I'm going to finish my ramen," Big Sis declared. All she had left was the broth, but she refused to be rushed or harried.

I walked around the table and threw my arms over both

girls' shoulders. Little Miss Sunshine brightened with stars in her eyes and even the other one looked at me with soft hope. The poor innocent little things.

Oh. This was going to be fun.

The park was a large expanse of greenery that hugged the river winding through the south side of the village. When I chose the location, I was trying to choose a place with enough room for a full out spar, but unfortunately, I forgot that it was summertime.

Families were sprawled out underneath tents as they fanned small grills, wafting smells of grilled fish, onigiri, and yakisoba across the park. Trees were lined with colorful streamers and kites clustered in the air, taking advantage of the windy day.

"Eh, I guess this is good enough," I said, once I found a relatively clear space underneath a tree, with branches so expansive that sunlight drizzled through the leaves. There was a group behind us having a whole family reunion, with their names written on a banner stretched between two trees. Their food sure did smell good.

"You don't think there's too many people?" Kayla asked, uncertainly.

"They'll get out the way soon enough." Or maybe not. I might have declared the fight a little too loud in the restaurant, as word was getting around, and people were beginning to gather.

"Get ready, girls," I told them as I waved my hands in the air, drying the nail polish. Kayla and Imani began whispering way too loudly to each other as they discussed their plan of action. I did a few lunges as I listened. Big Sis might always be complaining of her knees, but you're only as old as you feel.

"It's the both of us against one of her. We got this," Kayla said, with seemingly endless positivity. Imani, the quieter of the two, nodded. She set down her wheeled shoes. In turn, Kayla set down her backpack and patted the teddy bear on the head as if it was a pet.

Then the crowd parted, as if someone had cut through the

thick press of bodies with a large katana, and Big Sis strolled through the opening. Look who finally finished their ramen. Without a word, she sat against the large tree. She dropped her shades over her eyes and pillowed her hands behind her head.

"You have—" I paused and looked at the angle of the sun, trying to determine the time.

"Ten minutes," Big Sis said, oh so helpfully.

"You have ten minutes to impress me. Feel free to come at me one or two at a time. Whatever," I told them, and flicked my braids over my shoulder.

Kayla pulled out two fans, which were edged with daggers from her waistband and cut from a pattern of smiling sushi. The taller one, Imani, stood with a naginata poised in her hands. If they had graduated, they would have received the iconic pink katana & wakizashi of the clan. Too bad they never finished.

I reached towards my own pair of swords. Every time I touched one of my girls, it felt like coming home. I always regretted selling my last pair, but sometimes, a bad bitch got to eat.

I named my new pair the same as the last—Ghetto and Bougie. My gold dipped nails curled around the hilt, and slid my katana, Bougie, out of her sheath. She was a classy and uptight girl who demanded all of the finest things. Like her mama.

"Ten minutes," I reminded them with a tease as I balanced on one leg and wiggled my left foot to fan the toenail polish. I was going to be so pissed if I messed up my nails after just getting them done, but I also doubted this would be much of a challenge. I didn't even bother taking off my earrings.

They shuffled forward, looking solid in their fighting stances. They've had some sort of training, that was for sure. Still—I leaned out of range of Kayla's attack and with my free hand, redirected her momentum and sent her sprawling to the ground. The girl was already huffing.

I circled at the waist, under the down swing of Imani's

naginata. I whipped toward the sound of someone coming up behind me and my beaded braids whacked Kayla in the forearm.

"Hey!" she shouted, as I kicked a roundhouse into her shoulder. The cloth woven between my toes popped out, brushing against her face and flying into the grass.

I stabbed my elbow into Imani's stomach, staggering her back. Her right heel slid hard against the ground as she braced against the blow, but I stomped at the inside of Imani's knee. She folded to the ground, and I kicked the naginata away. She sat up, her bun now leaning lopsided atop her head.

Both girls glanced at each other, and I could see the realization settling into their faces. They were nowhere near the skills of a Sistah Samurai. I might as well put the sword away.

I sheathed my katana, then I waved my hands, drying the polish. Although Imani was better with her weapon than her friend, they were lucky my attention was split with making sure my nails didn't mess up. I'd even say I was going easy on them.

"Please," Kayla begged, her long white stockings now smeared with grass stains. Then, the girl sat there, in the middle of the park, and started crying. I could hardly believe it. Even the crowd was looking embarrassed for her. That boy who had run away before hid his face in his hands from where he stood in the crowd. Ah! The tour guide. I knew I'd seen him somewhere before. Definitely got to keep tabs on my baby gays, and make sure they're doing alright every now and then.

Big Sis said from where she was shaded underneath the tree, her eyes hidden behind her dark shades. "Five minutes."

That reminder gave the girls a second wind as they remembered that the fight wasn't over yet. Even though Kayla practically cried through it, both girls got back up. She wiped her wet face with the heels of her palms, and I had to give it to her—I've never seen a crybaby look so determined.

This time, she pulled out a talisman tucked inside of her large waist-bow. It was faded, but it still had some lingering ink. Even though I hadn't said they couldn't use magic, I was curious to see them go for it. I watched as she placed the talisman onto Imani's naginata.

Interesting. Was the tall one unable to activate a talisman herself?

The naginata flared bright with the four-stroked kanji for FIRE. No surprise, since it was the first kanji that apprentices practiced with to learn control. Fire had always been easy for me, but for the other students, it was one of the hardest to master. It wasn't the one I would have chosen in the middle of a park with so many people… but a little barbecue never hurt nobody.

If they were using factory ink, the resulting flare around the naginata's steel was surprisingly impressive. I held my hands out towards the blazing naginata and positioned my fingernails like marshmallows hovering over a fire. Kayla's jaw dropped, stupefied, that I would use her talisman to finish drying my nail polish, but let's see her try and stop me.

"Take us seriously!" she cried out.

"Take yourselves seriously," I challenged in turn.

Kayla sat cross-legged in the grass, focused on visualizing the fire, while Imani wielded the talisman. The naginata swiped towards me, and I evaded out the way of her attack. I casually spun and lifted my leg to use the heat of her weapon to dry my toenails. Then, I kicked her in the face when she got too close.

But Imani bounced back faster than I expected. She lunged forward and when she swiped the naginata over her head, I leapt out of range as she slammed it down and carved a crack into the grass before me. The grass curled and charred underneath the embers.

I stomped on the pole of her naginata, snapping it right out of her hands and pinning it to the ground. Then, I slipped my foot in a divot under the pole and kicked it up into my hand. It's been a while since I've used one of these things. I swirled it around my shoulder and then launched it like a competitive spear-thrower.

Right towards Kayla where she was sitting on the grass. The fire extinguished as she scrambled out of the way. The naginata stabbed the grass, the steel warm and smoking, joining one of many snaking towers rising from the multiple grills in the park.

"Finished," Big Sis announced as she got to her feet.

I tentatively touched the nail polish of my hands and feet. Tapping them as soft as possible, just in case. The polish felt hard and smooth, with no bubbles or smudges. Nice. My nails were finally dry.

"Thanks for the exercise," I told them. "But now it's time for us to go."

Kayla unfurled herself from her self-imposed imitation of a roly-poly to ask, "Wait, but, how did we do? Will you teach us?"

Imani helped her up from the ground. They held each other, as they looked at Big Sis and I. It was obvious the girls weren't lying about their background. Judging from what skills they had displayed during the fight, they have undergone training with the Salon, and if they traveled here by themselves, they've no doubt braved some demons and had actual combat experience. But compared to an actual Sistah Samurai? They were just flailing children trying to catch fireflies.

Still, there was potential.

I looked towards Big Sis for her decision. Ultimately, training the girls would mean bringing them to her home and revealing its location to essentially strangers. She was the one with everything at stake if this didn't work out, but I hoped she saw the potential of what these girls could offer. Having two girls who already had years of training come barreling into her ramen shop was a gift-wrapped box of mochi. We could rebuild the clan. We wouldn't have to scrape day by day anymore.

Big Sis approached them and asked, "Why weren't you at the Salon when it was attacked?"

I raised a brow at her astuteness. I was ready to take them on without further questions, but Big Sis, on the other hand, had peeped the fact that the girls weren't being entirely truthful. Perhaps it was the perk of having two young daughters herself.

Imani and Kayla looked at each other. It was Kayla who hung her head, looking sad and pitiful. "See, what had happened was…" She winced, and rushed through the words, "I had snuck a boy into the Salon and Imani got in trouble for covering for me. We were expelled a week before the attack."

"Oh ho," I said, amused. *The plot thickens.* According to clan rules, once a student was expelled from the Salon, they would never get another chance to become a Sistah Samurai.

"And was this boy worth it?" she asked.

Kayla flinched and then blew air out of her cheeks and pouted. "No. Definitely not." She looked at Imani. "If you won't take me, at least take her. She never did anything wrong. She should have been a Sistah Samurai. It was all my fault and I," she bit her lip. "I know I messed up, but Imani deserves a second chance. She's really good at so many different weapons."

"And Kayla is really good at visualization," Imani said. It was our first time hearing her speak as her words burst forth in defense of her friend. "If you take me, you have to take her too. It's just been the two of us for the longest and I won't be a Sistah Samurai without her. I won't. I'm sorry for interrupting your lunch. It was my fault that I didn't mind the time, and I am sorry. Please give us another chance. Please."

I felt sorry for the girls. After all, while I had friends among the Sistah Samurai, the older generation never truly accepted me. I was always talking too fast for them, testing out unorthodox talismans, and dancing to my own beat. I wasn't what they considered an "honorable" and "respectable" samurai.

Fuck them, I'd say.

Besides, how could anyone reject those bright and earnest faces?

"No," Big Sis said. She turned around and walked away, cutting a wedge through the chatter and laughter of the summer day.

AGE: 40

FAV FOOD:

SPICY MISO RAMEN

INTERESTS:

MIND YA BUSINESS

WILLPOWER: ★★★★★

VISUALIZATION: ★★★★★

KANJI PROFICIENCY: ★★★★★

WEAPON PROFICIENCY: ★★★★★

CHAPTER 4

ANXIETY

SISTAH MONIQUE

"*Come on,*" Sistah Simone argued, before jumping out of the way of the sharp tail that cracked the ground where she had been standing. She caught her breath to continue arguing, heedless of the demon over her shoulder, and continued, "An opportunity like this don't come around every day. They've already been trained on the basics."

"And they would still need at least a couple years more of training before they are ready to wear the headband," I told her. "What about the initiation ritual? What happens if something goes wrong? Is training them what's best for them, or what's best for you?"

I turned and sliced off one of the Fox Demon's nine tails, and the white furry limb cartwheeled into the air.

"Everything is dangerous!" she said. Punctuating her point, she jumped in front of me and slashed through another tail launched in our direction. Only seven more left, and in quick succession, we cut away each of the demon's remaining tails. But the severed limbs contracted and began to regenerate. She audibly sighed, loud enough to make sure I heard it. "Making this walk every day is dangerous and if we don't start planning contingencies now, then where will we be? This is our chance to rebuild the clan."

I got what she was saying.

But I hated to admit it, there was no *time* to think about the future. What the future demanded of me didn't matter before Sistah Simone arrived, not when I was out here too busy just trying to survive. When you're fighting to survive the day, you don't have space in your mind for tomorrow. You might know that everything is hanging by a wire, and just one mistake would be catastrophic, and yet, there was nothing to be done about it but put one foot in front of the other on that thin narrow line.

Should I dare risk the present for the promise of an uncertain future? Not only my present, but also that of my family, for a distant and unpromised hope?

You want to know the honest to god's truth? I was content. I was appreciative of the small gains and blessings that I have been afforded these past couple of months. I was satisfied with staying home one day out of the week while Sistah Simone traveled to the village and retrieved the ink, giving me more time with my husband and the girls. It wasn't much. It wasn't a lot. But it was more than I had before. Would I be too greedy to demand even more?

"If we can't force the inksmith to take on apprentices, then *we* take on apprentices," she insisted. "They can go into town in our place to grab the ink. Or maybe—"

She was interrupted by a second barrage of tails. With an annoyed roll of her eyes, she went low. I went high. We sliced through the tails a second time, and they fell to the road wriggling like fat white snakes. We both turned, and snapped at the demon, "Can't you see we're having a discussion here?!"

The Fox Demon's ears pricked up, and it clutched at its white furred chest, taken aback.

"With those girls here," she continued, "I could see to my own connections about procuring a more reliable source of ink. But I can't leave you here and—"

"*I never asked you to stay,*" I snapped, annoyed. I didn't ask her to base all of her decisions on my situation. I never asked her to hang around and care. And I certainly never asked her to push me to do all of this changin' too fast and too soon.

She jolted back, looking hurt, but only for a second before she lurched forward with more fierceness than before.

"I was *alone*," she hissed. "I thought I was the only one left. You thought I was just gonna get bored and abandon you after a few days? To abandon the only Sistah I've got, who is in obvious need of help? *No*." I opened my mouth to argue, but she always talked way too damn fast. She pointed her gold tipped fingernail at me and threw her words at me like a Speed Demon. "You might be too damned stubborn to admit it, but you are one really bad day from everything falling apart. One formidable demon you can't get through. One terrible injury you can't immediately heal from. One demon swarm attacking the village. Hell, one inconvenient fucking cold taking out the inksmith. You have been lucky so far, so damned fucking lucky, and I don't want to see everything you've worked so hard for be destroyed. My fucking bad for giving a shit."

I grew defensive at her tone, even though I know I should have been listening to her words. She stepped closer, and at that moment, I didn't want her nearness. I didn't want to face the truth that I kept shoving in to the back of my mind.

She stepped past the range of my wakizashi, and my hands itched at the discomfort of it. Undaunted by my defensiveness, she clutched my shoulders, and told me fiercely, "You are one of the baddest women I have ever known. You've made it this far and you have done an amazing job. Perhaps you don't see it, but life shouldn't be this hard. It's okay to need help. It's okay to *want* that help. I am *here*, and I ain't going nowhere."

Emotions swelled a knot in my throat. I turned from her as the corner of my eyes began to water. I hated to waste tears, especially when I could be using them for ink. I had been so preoccupied with keeping them in, that I hadn't realized how the stiffness in my shoulders had loosened.

An 'oomph' released from me when she shoved me into

her arms. I hated hugs. And it was summer. It was way too hot to be doing all of this.

But sometimes, I needed them. Sometimes, I needed that physical reminder that I wasn't alone in this. That I didn't have to carry everything by myself.

Over Sistah Simone's shoulder, the Fox Demon leaped towards us with sharp blood-red nails. As quick as a flash, she snapped out her foot in a back kick, slamming the straw heel of her sandals into the demon's face. The demon rolled along the ground, hitting its head and landing on its tails.

"Can't you see we're having an emotional moment here?!" she demanded.

She stomped towards the demon, planted her foot atop the Fox's furred belly, and she swiped her katana straight through the demon's jugular. It burst in a gold swell of souls, reminding me of club lights that used to frame her figure late night dancing in Edolanta's red lights district. They lit her face with that same maniacal glee. She flipped her braids over her shoulder and patted at an itch in her scalp.

With the demon taken care of, I sheathed my sword, feeling exhausted. I swore. There was something about summer that made the simplest of tasks twice as hard, taking twice the energy out of you.

"What do you say?" she asked.

"I'll think about it," I conceded. Besides, it was way too hot to keep standing around here and arguing. There was a bit of a breeze, but it was ducking and dodging me, giving me no relief from the harsh summer sun.

"That's all I'm asking," she said.

We continued down the road. Sistah Simone would have stayed in the village today, a routine she does every other day, but those girls had thrown her off schedule, and yet she seemed to take it in stride. We stopped when we reached the river and paused at the sight of the broken bridge.

It used to be a beautiful bridge, until it was destroyed by a warlord and his army a couple of months ago. Fixing it would save a whole hour that it took cutting through the bamboo forest and wading through the shallow crossing upriver, but it was a hard task for two people on a tight schedule. Despite the time it could save, we didn't have the current time to fix it. I sighed, catching the heavy meaning in her look.

"I know," was all I said as we made our way toward the forest.

Even if we fixed the bridge, we didn't have enough resources and knowledge to return it to its former glory. All I could do was build it well enough to reach the other side. Would rebuilding the clan be the same? Was serviceable good enough? It would be impossible to build the clan the same way it had been before. But does that mean any version wasn't necessary or useful? A bridge was a bridge, whether it was a beautiful curved red, or rickety wooden planks.

For once, Sistah Simone didn't talk much. Instead, she walked ahead, staying alert and giving me the chance to truly consider what the future might look like. 'Cause she had one thing right: I couldn't keep doing this forever.

"Did you see what type of ink they were using?" I asked.

"You really need to start wearing your glasses."

She laughed as I glared at her. She was the one person where my glaring never elicited the right response. Always laughing when I was trying to be serious. She grinned over her shoulder and answered, "It was factory ink."

For the crybaby to have produced that much fire while using factory ink meant she had a natural talent for visualization. The tall one had shown decent skill with her polearm and had acceptable physicality. Those were skills we could work with, certainly.

"It's a lot to ask of these girls," I said, softly. These young women should be enjoying the summer of their youth, not devoting their lives to some order that was past its prime and to most, a distant memory.

"But the world is going to ask it of them anyway," she said.

How painfully true.

"We could train them without making them Sistah Samurai," I said. "We could teach them how to hold a sword and then send them on their way."

"You saw those girls. They wanted to be a part of something."

"They were expelled."

"They were *kids*. We made dumb decisions all of the time too. We just didn't get caught. Who cares if they aren't perfect? All of the old guard is dead. It's just us now, and we've certainly made mistakes. Maybe that's exactly the type of teachers they need."

I hadn't thought of that. All of my mentors had seemed so perfect in my mind, so beyond transgression and human foibles. But perhaps I simply hadn't got the time to truly know them.

For some reason, the idea of rebuilding the clan weighed on me as if the ocean was pressing down on my chest, so mighty and overwhelming. Rebuild the clan? Me? The one who wasn't there when her Sistahs needed her? Then there was Sistah Simone—the one always talking back to her teachers and always in trouble. She was as loud and brash back then as she was now. Should we—the ones who survived by some lucky stroke of fate—carry on the clan's legacy simply because we were the last ones left?

Perhaps that was the wrong question.

Could we do right by those girls?

I thought of the altar that I had built to honor the clan, and all of the memorabilia I had reclaimed over the years. What was I collecting it for? Were they mementos collecting dust in a museum of memory, or tools for the next generation? Perhaps I've known what I've wanted all along, but I just had to admit it to myself first.

I smiled at the sudden thought, "Can you imagine what they'd say to see us as a senseis?"

"They'd spill their ink," she cackled.

"Why us?" I couldn't help but ask. For a moment I closed

my eyes, hoping for some sign or answer. But it was just the rustle of the trees, and the launch of black birds from a tree branch.

"If not us, then who?" she challenged. "Maybe this is why I survived that day. Maybe this is why you weren't at the capital. Maybe this is why those girls were expelled. Maybe, just maybe, the dead don't require a moment of vengeance, but instead, a lifetime of service. We rebuild the clan because we are here."

I stopped atop the height of a hill, beside a stripped and burnt tree leaning forcefully to its side. A badger had made its home at the base of the roots. I looked back at the valley that we had crossed, overgrown with lush grass spotted with wildflowers. I mused on how devastation didn't last forever.

"We'll teach the girls," I said finally. I was done feeling guilty or ashamed about my past, and I was done feeling helpless and stuck about my present. It was time to put my big girl panties on, sharpen my blades, and fight for our future. "We'll take them on as apprentices and when they're ready, they'll join us as Sistah Samurai. But those girls are going to need a lot of work. If we do this, I—" I sucked in a breath. Why was it so hard to ask for help? "I can't carry this on my own. If we do this, we do this together."

Little Sis clasped her hand in mine, a promise underneath that burnt stricken tree. Someday, its leaves will grow again.

"We rebuild the clan, together."

KAYLA

AGE: 22

FAV FOOD:
BROWN SUGAR MOCHI

INTERESTS:
FASHION DESIGN
CRAFTS
HANGING W/FRIENDS

WILLPOWER: ★★
VISUALIZATION: ★★★⯪
KANJI PROFICIENCY: ★★★
WEAPON PROFICIENCY: ★

CHAPTER 5

MISS SHINEY

KAYLA

I was *waaay* too excited to sleep. I couldn't believe that in the morning I would finally, after so long, like an eternity, resume my training to become a Sistah Samurai!

Unable to settle down, I picked up a thread and needle to embroider cherry blossoms onto a new skirt. For the first time, I chose the pink thread. I often wore baby blues, lavender purples, and honeysuckle yellows, but never pink. Pink was the color of the Sistah Samurai. Because it reminded me of my expulsion and failure, I never felt I deserved to wear it. But for the first time in years, I felt hope. I smiled at the pink flowers blooming along the hem and determined that I would finally wear the color when I became a Sistah Samurai, which might not be for a few years yet, of course, but it never hurt to be prepared.

Imani slept like a stone in the futon next to me. It was a sharp contrast to last night, when we had slept on the bare ground of an alley because we were out of ink to afford an inn. A nice mountain breeze flowed through the open shoji walls, cooling some of the stagnant summer heat. Shadowed tree limbs blocked my view of the moon as I worked by waning candlelight. The beeswax melted and dripped into the candle's stone basin. Before I knew it, I heard movement in other parts of the house and the morning birds had gathered a choir to sing good morning.

The door slammed open.

"Mommy said to wake you up!" Two girls screamed joyously into the room. Imani didn't move, who could sleep through anything. Little Ari, the one with the slight scar on her forehead, belly flopped onto Imani and shook her awake.

"These are your clothes!" Alex said brightly, handing me a fold of white fabric she had dutifully carried into the room. "You are our guests and daddy said that we must be good hosts."

"You're doing an amazing job!" I told her. Already, my cheeks hurt from smiling too much.

"Breakfast will be ready soon! We are going to help daddy cook!" Alex said and then tugged her sister by the arm. They both raced out of the room with all the chaos that they had brought into it. They were both sooo adorable!

I bounced on my toes as I got dressed in the white apprentice training robe. I absolutely despised wearing it when I was training in the Salon. It was unbelievably ugly, but just wearing this fashion disaster again brought back helpless feelings of nostalgia. As an orphan, the Salon had been one of the few places where I truly felt safe, so I guess I could endure this outfit for *now*, but I was determined to bedazzle it to my standards later. We were training to become Sistah Samurai, but that didn't mean we had to look so basic while doing so.

We got dressed, ate breakfast, and met the Sistah Samurai on the sprawling field of grass outside the house. Both Sistah Senseis stood before us like two ethereal goddesses crowned by a gilded sunrise. *Queens, the both of them.*

Imani stood alert beside me, but I felt ready to burst with all the anticipation fizzing through me. Were we going to practice magic first? Oh, I hoped so!

"I've only got two rules," Sensei Afro said without preamble.

"Number one—don't waste my time. Number two—keep your mouths shut about this place. No gossiping or blabbing to your friends if I allowed you to visit the village. If you can't keep this place a secret, if you dare to break this trust, there aren't any more second chances. You will never become a Sistah Samurai, understand?"

"YES, SENSEI!" I screamed, with all of my excitement, all of my enthusiasm, and all of my exhilaration exploding out in that moment. Flocks of birds fled from the trees, and Imani winced beside me.

There was an awkward silence in the follow-up, and I realized it might have been too much. It was just so hard not to be excited.

I've been vibrating with it ever since they told Imani and I that they would train us. I've been vibrating with it ever since they led us up the mountain to Sensei Afro's *adorable* home, and introduced us to her *daddy* of a husband, and to the *cutest* little twin girls I have ever met in my entire life! I could hardly get any sleep last night because of my excitement, and now I was finally here, ready to finish my training and become a Sistah Samurai. I have been waiting for this moment my entire life!

Sensei Afro glared at me, and I hunched apologetically under her ire. She said, "It's too early in the morning for all that noise. Tone it down, girl."

"Yes, sensei!" I said, hopefully at a more acceptable volume. Do you think she hated me after this? What if she didn't want to train me anymore? What if I've messed everything up and destroyed my chances of becoming a Sistah Samurai?!

While I was internally panicking, Sensei Afro turned to Sensei Braids. "You got anything?"

"Nah, I'm good." Sensei Braids shrugged.

"Come on, then." Sensei Afro rested her hand on the hilt of her katana and then started on the path down the mountain. Imani and I followed behind her, not knowing what to expect from our first day of training. Sensei Braids slapped a hand onto my shoulder.

"It's okay to be excited," she said, "but not too excited for the demons to hear, know what I mean?"

"I'm sorry," I apologized, and bowed so deep her hand slipped off my shoulder. I quickly added, "Please don't abandon me in the middle of nowhere, and leave me to fend for myself, and refuse to let me become a Sistah Samurai. Give me one more chance, pretty pretty please?"

"You think we'd refuse to train you for being too loud?" Sensei Braids laughed. "If that was the case, I wouldn't be here." She patted me on the shoulder again. "It'll be growing pains for all of us, I'm sure."

I bobbed my head. She winked at me, and then lagged behind, taking up the last position as we formed a duckling trail down the mountain.

We made it halfway down when my leg buckled, and my foot landed in a puddle of mud. I quickly slapped my hands over my mouth, and clamped down on the scream like a peach pit I didn't have anywhere to spit out. I was so proud of myself. But everyone had stopped anyways, because I had stopped, and I had messed up the line.

In explanation, I lifted my foot to show the mud covering the ugly straw sandals we had been given that morning.

Sensei Afro only shook her head and continued down the trail.

I felt bad for the pause, and I hoped she didn't hate me for it. My feet were sore, my thighs chafed together, and my toes were crusty with mud. Despite all of these inconveniences, I marched down the mountain even faster than before, hoping that she would see me trying.

I was a people pleaser, okay? I didn't know how to turn it off.

We stopped when we reached the river. I was surprised when Sensei Braids gave us a wink before parting, leaving along the upriver trail. I was sad to see her go, because even though she had kicked my butt in the most embarrassing way ever, I was definitely more intimidated by the other sensei. There was just something about Sensei Afro, you know? An attitude that was stamped on the lens of her shades that screamed: *Do not fuck with me.*

She turned to both Imani and me and said, "There used to be a bridge here. We're going to come here every day until that bridge is rebuilt. I suggest you get to cutting some trees."

She tossed us a bag that spilled with various tools we would need to accomplish the task: a saw, a hammer, and several nails. Construction? That was what was going to be our first day of training? How…underwhelming.

"But-but we're sixth-years," I said, thinking maybe she might have forgotten. Imani and I were no longer first-year trainees who spent the entire year on physical conditioning before they were allowed to touch a practice sword. I shuddered at the memory of it.

I couldn't see her eyes behind the shades, but I could hear her condescension as she said, "*This* from the girl who could only last a minute in a fight without huffing and puffing? What's the point of teaching you how to wield a sword if you can't wield it for long?"

Okaaay. Fair point. Maybe the tailor shop had made me a little soft.

"Get to work," she ordered. "I'll keep a lookout for any demons."

Apparently, her definition of keeping a 'lookout' meant finding a nice spot against a tree to set up a fishing line and then closing her eyes to take a nap. It was certainly different than my definition of it, but I wasn't going to be the one to tell her otherwise.

This wasn't at all what I had imagined for my first day back to training. I wanted to learn new kanji and practice harder visualization spells. But, fine, I guess. If she wanted me to chop trees, then I would be the best tree-chopper she had ever seen!

I grabbed the handle of the axe, and it wobbled in my grip

as I attempted to lift it. Why was it so heavy?!?! I dragged it along the ground and picked a tree that looked like it wanted to be a bridge in the same way a piece of fabric told me it wanted to be a kimono. You just know, you know?

I picked up the axe, closed my eyes, and hit the tree as hard as I could. Did I do it? I peeked an eye open and slumped at the sight of a small chip in the bark. At this rate, building a bridge was going to take *forever*. I could feel the tears welling up in my eyes, but I wiped them away and kept going. I didn't wait a lifetime to be denied by some stupid tree.

I. AM. GOING. TO. BE. THE. BEST. TREE. CHOPPER. EVER!

After the tenth swing, my arms felt like jelly. I released the axe and collapsed against the tree trunk, hugging it with my whole arms in my despair. The bark dug into my cheek as I looked over to where Imani made solid chops into her trunk, really losing herself to it, and putting my work to shame.

Someone sighed over my shoulder. I turned to find Sensei Afro glaring balefully at my progress. I almost bowed to my knees as an apology for my sheer inadequacy, but before I could do so, she reached out her hand. She had a thick callus between her thumb and index finger, formed against the hilt of her katana. Uncertain, I gave her the axe.

"Similar to when you're holding a katana, widen your legs and dip into your knees. Don't swing at the tree, but through the tree," she instructed.

She lifted the axe, and her sleeves dropped down to her shoulders, showing off toned muscles that cut like glass on the sun. I nodded eagerly and watched her demonstration as she swung the axe. With a shout, she cut into the tree, slicing straight through all of my previous attempts.

"Certainly, you can do better than this old lady," she said.

"Why do you do that?"

With a gasp, I closed my hands over my traitorous mouth, not meaning to let those words tumble out. She paused to look at me, with an expectant eyebrow, and I cautiously explained,

"You're always complaining about your age, but you're," I flapped my hands around, hoping she would get my meaning, "You're… you're… fit enough to kick the ass of most people *my* age. I seriously *can't* do better than you."

She certainly had way more arm strength than I did, and in the bath last night, I spied abs as mighty as katana steel. Sensei Afro was *fit*, but she never seemed to act like it. As if the way she saw herself was very different from reality.

Shockingly, a small smile tugged at the corner of her lips. I slumped in relief. The Salon Senseis would never have allowed me to question them. She cocked her head and said, "Sometimes, self-deprecation is easier than the knowledge you aren't as fast or strong as you used to be."

It was my understanding that Sensei Afro was of Captain rank. While I certainly couldn't imagine what she was like in her prime, there were many Sistah Samurai who never achieved that rank in their lifetimes.

"But you shouldn't do that," I told her. "For one day, you'll start believing it."

"Hmm," she hummed, thoughtfully. "That's enough chit-chat. Get to work, and I'll see if I can catch us some fish for lunch."

I watched her walk away and—random aside, but her afro was really really glorious. Look at that *length*! One of these days, I'd work up the courage to ask about her hair care routine, but right now, I should probably get back to work.

I lifted the axe with renewed energy, ready to take my own advice. *I can do this. I can do this.* I widened my stance, set my feet, and swung the axe with a shout.

It cut deeper than before.

Look at that! Dropping the axe, I lifted my hands in the air and danced in celebration.

When I looked over my shoulder, I was immediately embarrassed to find Sensei Afro had been watching me, but she gave me a nod, and that sign of approval sent a jolt of energy coursing through me. I felt like I could do anything!

But by the time Sensei Braids returned from the village, the heat and my exhaustion had tempered all of the excitement that I could possibly muster. Imani and I succeeded in felling two trees and had begun cutting off the branches. Eventually, we would make planks to create a rope bridge across the river, but it was going to take *forever times infinity*.

We returned up the mountain, and as we drew close, I could smell the delicious food wafting from the house. I almost floated towards it, but Sensei Afro snapped her fingers and demanded, "Ten laps."

"What?!" I gasped.

She raised that ever-demanding eyebrow, and too tired to keep holding it together, I burst into tears as I ran off to make the laps around the house. By the end of the first lap, there were grass stains all over the apprentice robes from where I had given up and crawled across the ground. The ribbons I had tied into my hair were sad and sagging, no longer perky like my confidence. I was woefully out of shape, and I was a thick girl, and it was the beginning of summer, and I was *dying*.

"Come on, Kayla," Imani insisted as she pulled at my arm. "We can do this."

Her long legs had already loped past me and lapped me once. She had always been the more athletic of the two of us, and there were definitely multiple times in my life that, without her, I didn't know if I was going to make it. Imani pulled me to my feet, and she held my hand as we made another lap.

When I had finished all ten laps, not all of them on my feet, honestly, I collapsed against the ground. Imani curled into the grass beside me. We glanced at each other through the blades of grass. A yellow ladybug clung to a swaying wildflower. We shared a soft smile. Everything hurt, but we've been through worse.

I hadn't known Sensei Afro was standing over us, until she said something, "You're not done yet."

I glanced up to see her eating a skewer of yakitori, and the spices smelled so divine that I naturally sat up to get closer to it.

"What about dinner?" I asked.

She pointed over her shoulder at a pair of low desks that had been moved to the deck of the house. "Kanji practice, then dinner."

"But that means we won't be eating until late!"

Her face gave nothing away, just a mask of indifference as she said, "Run faster tomorrow."

I dropped back onto the grass, heavy with my horror. Imani had to grab both of my hands to peel me up from the ground. We trudged over to the two desks where Sensei Afro waited. We sat underneath a hanging lamp with a light that attracted a buzzing cloud of bugs.

"But I'm tired," I mumbled.

"You think you're always going to be ready in the middle of a battle? You think you're always going to have ideal conditions to create talismans? I thought you were sixth-years?" she asked, using my earlier words against me.

I swore, she was more terrifying than all of the Salon senseis put together. She tested us on the standard—the one hundred and fifty kanji that were most commonly used for talismans. Usually, I was confident in my kanji abilities, but my hands shook nervously before her withering glare. I licked at the sweat budding at the top of my lip and glided my calligraphy brush over the solid bar of suumi ink.

Any wobble or mistake could render a talisman ineffective at the least, and explosive at the worst. From the outside, people always thought that shodou-jujutsu was easy, but when there were so many kanji you had to memorize by exact form and brush order, it was harder than you'd think.

"Time's up," Sensei Afro declared.

I slammed down the brush and looked at my paper triumphantly. I didn't manage to finish them all, but the ones I did finish were all clean. I glanced over at Imani's paper and saw that although she hadn't completed as many kanji as I did, hers also looked really good. Then again, drawing the kanji had never been her problem.

Sensei Afro snatched the scroll of paper from my small desk. Then, she snatched up Imani's. I looked up and tried to interpret her expression, but her face was as placid as creek water.

"Again," she stated.

Uncertain of what would please her, this time, I finished the entire standard set within the time limit, but the increased speed led to mistakes in several of the kanji. I was developing a cramp in my hands, my legs were falling asleep, and my booty was growing numb. She reviewed them and said, "Again."

I wanted to groan, but my stomach did it for me. I helplessly waited for it to finish rumbling, before I responded with, "Yes, Sistah Sensei!"

I longed to complain but the initial years at the Salon had been worse, where conditioning training often meant skipping meals and little sleep. With a yawn, I picked up the calligraphy brush and poised it over the paper, waiting for Sensei Afro to tell us to begin. When she didn't, I looked up and found her staring at me with a frustrated fluster on her face. Did I do something? Was my stomach grumbling too much?

"No," she said finally. "We'll work more on kanji tomorrow. We will be working on improving your speed while maintaining the quality of your strokes, but for right now, go wash up and eat."

I shot up to my feet and bowed in thanks. "Thank you so much, Sistah Sensei!"

"This isn't the Salon. No girls will go hungry in my house," she replied. She turned away from us. The lamplight shaded most of her face but edged her afro in a soft glow. Then she walked out into the night, beyond the light of the lamp, to a glittering darkness where a thousand stars cloaked her head.

I didn't have to be told twice. I skipped into the house where her husband had dinner waiting for us. After we had bathed and eaten, we settled back into our room. I bemoaned how I could barely move my body. No doubt I will be feeling sore tomorrow. Even tying up my hair with a silk scarf for the night caused my arms to ache.

"Kayla," Imani said softly. I turned to look at her. She had been quiet all day, but I had expected that as it usually took her a while to break out of her shell around strangers. She clutched the purple transparent Tamagotchi in her hands, and spoke as she stared at it, "What do you think they're going to do when they find out I can't do magic?"

"*Yet,*" I said insistently. "That's the whole reason why we're here. To learn the stuff that we weren't able to. You heard them. They don't expect us to become Sistah Samurai immediately. You've got time to learn. It'll be fine."

Imani gave an uncertain smile, but tucked her little egg monster beside her pillow, and settled into her bedroll. I nestled my arm under my head, intending with all of my might to follow after her into sleep. No doubt I was exhausted. I haven't really slept for two days. But I worried too. Imani wasn't the only one with a secret.

What would happen if they found out that the boy I snuck into the Salon had sold information about the secret entrance to the local warlord? Who dumped dead bodies in the training yard and attracted a swarm of demons? That I was the reason all my former teachers and friends were dead?

I had broken the rules, and the consequences have haunted me ever since. I curled myself into a ball, and reached to pull Teddy-san against my chest so he could suck out all my bad feelings and emotions.

Imani often told me that it wasn't my fault, that I had been tricked and manipulated by a boy who cared more about achieving his dreams than seeing me achieve my own.

This time, I refused to let anyone—not no boy, not no demons, and especially not myself—keep me from reaching my dreams any longer.

I *will* become a Sistah Samurai.

Believe it!

AGE: 23

FAV FOOD:

SOUP CURRY

INTERESTS:

ROLLER SKATING

CARD COLLECTING

NATURE

IMANI

WILLPOWER: ★★

VISUALIZATION:

KANJI PROFICIENCY: ★★

WEAPON PROFICIENCY: ★★★

CHAPTER 6

BLACKGIRLMAGIC
SISTAH IMANI

The summer days were slow and congenial, all languid and crystal, like bright blue skies. It felt like we had stumbled into a portal on top of that mountain, where family meant warm conversations around the dinner table and playing with the twins down by the creek. Sensei Afro would let us take one day a week off from training, and I would explore the surrounding forest, and grow familiar with every tree and rock that was my new home. My favorite moments were when we would sit on the deck and eat watermelon, spitting out glossy black seeds in communal existence, while watching the evenings turn gold.

But no matter how gentle the touch, all bubbles pop.

Now that we had finished building the bridge, we were to start practicing our magic. But what the Sistah Senseis didn't know was that I had never managed to get a talisman to work. None of the teachers at the Salon could figure out what I was doing wrong, and even though I went through the motions of studying, and practicing, and sparring, I knew that I would never become a Sistah Samurai.

The Salon might have expelled me for lying about Kayla being sick while she rendezvoused with her boyfriend, but I knew the truth. They expelled me because I was a lost cause, and they had finally found their excuse.

I've had four weeks to tell the Sistah Senseis the truth, but I never found the words. Now we were here, practicing magic for the first time, and my silence had stretched enough to feel like a lie. It was inevitable that they would let me go once they discovered the truth, but this time, I would deserve it. As I sat down at the low table placed underneath the shade of the front yard tree, I knew I would miss this place—this fragile bubble of peace swaddled by their protection talismans.

"You can write the perfect kanji, have the best quality ink, but ain't none of that gonna matter if you don't have enough willpower and strong visualization skills," said Sensei Braids, as Kayla had begun to call her. She led today's lecture as the senseis alternated their teaching days. "Any effect you can visualize within the limits of the talisman will occur. The spell is stronger when attached to the object affected by the visualization, but it can also be used at a distance, although to a weakened effect."

Sensei Braids held up a talisman with the kanji for FIRE written onto it. "For example, if I visualize my katana lighting up with fire, it will occur. If I visualize this dumb ass mosquito that keeps biting me lighting up with fire, it will also occur, although not as strong depending how far away—" Sistah Braids suddenly slapped her hands together. "Ha! Anyways, as I was saying, the effect will not be as strong depending on the distance from your visualization to the talisman."

"For the same amount of strength, you would need to attach the talisman to your target of visualization—disregarding willpower rate and an individual's natural talent for visualization, of course," Kayla added. Both Senseis have now learned to expect her eager interruptions.

"Correct." Sensei Braids nodded. "There are many things to watch out for when using shodou-jujutsu. When using a fire talisman, if I visualize fire, the effect will happen. But if I visualize, let's say…water with a fire talisman, then the effect will not happen. You've got to make sure that what you visualize is within the realm of the kanji being used. Sounds easy, but as you two know, not as easy in the middle of a battle. A wasted second on accidentally visualizing the wrong thing or not visualizing fast enough…then that's it, bam! You're dead. Finished. *Fatality*. So, let's practice and make sure that doesn't happen. And don't forget, you can visualize the biggest flame possible, but the power of the spell can still be limited by the type of ink, the execution of your kanji, and your own willpower. So yeah, I think I covered everything. Any questions?"

Most of the information she relayed was the basics we had already learned in the Salon, but I had listened intently in case somewhere in her words was the key to unlocking my magic that I have been missing for so long. But I hadn't heard anything I didn't already know.

Kayla shot her hand up, fluttering it for attention with the speed of a hummingbird's wings. "What about how you use two or three kanji at a time on one talisman?"

I straightened, wanting to know the answer to this too. I have never seen anyone in the Salon use Sensei Braids' technique of multiple kanji on one talisman.

"Oh, we're just skipping over everything now?" She asked, planting her hands on her hips. "I guess y'all have already heard the basics before, hmm? Well, a multi-kanji talisman is a more advanced technique that I like to call…" She raised her finger and winked, "a braided talisman. The base power of the effect is the same but because there are more kanji on the talisman, the effect lasts longer. But with many kanji, there is a limit on what you can visualize. With one kanji, you can be broader. But with multiple kanji, you have to be more specific. And of course, it uses more ink, so there are cons."

Kayla fluttered her hand in the air again. "So, let's say I'm using a trap talisman, and I use the kanji for, "Yellow" "Circle" and "Trap," as long as I visualize a round yellow trap, it would work? And it would last three times the length of a regular talisman?"

"Pretty much. That's the concept."

"Then that would minimize the importance of the standard nouns for attacks and place a new emphasis on adjectives and adverbs. It's a whole new set of kanji we would need to practice and learn! We could even establish popular combinations," she said, then gasped, and immediately began writing possible combinations down into her notebook.

With her preoccupied, I uncertainly pushed my arm into the air. Sensei Braids' attention turned toward me, and I avoided her gaze, instead drifting my eyes toward a line of ants crawling up the tree bark.

"Could you double-up the kanji?" I asked. "Use the same kanji on the braided talisman, I mean."

"Yeah, don't do that," she said immediately, and I could hear the wince in her voice, rooted there by experience. "Not unless you want to cause an explosion in the east dormitory of the Salon. Luckily, all the other girls were at class, and no one got hurt, but I don't know if they ever patched that hole."

"Wait, that was *you*?!" Kayla exclaimed.

Sistah Braids laughed. Because of the heat, she wore her braids in a high ponytail, and the beads at the end clacked together at the motion. "Okay, okay, any more questions before we actually start practicing?"

A sinking feeling landed in my gut, and I scrambled at anything to delay the inevitable, even if that meant asking another question. I pushed my hand into the air again, almost outside of myself at the motion. "Is it possible to use two different talismans at the same time? Our teachers at the Salon always said no, but there was a rumor that those of Captain rank could do so."

"Oh yeah, that's a load of bullshit. There are some samurai who can visualize between two talismans so fast that it seems like they are using them at the same time, but to visualize two effects using two different talismans at the same time is unstable, at best. Those samurai who can visualize that fast are the ones typically promoted to Captain, like Big Sis, which is where you get those rumors from. To visualize with that sort of speed gives me a headache honestly and was never my particular specialty."

"What is your specialty?" Kayla asked curiously.

She tapped her finger against her glossy lip and said cheekily, "Creative applications."

"Oooh, you haven't talked about group visualizations yet!" Kayla said, brightly.

Sensei Braid squinted towards her. "But you already know what it is."

"*Yeeeah*, but I'm starting a new notebook," she said, raising the bound sheet of papers where she had doodled in the margins. She had drawn a cute sketch of Sensei Braids with butterflies fluttering around her.

We definitely already knew about group visualizations. As a first year, the first visualization we were taught was how to envision a shield in our mind's eye. After doing this for six years, it was to help us immediately join a Sistah Samurai formation and group visualize the shield talisman. There were more group visualizations they would teach us once we graduated and became a member of the clan, but the shield was always the first one taught to new apprentices.

"A group visualization is when two or more individuals visualize the same thing with matching talismans. The effect is exponentially more powerful, but it is an extremely difficult technique to pull off. For example," Sistah Braids held up the fire talisman again. "If I tell us all to visualize fire, no doubt what we imagine will all be different—from the size of it, to the color, to its heat. Which means we need to practice visualizing the same thing, which takes a lot of patience, discipline, and years of training. I assume you two have practiced with the 'shield' talisman, and maybe we'll start with that one when you're ready, but other group visualizations aren't anything you need to worry about right now. You've got to master the basics first, like actually holding your visualization under pressure," she looked at Kayla meaningfully. I remembered how, during our spar, the fire had disappeared from my naginata before the ink had run out because Kayla's concentration had broken.

I knew that holding a basic visualization could be difficult. I've seen fellow apprentices who could visualize a flaming sword no problem but struggle with maintaining it while watching their opponent for an attack. It took years for apprentices to master just that, and my head dropped at the thought that I'd never gotten further than the starting line.

"Now." Sistah Braids clapped her hands. "Enough yapping, let's get to it. I've got some factory ink for us to practice with today. We'll start with some simple kanji and work our way up to the more advanced ones by stroke count. Then, we'll practice regulating the strength of the effects with our willpower. There are times when you want a candle instead of a blaze. We'll also start drills to increase your visualization speed. But first, I need to see where you two are at. I placed a bowl on each of your desks. Make a water talisman and fill it up. Chop chop. Let's go."

As instructed, I drew the kanji for WATER onto the paper. It was a kanji that I have written at least a thousand times in my lifetime. I placed it at the bottom of the bowl, unconcerned as tamashii ink never smeared or ran runny once dry. I closed my eyes and visualized a bowl full of water.

I saw nothing.

As hard as I tried, I couldn't *see* anything.

I was at the top of my class with weapon proficiency, my kanji skills were solid, but no matter how hard I tried, I kept failing at magic. All of the other girls could do magic, but for some reason, I couldn't. Why wasn't it in me? What was wrong with me? Why didn't it ever work?

I glanced over at Kayla. She had easily filled her bowl with water and was now drinking from it. Then she poured it over her shoulders and chest as a relief from the summer heat. I tamped down on the ugly jealousy in my gut, because that would be unfair. I was better at other things than Kayla was, and I was happy for her, that she was so talented at something that I struggled with. But it still hurt as I desolately looked at my empty bowl.

Where was *my* magic?

I could hear the voice of my father creeping in through the cracks of my doubt. *Girls wouldn't do that. Girls couldn't be that. Girls shouldn't act that way.* All I've wanted to do was become a Sistah Samurai, because they embodied everything my father said I shouldn't be. I wanted to be strong. I wanted to protect people. I wanted magic to come easily to me. After all this time, I had desperately hoped that if I wanted it badly enough that it would finally work.

But wanting something badly enough didn't always make it true.

I sat there, with the sting of the sun on my neck, and a mosquito buzzing around me as I stared at that bowl. The image of it began to blur. Tears sprouted from my eyes, falling inside of the earthenware, and leaving damp drops on the blank talisman.

I shot to my feet, feeling so foolish for trying. I didn't mind trekking all this way for Kayla to have her second chance, but I should have known there would never be a second chance for me. I wasn't fit to be a samurai. My father was right.

"Imani-chan!" Kayla called after me as I ran back into the house.

I ran into our room with all the intent to start packing, but felt immediately overwhelmed and instead, collapsed into my cot. I curled, tucking my arms around my knees, and stared at the wall for some time.

My bamboo scroll lay in the corner of my eye. I reached out for it and dragged it towards me. One by one, I brushed my hands over the pretty artwork of the cards inside. I reached the one at the end, the one torn into two that I had glued together. My older brother had found it, sometime after the beating, and I'll never forget the viciousness on his face when he had ripped the card in two.

How could someone take so much joy in ripping apart

people's small joys?

A ragged line scarred down the body of the cute orange little creature with a flame at the end of its tail. Like the card, I felt ripped apart, broken like kintsugi pottery. I held the card to my chest, holding us both together.

"Hey, baby doll, you okay?"

I pushed myself off of the floor and shouted, "I am not a baby doll!"

Then I froze, in shock, that I had raised my voice at a sensei. But Sensei Braids didn't seem angry or taken aback as she leaned against the inside of the door. Instead, she challenged, "What are you then?"

I looked at the little creature in my hand, and then I answered, "a dragon."

Soon after, I realized how odd that sounded, and I bowed my head in embarrassment. I wanted to sink through the floor and never come up. In atonement for my behavior, the truth poured out of me, "I can't visualize. All I see is darkness. None of the teachers could ever help me. I always knew they were letting me go by the end of the year. I'm so sorry for wasting your time. I was never meant to be a Sistah Samurai."

"You think I'm a Sistah Samurai just because I can do magic? Or because I can wield a katana?" she asked. "Perhaps when I was younger, I thought those things were important too. But you know, I was there in Edolanta when the capital fell. No amount of magic saved them. No amount of sword skills saved them. None of it mattered. What matters is how much you're willing to fight. I'm a Sistah Samurai because when all my Sistahs were gone, I kept going. Sistah Samurai is what's in here," she said, touching my chest with a glittery honey-colored nail. "You've got soul, kid. You and Kayla proved yourselves to me back during our spar when she put that talisman on your naginata, and you wielded it to protect her. You fight for one another. You stand for one another. You defend one another. You have always had the heart of a Sistah Samurai."

I burst into tears. When she hugged me, I broke down further, as she reminded me of long-ago hugs with my mother, who had not survived my father. Her death was the defining motivation that spurred me to run away from the compound. I had refused to be another one of my father's broken dolls.

"I can be a samurai even if I can't do magic?" I asked.

She shrugged, and I felt it against my chest. "Yeah, I don't see why not. Big Sis and I have discussed the possibility that you might not be able to. It was in your student notes in the records that Big Sis had salvaged from the Salon." I tensed, in shock. This whole time, they knew. "But you don't need magic for the initiation ritual, and as long as you and Kayla plan on sticking together, we figured you would be alright."

As long as we stuck together, Kayla and I would be alright. No statement rang truer. I wiped at my runaway snot with my forearm and nodded. "Kayla is a good friend."

It was surreal how one person, one chance meeting, could change the trajectory of your entire life. One best friend truly had the power to terraform your world.

"Ah, now your crying got me crying," she said. She pulled away and wiped her sleeve against her face. "Gonna mess up my liner."

Kayla cried all of the time, but I couldn't remember the last time I had done so. It felt refreshing in a way, like a weight had lifted off of me. I found myself looking into sensei's eyes, brown like fuzzy cattails, and I bashfully picked at a loose thread of my apprentice robe.

"What now?" I asked.

"Maybe you might never do magic, but that doesn't mean we should stop trying to figure out what is going on with you. Besides," she leaned in to whisper conspiratorially. "I think I know how to fix it for I have the exact same problem."

She had the same problem? But that was impossible. She could do magic.

"When I try to visualize magic, all I see is darkness too. There are a lot of people the Salon have turned away because of a 'lack of innate magical talent,' but sometimes I wonder how many of those people were like me? People who see in words, instead of images. Those old teachers thought they knew everything, that there was only one way of doing things. Bah. There was so much they didn't know. Close your eyes."

I followed her instructions with fledgling hope, and she placed the weighty wrapped hilt of her katana into my hands.

"I've gotten accustomed to saying the words in my head, but starting out, it's easier to say the words out loud. Let's practice for right now. Describe what the katana would look like on fire. Give me all of the descriptions. How does it feel? What does it sound like? What would you hear?"

Hearing my own voice sounded weird. I didn't know why, maybe it was because of growing up in a compound full of siblings where I didn't want to attract too much attention, but stringing together more than a couple of words seemed so hard at that moment. But if I wanted to find my magic, then I needed to find my voice.

I clutched that hilt, closed my eyes tightly, and spoke aloud what I wanted, "The fire is large enough to where I can feel the heat on my face. It crackles like a campfire. When I swing the sword, the light of it smears the air. It's hot enough to burn my opponent, but not enough to melt the blade. The fire is powerful, so much so, that I can't see the blade inside of it. It—"

My eyes snapped open at the sudden and real heat of fire on my face. The katana, the one that I held in my hand, was on fire. Sensei had placed a talisman on the blade while my eyes had been closed. And it was on *fire*.

I found my magic.

It was inside of me all along.

SISTAH SIMONE

AGE: 36

FAV FOOD:

DANCING SQUID SASHIMI

INTERESTS:

FIGHTING

DANCING

MUSIC

WILLPOWER: ★★★☆

VISUALIZATION: ★★★★⯪

KANJI PROFICIENCY: ★★★★⯪

WEAPON PROFICIENCY: ★★★★★

BOOTY BRAIDS

SISTAH SIMONE

Look. I enjoyed a good bowl of ramen as much as the next girl, but everybody knew that variety was the spice of life. I loved trying out new places, and there was always a new restaurant popping up in Chigakure every time I turned the corner. While the burgeoning city wasn't as rich and diverse as Edolanta, it still had some of the best food I've had in a long time compared to down south, where communities had been so ravaged that people were more concerned about their own survival than their contributions to the food industry. It was a gift to have the opportunity to discover a new favorite dish, and if Big Sis didn't want to take advantage? Good. More for me, then.

Today's restaurant was a place that delivered sushi to you along a rotating belt, inspired by a conversation the owner had with the village's Street Prophet. The chef worked at a counter in the center of the restaurant while one of the workers cranked the conveyor belt nonstop to deliver sushi straight to your table with the sort of speed and strength of iron-thighed rickshaw pullers. The novelty of it had people lining out the door.

I grabbed the restaurant's signature dish off the belt, which featured two slices of tuna: a raw fatty pink and a fried well-done posing all fancy-like atop a bed of white rice. I dipped the well-done sushi into the soy sauce and stuffed the whole thing in my mouth, and—hmph—the seasoned batter crumbled with a delightful crunch. I stuffed the second piece of tuna into my mouth, and it was so good, I had to close my eyes to eat it. The flavor was light and refreshing, with a crunch of shaved leek, and a hint of wasabi.

Both pieces were good separately, but it was the combination, how the opposing flavors worked together, that elevated the dish and sent my taste buds soaring to proclaim its divinity. Yeah, I was coming back here again. Some places were all aesthetics and fancy gimmicks, but in truth, all you needed was good food to keep people coming back.

I looked up just as Lisa came through the door, and I smiled as butterflies set loose in my stomach. Her beauty was breathtaking, and for a moment, I admired the way her hyper-melanated skin absorbed light, all shiny and smooth like black pearls. Her hair wasn't done up yet, but she looked just as beautiful wearing the elaborate bun of a geisha as she did with a scarf covering her hair and knotted at the center of her forehead. She smiled at me, revealing a shock of white teeth in contrast to her dark skin.

I was waiting for the right moment to ask her to be my girlfriend, but I had half a mind to do it right then and there, with my mouth stuffed full of sushi. Instead, I waved her over and shifted my chair for her to fill the empty seat next to me. As a geisha, she worked as a hostess at a local tea house and entertained patrons with conversation, dance, and games. She wasn't completely dressed in her work attire yet since the tea house didn't open until the evenings, which was why she was often free to join me for lunch when I visited the village.

I asked after her day as she considered which plate she should choose. I picked the shrimp sushi, which was accompanied by its spindly head placed like a half-moon onto the plate. I stuffed the sushi into my mouth, pulling away with the tail, and the pale pink shellfish melted onto my tongue. I sucked the butter juices out of the head, and nodded as I ate, smacking in my enjoyment.

"I've started training my maikos in dance, and let me tell you, I've never seen a girl with a worst pair of left feet. The other one has the opposite problem. She's too talented, enough to think she knows everything," Lisa said with sigh, but I could hear the fondness she had for her apprentices.

"I know what you mean. Give Kayla a sword and she's more likely to trip on it than actually hit anything and Imani can barely get a talisman working half the time but… they're good girls," I said. When I began this budding courtship, I hadn't expected how much we would bond over our shared experiences of being a mentor to young women. It was nice to have someone else besides Big Sis to talk to about my doubts and uncertainties or share tips and methods on how to best advise our students. There were certainly times when I failed to have the patience that Imani needed or when I wanted to stick a SILENCE talisman on Kayla's forehead, but there was nothing more satisfying than seeing their gradual improvement—like building a fire one stick at a time and knowing that you had a hand in helping it glow.

Lisa nodded and agreed regarding her own apprentices, "They're good girls."

I chased the sushi down with a refreshing cup of yuzu lemonade. Then I asked, "Have you thought about it yet? Will you come to the summer festival with me?"

I could already imagine it now—us walking hand in hand through the food stalls, playing festival games, and asking her to be my girlfriend under a firework sky. We could even write our names on one of those couple's talismans and tie it to the bridge in the park.

"I don't know," she said, uncertainly, while I watched her lips consume the black roll of uni and salmon roe, her lipstick as red as the opalescent eggs. "I'm organizing the geishas' dance performance at the festival. I don't know how much time I'll have."

I tried not to show my disappointment, but sometimes my insecurity whispered that she may not be as into me as I was into her, and that she was just entertaining me with conversation like one of her teahouse patrons. Nothing ventured, nothing gained, as they said, but damn, dating women could be so intimidating and terrifying sometimes.

"We can meet up afterwards," I suggested. Admittedly, I was afraid that maybe I was coming on too hard, but I always found it difficult not to throw myself all in. Nervously, I changed my words, trying to be more considerate. "You're right. You'll probably be tired afterwards. Maybe you can join me up in the mountains when you get a day off?"

Of course, I'd have to convince Big Sis to let me bring Lisa up the mountain for a day. There had to be a romantic bone somewhere in her body. I've seen her drinking tea at night with her husband, all cozied up on the porch. Certainly, she wouldn't deny me a perfect evening of strolling the starry mountainside as I asked Lisa to be my girlfriend?

Her expression shifted. She glanced away but looked back towards me, looking nervous all of a sudden, and I've never seen this woman look nervous. Not even that time I saw her talk down two drunks with nothing but words and a shamisen she was ready to make into a bludgeoning weapon.

"You've said that's where you've been staying with the other Sistah Samurai?" she asked. "A day's walk up the mountain?"

"It's not too far," I assured her. "We could be back in the village the next day before the teahouse opens."

"I'll think about it," she said, sounding a little distant now. She was pulling back, and I felt like I was losing her without really understanding why. If she broke up with me, I would respect her decision, but I was definitely going to get drunk for a couple of days.

I bit the inside of my lip. Yeah, a bad habit I know, but I couldn't stop myself from doing it when the tension ratcheted up in moments like these. I've laughed in the face of demons but on the field of dating? That was where the real battles were won or lost.

I forced the words out of my mouth. "If you're not interested, I understand."

"I—" She licked her lips nervously. Then, she looked over her shoulder, and I followed her gaze to the throng of customers on the other side of the restaurant. She lowered her voice as she leaned towards me. Fear pressed against her lips until they thinned, and a foreboding twisted my stomach. "He threatened my girls. I'm sorry, I—I had to protect them."

"Wait, what? Who threatened your girls? What are you—"

Suddenly, my arm seized. I stared at my hand, and the sensation tingled up my arm and traveled through my body. Before the sensation crept up my throat, I croaked out, "Something's wrong."

I expected Lisa to look startled or concerned, but she hung her head like a neglected rose that desperately needed watering.

Over her shoulder, a movement caught my attention—a movement in the same direction Lisa had been glancing toward during our conversation. On the other side of the conveyor belt, a woman stood up. I hadn't noticed her before. There was no reason for me to, but I did now as she yanked up a loose neck collar over the lower half of her face like a mask, and pulled a hood over her head, leaving thick strands of jumbo braids to drape either side of her chest.

Fucking shit.

Hood ninjas.

I tried to scream at Lisa to run as the hood ninja walked right towards us. She shot out of her chair, knocking it over and the clang of it against the floor caught everyone's attention.

"I did everything your boss wanted. He said he would leave the tea house alone. He—" she screamed, a glass shattering sound as the ninja yanked her by the arm. She flailed and knocked over my sushi plate to the floor.

It fell on its face and revealed a paper talisman attached to the bottom, written with the kanji for FREEZE—the magic holding me captive. The ninja held a kunai to Lisa's throat, and she immediately stopped screaming.

"This wasn't the deal," she hissed.

"Cry to someone who gives a shit," The ninja answered with a bored voice, as if kidnapping women was an everyday occurrence. The ninja looked at me and relayed the words, "Warlord Scrubs hears you've been looking for him. He gives his regards."

Then the ninja slammed the hilt of their kunai against Lisa's temple and knocked her out. She pasted a talisman on Lisa's forehead, activated it, and lifted her over her shoulder as easy as a sack of rice. The ninja looked back at me and cocked her head.

"You've got a look about you," she said. She crouched and yanked at my collar to expose my back. I wanted nothing more than to move and stab my nails into her eyeballs. She found what she was looking for as a jagged nail traced the tattoo of flames on my back. "Fire clan, are you?"

I fought against the talisman, and painstakingly pushed the words from my throat, "I left the hood a long time ago."

The ninja scoffed. She stood and with her free hand, adjusted the black hood over her face, before declaring, "Once a hood ninja, always a hood ninja."

Then she carried Lisa away.

Other patrons had jumped to their feet, but none of their cowardly asses went after the ninja, or ripped up the fucking paper talisman no matter how much I screamed at them. I could only watch helplessly as the ink of the talisman slowly faded.

I was hurt and angry that Lisa had betrayed me, but all I knew was that despite it all, I would go through an army of ninjas to get her back.

When the talisman finally expired, I jolted into action. I pushed aside the line of people as I raced out of the door. My heart screamed in my ears as I skidded to a stop before the crowds that congested the streets. I asked the street regulars if they knew what direction the ninja had gone, but no one could tell me anything. There was a culture of silence when it came to the ninjas—to look the other way—and the dead-end answers filled me with frustration.

This couldn't be happening. How could she just slip through my fingers?

I clutched at my shoulder where that ninja had the audacity to touch me. I was born of the fire clan, but a Pestilence Demon had wiped most of them out. The lone survivor, I knew how to do magic and kill people. With those sorts of skills, joining the Sistah Samurai seemed the most logical step. Maybe I was going soft. If only I hadn't gotten too comfortable. If only I hadn't gotten too complacent in this village that I was beginning to consider my stomping grounds. If only I was paying more attention. If only. *Shit.*

I reached into my pocket for the daily vial of ink. I had already created the daily talismans before Lisa arrived at the restaurant, but none of those kanji could help me. The only ink left was the ink for the protection talismans to protect Big Sis' home.

With a curse and a quick apology, I pressed a sheet of paper against the wall of the sushi restaurant, atop a discount poster, and wrote three kanji onto the talisman. I threw it up in the air, and everyone in my proximity bowed in fear when the talisman shot up into the sky and exploded into pink fireworks—an SOS signal Big Sis and I had established a while ago.

If hood ninjas were in town, I needed back up.

AGE: 40

FAV FOOD:

SPICY MISO RAMEN

INTERESTS:

MIND YA BUSINESS

WILLPOWER: ★★★★★

VISUALIZATION: ★★★★★

KANJI PROFICIENCY: ★★★★★

WEAPON PROFICIENCY: ★★★★★

CHAPTER 8

PROTECTOR
SISTAH MONIQUE

"When should we tell the girls?" My husband asked as we sat within the shade of the curved eaves. Afro puffs bobbed above the grass as the twins played with Kayla's teddy bear, ushering him around the yard as they gathered the dandelions that seemed to have popped up in the field overnight. It was a hot muggy day, and their cheeks reddened in the heat.

Or was he referring to not just our girls, but also the ones we have seemingly adopted?

I looked past the twins toward the young women sitting underneath the shade of the tall and sprawling cherry blossom tree as they practiced their kanji. The pink flowers had long since shed, but the edges of its bright green leaves shone gold in the sunlight. Just a week ago, Hubby hung a swing from the tree's boughs, so the twins could enjoy a rush of air in the summer heat. Kayla was leaning an arm against the wooden plank as she studied the results of her kanji practice.

Kayla and Imani have been with us for half the summer now. Imani was getting better at visualizing her magic, and Kayla was getting more confident with sparring, but they still had a long way to go before their skills could compare with a Sistah Samurai. They were hard workers, though, once you got past all of Kayla's crying and Imani's reticence.

"Not yet," I said, and looked down to where I had rested my hand against my belly. It was nice to spend more time with my daughters and my husband these past few months but that also came with…other consequences.

I had thought I was finally going through menopause, but of course life had one last laugh for me. *Forty years old and pregnant.*

I was too damned old for this shit.

Little Sis had known that something was coming, something that would disrupt everything. But this was the very last outcome I had ever expected.

With a sigh, I leaned back against my husband's chest as he waved a paper hand-fan, pushing air across our faces. At first, I had panicked upon realizing that my recent bouts of exhaustion were definitely NOT menopause, but after some days of processing my emotions, in all the tangled web of mess that I was feeling, I was surprised to realize I was looking forward to this baby.

My first pregnancy had been marked with secrecy, shame, and so much stress that I barely remembered it. I had never gotten the chance to enjoy it, and this second go round was a chance to do better. And yet, there was still fear in me. An uncertainty. An unknowing if I would get to have this.

"Not yet," I repeated and said cautiously, "It's too early."

I was thirty-four when I got pregnant with the twins, and I am much older now. I knew it was still too early for it to be a certain thing, and I didn't want to get the twins' hopes up.

I straightened when they ran over in their yukatas, cut from the fabric I had purchased at the beginning of spring. The twins wore the outfit so much that those white cats had permanent smudges of dirt on their cheeks. Ari carried the teddy bear in her arms while Alex thrust one of the dandelions toward me.

"Mommy. You try!"

I leaned forward and sucked in a breath.

"Don't forget to make a wish!" Ari reminded me.

I learned dandelions didn't grant wishes when I had wished my parents were still alive at eight years old. But I wanted my daughters to hold their innocence for as long as possible, so I closed my eyes, and wished for protection for my family and the clan. I would make that wish on a thousand dandelion seeds if I thought it would make a difference. I puckered my lips and blew.

The girls squealed and danced as the fluffy seeds scattered into the wind.

Further beyond, a pink firework lit up the sky.

I shoved off against the deck, but my husband was already there, helping me to my feet. My hip had been bothering me lately, and I didn't know if it was because of the added strain of the pregnancy or my body doing its usual misbehaving .

"What's wrong?" Hubby asked. "What does the firework mean?"

"It's a distress signal. Something is wrong in the village."

Little Sis wouldn't have sent that alarm if it wasn't an emergency. I knew it was her as it was the braided talisman we had uniquely established as a signal. I touched the girls atop their heads, their scalps hot from the summer sun, and walked around the house to the study. I retrieved the unused talismans that Little Sis and I have been storing from days of little demon activity. I stuffed them into my obi and decided to leave behind the emergency stash of ink. I hoped I wouldn't regret doing so. When I returned to the front of the house, my dear husband had my swords waiting for me.

"Be careful," he cautioned. I settled my hand on his chest and kissed my favorite corner of lips. Then, I strode to where Kayla and Imani had allowed their calligraphy brushes to droop in their hands.

"Was that Sensei Braids?" Kayla asked.

"Sensei *what?*"

"Oh, nothing. Forget it. Is she in trouble?"

"I don't know. I'm headed into the village to see what's going on. Stay on alert and stay behind the protection talismans."

With a stomp, I activated a talisman and leapt UP over the treetops and off into the air. My heart thudded anxiously, an annoying woodpecker hammering at the inside of my chest. I knew it. I just knew I had a gut feeling that something was bound to go wrong. Not because I had any evidence of it, but because I was too happy and life always had a way of humbling you down.

Whatever was going on, I wished the storm clouds of danger would pass us by or move on quickly.

Because I knew summer had the possibility of producing typhoons.

KAYLA

AGE: 22

FAV FOOD:
BROWN SUGAR MOCHI

INTERESTS:
FASHION DESIGN
CRAFTS
HANGING W/FRIENDS

WILLPOWER: ★★☆

VISUALIZATION: ★★★⯪

KANJI PROFICIENCY: ★★★

WEAPON PROFICIENCY: ★

CHAPTER 9

WHO'S GOT THE BOOM
KAYLA

Why couldn't trouble wait to happen when it wasn't sooo hot outside? The heat was so unbearable that even standing still meant I was sweating out every one of my crevices. I was glad when we flipped to doing sword drills in the morning and practicing kanji throughout the day. Although, performing a fire talisman yesterday had me close to passing out. I was a delicate and fragile daisy, and I was definitely not made for this heat.

"What do you think is going on?" I asked Imani as we carried our desks closer to the house as Sensei had ordered. We left the safety of the shade, and I squinted when the sun hit us with the shock of a jump scare. It had no business being this bright, honestly.

"Nothing good," Imani answered. We carried our desks past the glowing protection talisman adhered to the stone gate and through the vegetable garden. The twins kicked their feet in the pond while Uncle stood on the deck, gazing out in the direction of Chigakure, looking concerned and nervous for his wife.

Uncle looked at our anxious expressions and suggested, "Want a snack?"

"That would be great!" I eagerly accepted.

Certainly, Sistah Afro wouldn't begrudge us a small break from our studies while she was away? We joined the twins for a snack of salted watermelon cubes. Imani spat out her seeds while I meticulously picked the glossy black seeds out with my chopsticks so that I could enjoy the entire cube in one refreshing bite.

Something in the corner of my eye caught my attention—a movement in the trees. I craned my head to get a better look, and nudged Imani since she was taller and might be able to see what I could not. Was that a rustle of wind, or were the bushes moving?

My molars crunched on a watermelon seed as a horde of hooded ninjas appeared from the trees. They wore deep green uniforms that camouflaged with the forest, and their hitai-ate flashed in the sun; the metal engraved with the symbol of their clan—a great roaring wave.

I've heard about the hood ninjas before. Everyone has heard about the hood ninjas, whose services had once been commissioned by various daimyos to help achieve their political ambitions, but who now loaned out their services to the many regional warlords. I should have been full of terror at that moment, but I only had one question at the forefront of my mind, *"Weren't they hot in all of those clothes?"*

"Daddy!" Alex shrieked, once she noticed the ninjas. I glanced at the protection talismans activated around the house. If the ninjas tried to enter with bad intentions, the talismans should work against them as they did against demons.

"Well," Uncle said, coming out onto the deck with a cloth to wipe the sticky watermelon juice from the twin's glistening cheeks. The sun smeared a glare across Uncle's glasses. "That's a problem."

I didn't know how he wasn't freaking out right now. The ninjas were lining up in front of the house. My heart drummed in panic. *It was happening again.*

Once again, destruction had found me, poised to take

everything away.

"Maybe we can make a talisman to alert Sensei Afro?" I suggested, as I got to my feet, ready to fight. I would not let another place be taken away from me. "Maybe I could make something like that pink firework? It's not one of the standard kanji, but I think I can do it."

"Just a moment," Uncle said, before he calmly walked back into the house.

Together, the ninjas stretched out their hands with the kanji for WATER tattooed onto their palms.

Each ninja clan had a specialty, often identified by the kanji inked into their skin. Ink directly applied to a person's skin was said to be twice as strong as ink applied to paper. I stumbled over the bamboo watermelon pan as I scooted back, splashing juice and seeds all along the deck.

Blasts of water shot out of the ninjas' hands and the protection talismans glowed to stop them. It was so much water that you would think they were throwing the entire ocean at us. The water enveloped us and trapped us in a fish bowl. The protection talismans around the house glowed brighter, straining. At this rate, the ink of the protection talismans would be depleted in a handful of minutes.

The twins stepped forward in awe, and I grabbed them by the scruff of their kitty-kat yukatas and pulled them back towards me.

"What is that?" Imani asked.

Uncle had returned, and my eyes widened at the mechanical contraption he carried over his shoulder. The shapes, "RPG" was written across the foreign object's extended pole, elongated in a way that reminded me of eating noodles on a bamboo slide. But I doubt it shot out noodles.

"It's a demon drop. Wifey figured it might come in handy if we were ever attacked." He bent to his knee and pointed the RPG toward the wall of water that gushed against the protection barrier.

He adjusted his glasses, aimed, and fired.

It caused an explosion of sound and heat so powerful, that the ground shook as if the mountain had shuddered. Because of the wall of water the ninjas had erected, they hadn't seen the attack coming. The explosion devastated their numbers. Those on the edge of the blast had been blown off their feet, heat puckering at their skin. But for those at the center—blackened grass replaced whole persons who had just been standing in front of us. So completely gone in an instant.

The ninjas that remained picked themselves up uneasily. They assessed Uncle and the foreign weapon that he rolled off of his shoulder and to the ground, seemingly out of ammo. I counted their slimmed down numbers, and brightened with hope that we might make it out of this alive.

Then, all that hope frayed when more ninjas stepped out of the trees. How many were there?!

They resumed their attack against the protection talismans. A few began dousing the flames that had erupted after the explosion, and I wondered why when the air was so humid that a fire would struggle to spread on its own. Then I realized that the ninjas didn't want to give the smoke a chance to rise too high. They didn't want Sensei Afro to see it and turn back.

Uncle reached into the fold of his yukata and pulled out a metal bar. I wondered what he was going to do with it. He held the metal bar like a sword-hilt, with all of the confidence of someone who had been trained in kendo. At the sound of an electric *zrrrr*, blue light burst forth from the metal.

"What is that?" Imani asked, the same time I asked, "*Who are you?*"

"It's a light…sword? Supposedly, it glowed red when the demon was wielding it. I don't know why it's blue now." He shrugged. "I admit, I am a little rusty. There should be some tamashii ink in the office. Take the girls and try to get a signal off to Wifey if you can."

"What about you?"

"Protect the girls," he said. He looked at the both of us, and my heart stopped as I've seen that expression before—the face of someone who didn't expect to survive. The blue light from his sword reflected off of his obsidian angles, way too beautiful to be broken. "And if I don't get the chance, tell Wifey I have never regretted my love for her. In any life, I choose her."

Tears blurred my sight, and I found myself unable to move, unable to force myself to leave someone behind yet again.

Then the protective shield audibly cracked, and hundreds of spiderwebs weaved along the barrier. I snatched the hand of the twin closest to me and ran as a mechanical sort of calm and distance descended over me. In the corner of my eye, I spied Teddy-san sprawled atop the kitchen table, but there was no time to go back for him.

"I'll grab the ink from the office. Imani, go grab our weapons from our room," I told her. She nodded. With the other twin strapped to her chest, she overtook me to reach our room, which was further away.

I turned into the office and dropped—I looked to see which one I had grabbed—Ari onto the tatami mats and raced to Sensei Afro's desk.

The protection talismans popped, followed by an inhale of silence, right before a crash of water thundered against the house.

I scrambled through the drawers. When I found the ink and paper, I stuffed it into my belt. I snatched up Ari and ran with her back out of the door. As we exited, Imani had just turned the corner with our weapons, returning to come and get me with Alex riding piggy-back. She held her naginata in one hand, and handed me my bow and string with the other. I dropped to my knee in a growing pool of water to string it. Once I finished, I swung it over my chest and stuffed the bladed fan Imani gave me into my belt.

We sprinted off into the forest and were startled when we found three ninjas waiting for us behind the house. One of them had a collar popped so high that it covered their face, another had microbraids falling out the sides of their hood, and the last had a hood so low that it fell over their eyes, and I couldn't help but wonder how they could see. Why did they all look so stylish and dangerous at the same time?

I tripped on a tree root during my attempt to come to a stop. I fell on my butt with Ari in my lap as a shuriken zipped over my head. Imani deflected hers with quick metal dings.

"Hey! Watch the hair!" I cried out, outraged, and clutched the bantu knots that had taken so long for me to twirl and wrap this morning.

They brandished their shuriken, fanning sharp stars between their fingers.

Why weren't they attacking us with large magical attacks? Were they trying to capture us? Wait, no, that doesn't make sense. They weren't trying to capture *us*. They were trying to capture the twins. That was why they were desperate to avoid Sensei Afro's attention. She might have seen some of the smoke from the explosion before they stamped it out, but it might not have been enough, and we needed to somehow get a signal to her.

"Kayla!"

I turned, and Imani tossed me her twin. I had them both in my arms and she stepped, protectively, before us. Without words, I understood her plan. Since she was the best at physical combat, it made sense for her to try and create an opening, slowing them down and giving me time to escape with the girls.

The ninjas threw a wave of shuriken, but Imani twirled her polearm, deflecting them. She thrust toward the closest, who evaded, but she immediately swiveled and swept the naginata across the ankles of the ninja closest to me.

Now.

I hitched the girls on either side of my hips and ran for it. I made it past their defensive line. The sounds of fighting—the grunts and cries and the pinging of steel all faded behind me.

I was running as fast as my legs could carry me, but I was short, okay? I wasn't getting anywhere fast, and these twins were heavier than they looked. But I refused to fail Sensei Afro and fail at protecting her family. I had to keep going!

I chanted to myself, "Go, go, Kayla, go! Go, go, Kayla, go!"

When I had absolutely nothing left in me, I collapsed against a tree and pressed my face against it with a sob. Seriously, though. What type of cruel person decided to attack people in the middle of the summer?! The humidity was so thick I felt like I couldn't catch my breath. I was crying as I reached into my belt and pressed the rectangular sheet of paper against the tree. No, that wouldn't work. The grooves of the tree were going to mess up the kanji.

I looked around, desperate. Then I jumped forward, slipping in foliage and landing hard against my knee, but crawled toward a smooth stone jutting out of the ground.

Two kanji, flower (花) and fire (火), made up the word for 'firework.' An eleven-stroke count. What kanji did I use for pink? Wait, I could just keep it simple. No doubt Sensei Afro would turn back at the sight of any explosion over her house. All I needed was the two kanji. If I made it out of this alive, I would have to ask Sensei Braids about the third kanji. Okay. I was ready.

I looked down and my entire heart froze at the black stain spreading across my belt.

"Nonononono," A keening whine escaped me when I pulled out the ink and found the vial had shattered. Black ink, someone's soul, was smeared across my hand. *Why was I so terribly and unluckily clumsy??? WHY ME????*

No. I had to pull myself together. I dipped the brush against the ink of my palm and hovered it over the paper. My hand shook uncontrollably, and my vision blurred, tears springing up automatically at the growing panic. It was a four-stroke kanji. An easy kanji. One that I've written a bajillion times. But I couldn't stop my hand from shaking. How did Sensei Afro manage to create talismans in the middle of a battle and not lose her ever-loving shit?!

"You can do it!" Ari cheered beside me, reminding me what

was at stake and that I needed to get my act together.

"You got this!" Alex cheered at my other side as she clutched onto the white fabric of my apprentice robe.

I wiped my tears with my arms so that I could see. I stared down at the piece of paper as if it was a newly cut pattern that needed to be sewed for a next day rush order. I lifted the brush, determined, and attacked the paper with ink. Muscle memory knew what to do. Stroke by stroke. Perfect.

Twigs snapped beneath a heavy footfall. I snatched up the talisman, attached it to an arrowhead, and rose to my feet as I nocked the arrow to the bow and aimed.

"Don't come any closer or I will pop you like a firework!"

Despite my warning, a shadow came forward with raised hands and stepped out into the light of the sun. He wore a custom cut kimono and a high taper fade that transitioned to the skin like smooth silk. An ice-cold chill raced down my spine at that familiar crooked smile.

"Hey, Kaybunny, don't you look good?"

"Xavier?" I asked. In my utter shock, the bow drifted down and the tension in the string laxed. I hadn't seen Xavier, my ex-boyfriend, since that misty night I confronted him about the Salon.

He stepped forward and I trained the bow back on him as quickly as possible. I intended to sound commanding like Sensei Afro, but my voice came out all soft and wobbly as I asked, "How are you here?"

He raised both hands and shrugged, all lackadaisical as if we weren't surrounded by ninjas in the middle of the forest. "Heard you were in the area. Wanted to see you is all. Catch up, you know?"

"*Catch up?!* I told you that I never wanted to see you again."

"Come on. Is that how you're gon' act? We haven't seen each other in years."

"Yeah, because you *betrayed me!*" I yelled. "You told the warlords how to get into the Salon!"

"Aye, but how was I supposed to know they'd do what they

did? They just told me they were going to steal and smash some stuff. No harm no foul, you know? Besides, you were the one always complaining about that place—complaining about how much they made you run, complaining about how nasty the food was, or complaining about the other girls. That's all you did!"

My words choked my throat. I didn't remember it like that. Maybe I complained sometimes, but had I really given the impression that I hated the place? Had what happened been even more of my fault than I thought? My arms weakened with doubt.

"*They expelled you, Kayla*. And for what? For sneaking me in the backdoor? We'd been friends before you ever went to that place. As far as I'm concerned, they deserved what they got. They abandoned you. What loyalty did you ever owe to them when I was the one trying to make a better life for us? Look at me," he said, and showed off his graffiti-sprayed cloak with built-in pauldrons. He spun around, displaying the titanium on his fingers, and the silver in his teeth. "I'm a warlord now. I killed the one that did all that shit to the Salon and took over his territory. I've got money now. I could take care of you. I could even help you open up that tailor shop you were always talking about."

I was so confused. For so long, I had blamed him, but now he was telling me that everything he did was for me?

"The other warlords, all they want to do is divide this territory amongst themselves, but I know that the Big Guy is going to betray us and take it all for himself. That motherfucker is crazy strong like you wouldn't believe. But we could run away together, Kaybunny. We could get out of here. It'll be you and me against the world. Just like old times. All you've got to do is hand over those girls."

I didn't remember my parents. I was an orphan as long as I could remember and grew up on the streets with Xavier, until it was *his* idea that I enroll with the Salon for the free meals so I could sneak him out some food. But somewhere along the way, I had fallen in love with the Sistah Samurai and everything they represented. I missed the laughter, the camaraderie, the happiness, and the sheer light that I found within those walls. I might have complained about it, but I fucking loved that place. And he *knew* that. He knew me long enough to know all of my complaints were just hot air, and how I wrapped them in a little bow of love.

No. I would not fall for his gaslighting. Fuck his plans and whatever plot he was hustling. This time, I refused to be an accomplice to his betrayal. With my leg, I pushed the girls behind me. I told him decisively, "No!"

"Fuck you then, bitch." He snapped, transforming almost instantly into a different person. He finally looked like the same monster on the outside as he was on the inside. He clicked his tongue as he swayed back with disgust. "Never knew a good thing when it was standing right in front of you."

"I would rather get my soul eaten by a demon than to see your stupid face one second longer!" I yelled at him. I wanted him gone. I didn't want to deal with him and all of the emotions he stirred up inside of me. I could feel the anger bubbling up and immediately suctioned away, leaving me with all of the rest—the grief, the hurt, and the disappointment that I wanted to shove aside so that I could get back to being happy. But my happiness was stripped from my words as I screamed at him. "I am done with your lies! It was never about me, and you know it! You sold the information to the warlord for your own greed and your own ambition! You used me! You hurt me! You said you loved me!"

"Why you always gotta to be so dramatic?" Xavier asked. "You know I got love for you, girl. I always will."

He moved towards me.

I lifted the bow and pressed the string against my lip. Instead of being intimidated, he looked at my body with a roguish grin, sweeping his eyes down as if I had posed for a painting instead of aiming an arrow at his face. The heat of his gaze caused my cheeks to warm in shame and embarrassment that I had let this lying cheating ass be my first.

"You were always so cute, Kaybunny. I—"

UGH!

I aimed the arrow up and released it into the sky. It soared and the fire talisman exploded into the air as big and loud and bright as I could visualize it.

BOOM!

I smiled to see the ashen look come over his face. He glanced at me and then at the twins, and I saw him doing what he did best: calculating how to save his own skin. But whatever the calculation, he decided that staying and trying to capture the twins was worth the risk.

He lunged towards me, and I dropped the bow. I snatched the bladed fan from my belt and with a twist of my wrists, I fluttered them open and stood against him.

He laughed at me. "Really?"

He'd never had the chance to get to know this Kayla— the one he didn't have to protect. I didn't blame him for his disbelief, but I was determined to show him that I wasn't that crybaby any longer… okay, fine, still a crybaby, but one who could finally take care of herself.

He grabbed a red pole from out of his belt and it extended in his hand. It elongated unnaturally, longer than any staff had any right to be. A demon drop? When it didn't stop growing, I threw my fans in front of me. The butt-end hit the fans, cracking the bamboo frame, slamming against my chest and shoving me to the ground.

I threw the cracked fans at him, and one smacked him right in the forehead. Beside me, the twins picked up rocks to throw as well. He raised his cloak before him in defense and then a SHIELD talisman sprouted around him. A rock that rebounded off the barrier clipped my shoulder.

He dropped the shield and the drum of his feet pounded the dirt. I looked around desperately for anything I could use as a weapon. I surged up from the ground and whacked him in the face with my bow. His head was so hard the wood cracked.

He stumbled back as I turned to the twins and told them, "Run!"

They looked at me uncertainly, unwilling to leave me. But I had no more weapons, no more magic, and the best I could hope for was to buy time. "Run or I won't play Double Dutch with you anymore!"

Startled, the twins ran off. I turned as Xavier lunged towards me. I tried to whack him again, but he was close enough to grab my wrist. My feet flew out from under me as he slammed me to the ground. He reached into the fold of his cloak for a talisman. The EARTH shifted and clasped around my wrists. I tried kicking but his weight held down my knees.

"Just like old times, huh?" He smirked above me.

I screamed at him, but even as I did so, I could feel all of my anger being sucked away, leaving me with nothing but tears.

"Maybe next time you'll realize how much you missed me." He winked. I watched as he threw the glowing talisman at me before strolling away. I watched as that earth talisman landed, and tried to calculate how long it would take for the ink to fade. He only locked my wrists to the ground, using a small amount of earth. It would grow weaker with distance but, at my estimate, it would take an hour before the talisman faded if he decided to hold it that long.

Xavier chased after the twins, and I heard their screams in the distance as he caught up to them.

An audible sob hiccupped from my lips. I couldn't protect them. I failed to save everyone, *again*. I spent years studying and working to become a Sistah Samurai. I spent this past month sweating my ass off and for what? So that I could lose to my stupid ex-boyfriend and let him take everything away from me again?

Absolutely not! Get your ass up, Kayla!

I pulled my right hand against the restraints. The pain was *sooo* excruciating, more painful than someone stepping on your hand, or punching you in the gut, or crossing shins during a spar. But finally, my right hand slipped through. I clutched it to my chest, and I swear I could feel the throbbing pain of it pulse through my veins. I glanced over at the left hand.

One more to go.

This was the worst day ever. But I gritted my teeth and embraced the pain, and hugged it like a ratty alleyway blanket. My left hand finally slipped free with sobbing and sweaty relief. I whimpered as I got to my feet and glared in the direction Xavier had gone. I could still hear the twins screaming.

I sucked in a determined breath, snatched that earth talisman off the ground, and then I raced after them. I hated running. My entire body pulsed with pain. It was sooo hot. But despite all of these impossible discomforts, they faded away to nothing as I focused on the back of my good-for-nothing ex.

I was NOT going to let him take this home away from me too. I activated the ink left in the talisman and a nice rock lifted up underneath my feet and carried me forward, chewing up distance. Even when the talisman ran out ink, I kept running.

Go, go. Kayla, Go!

AGE: 23

FAV FOOD:

SOUP CURRY

INTERESTS:

ROLLER SKATING

CARD COLLECTING

NATURE

IMANI

WILLPOWER: ★★

VISUALIZATION:

KANJI PROFICIENCY: ★★

WEAPON PROFICIENCY: ★★★

CHAPTER 10

ZOOM

IMANI

I faced the three ninjas with my stalwart naginata, as faithful a companion to me as the Tamagotchi clipped to my hip. In some ways, it was easier that I could not see the ninjas' faces, shaded by their hoods. The ninjas might outnumber me, but I have been up against bigger demons.

I held no fear of them.

I ducked underneath the ninjas' jet of water and raced closer, bringing the fight to them and making it more difficult for them to use their magic. I pushed the polearm against a ninja's forearm as he sliced down with a kunai, then I slammed the butt-end of my naginata across the ninja's face, knocking him out. Like skating, I leaned into the momentum of the attack, swiveled around, and sliced across the ninja's chest approaching from behind.

A wave of water crashed over me.

I stabbed the end of the naginata into the grass and dropped to my knee to withstand the force of it. When it was over, the ninja who I had cut across the chest had been thrown to the ground in the attack, their head bleeding against a rock. I was surprised for a moment—that the ninja would so carelessly attack one of their own.

I raised my head to my attacker, her arms outstretched. Her eyes met my own. Eyes said too much. I saw her surprise that I was still standing, and then her intent.

I snatched up a kunai fallen from the dead ninja and threw it. It lodged into the ninja's hand, and she jerked up her arm at the pain. I thrust off my back foot and stabbed my naginata through the ninja's chest and into the tree behind her. I twisted it, and kicked against the ninja's belly, to dislodge her from my blade. Her body dropped and her eyes were now dark shattered voids. The death sat heavy on me, thicker than the humid pressure of summer.

"Not bad, little sister."

My limbs locked still—at that voice, at those words.

I turned and my older brother floated down from the sky. His cloak fluttered like a wave behind him—a demon drop?— and stopped a hand's length above the ground, careful to make sure his white shoes avoided the dirt. Thick locs framed his face like mighty tree branches, dyed blonde at the bottom.

Our hair matched, and that small detail tugged at me like a fishing hook caught in my skin. So many years apart—and we still looked undeniably like family.

I stared at this ghost, this haunting, as my past and present collided together as forceful as exploding stars. I hadn't seen my older brother since I left home and joined the Salon. I felt pulled in different directions, as if the core of my being was imploding.

"Father is disappointed in you," he said, gravely.

"Is he-he here?" I stuttered, hoarsely, terrified by the mention of him and the possibility that he could be just around the next tree. Seeing my older brother brought back all of the helpless feelings that I felt as a child, trapped by what seemed like my father's impossible demands. *Girls are supposed to be seen, not heard. Girls are weak and are supposed to be protected. Girls are supposed to be polite and gentle. Look adults in the eyes when they are talking to you!*

My older brother looked over my shoulder and I turned

in that direction, terrified to see the shadow of a man that haunted my waking. But no one was there. I sighed in relief, but when I turned around, I found only danger as he jammed a fist into my gut. I internally screamed when I slumped forward, and he wrapped me in a hug. As if we were estranged siblings reunited once again.

"It's been too long," he said, patting my back consolingly. It reminded me of all the well-meaning touches I had to endure as a child—cheek pinches and hugs I never asked for but was forced to endure because it made the adults comfortable, when all I wanted was to stay in my corner. "But you should have stayed out of the way. Father wants this land, and he wants to destroy the Sistah Samurai, and you know father always gets what he wants."

He hovered taller than me, even though I was the tallest of the two of us. Perhaps he refused to put his feet on the ground to face that small insignificant piece of reality, which seemed like a lifeline right now. Tears slid from my eyes, and I opened my mouth to croak. I shut my eyes and tried again. "Why? You let me go that night."

And why return now?

A bright brilliant explosion detonated over our heads. I looked up and my heart cheered at the sight of it. Kayla got off the signal!

My older brother jolted back and hissed to himself. "What is that fool doing? Father was right. If you want a thing done, you've got to do it yourself." He turned to me and said, "If you don't want father to find you, leave the Sistah Samurai. Run away. You're good at that, aren't you?"

Then, he made to rise back into the air. Alarmed at whatever horror our father had him up to, I tossed my naginata and lunged towards him. I caught him by the waist, and while my weight slowed him down, we still lifted into the air. Around us, white clouds smeared the sky like melted marshmallows.

"What—Let go of me!" He said as he rose higher than the treetops. He pushed me with his hands, but at a certain height, he stopped. I wondered why but then I realized he didn't want to risk me falling and dying now that we were so high above the trees. Did he still care about me, or was he going through the motions of the big brother beaten into him?

As we rose higher, the sun seared my skin. We came from harsh northern winters, and even though the summer heat was something I still struggled with, I'd always preferred the sun.

"There that fool is," my older brother said. He grabbed me around the waist as we made a sudden descent. Leaf litter flew up, but somehow, no dirt managed to get on his shoes as he halted an inch above the ground.

Someone stopped abruptly before us and my breath hitched at the sight of some stranger holding the twins, who were crying and screaming in his arms. What happened to Kayla? How could I save the twins? My grip loosened, and my knees landed in a crunch of leaves.

"Hey, what the fuck you got Imani for? She wasn't one of the targets," the stranger said my name as if he knew me.

This time, I forced myself to look at his face and realized that I did recognize him. That was Kayla's ex-boyfriend, Xavier. The one who had sold out the Salon's back door entrance and got everyone killed. How was he here as well?

Older brother jolted back for a moment and glanced between Xavier and I. He adopted that telltale protective big brother pose. "How do you know my sister?"

"Your sister? *Your sister?!*" Xavier threw his head back and cackled. "That's my ex's best friend. They went to the Salon together. Daddy didn't tell you? I'm the reason there ain't no Sistah Samurai anymore," he said, pointing his thumb against his chest, as if boasting about mass murder added to his street cred. "I got my opps fair. What about you, nepo boy?"

The tension between the two men made me uncomfortable. Arguments between two people always did. I glanced at the twins, and they looked at me with wide hopeful eyes. Perhaps, I could do something while they were distracted.

"At least I can follow orders," my older brother sneered.

"You and the ninjas were to obtain all three targets. You've only got two of them."

"I don't take fucking orders from you."

"My father—"

"Oh yeah, that's right. You can't piss unless your daddy tells you to."

"AHHHHHHHHH!!!!!!!!!"

Everyone turned as a high-pitched monster charged out of the forest—a grass-stained, yukata-ripped, missing a shoe, branches accessorizing her bright purple hair, forest creature that slammed straight into Xavier, knocking him over and releasing the girls from his grasp. Kayla whacked a tree branch over the barrier of his forearms, which he had defensively lifted to protect his head.

With the sudden distraction, I ran forward and grabbed the girls. Xavier had grabbed Kayla by the arms, and now she was trying to unsuccessfully pull out of his grip. "Let me go, X. Let me go!"

Then, Ari slipped from my fingers. She curled her little fists and beat them over Xavier's head.

Annoyed, Xavier released Kayla to shove Ari down. She oomphed into the soft dirt and then yelled, pointing, "My mommy is going to kick your ass!"

I grabbed Ari around the waist and pulled her away as Kayla kicked his face and twisted her trapped arm, snatching it out of Xavier's grip. She crawled backwards, and I helped her to her feet. We shoved the girls behind us and together, we raised our fists, ready to do anything we could to protect them from these unwanted relics of our past. I had left my naginata behind, and Kayla didn't seem to have her bow any longer. No ink. No weapons. But we'd face them together.

Xavier grumpily brushed leaves off of his clothing. Over his shoulder, my older brother just shook his head, disappointed by his incompetence.

Then, a whooshing sound plummeted out of the sky. I raised my arm to block the leaf litter and dirt that had dispersed into the air. When the dirt settled, I looked up at the back of Sensei Afro's summer yukata, blooming with sunflowers.

Ari shouted, "Mommy! He hit me!"

Sensei Afro looked at her daughters and then toward Xavier. His eyes widened for a moment. Then he activated a talisman and bolted away, speeding off with a blur.

"Scaredy ass nigga," my older brother spat, not at all impressed, and began to rise from the ground.

He pressed a COMMUNICATION talisman to his lips and spoke against the paper, "Ninjas, converge on my positi—."

By lifting into the air, he tried escaping the reach of Sistah Afro but she jumped, grabbed him by the ankle, and then slammed him to the ground. He reached for a talisman to save himself, but his arm audibly cracked when Sensei Afro stomped on it, cracking the wood of her getas.

Did I want my older brother to die? He was a dickhead, but like me, he didn't choose his father.

She lifted her katana above her head.

"Wait!" I didn't know when I moved. I trembled as I wrapped my arms around her waist from behind. "He's my older brother. He's dumb but don't…"

She paused. There was a terrifying shadow in her expression, but it lifted when she looked over her shoulder to where the twins watched against Kayla's leg. In that moment of hesitation, I moved around her.

I looked down at my brother—the one punished for not taking care of me, the one who hated and bullied me, and the one who let me go.

"Tell our father that I'm done running away," I told him. Then, I cocked back my leg and kicked loose dirt onto his front-laced white shoes.

"NO!!!!!!!!!" he cried out like a wounded animal.

Then the hood ninjas swarmed.

Sensei Afro grabbed my arm, and we backed up toward Kayla and the twins. A hard darkness descended over all of us. Rushing water crashed against a distant shore, as Sensei Afro held a single trap talisman in her hand, which glowed bright gold in the darkness.

"Did you just use a trap talisman as a shield?" Kayla asked in awe. When the impenetrable TRAP fell away, my older brother had disappeared, to be replaced by six ninjas.

Sensei Afro narrowed her eyes and glared at the ninjas as if they were a colony of annoying ants ruining our picnic. She declared, "No amount of money is worth your life. Turn back now, and maybe I won't crush you."

"You're just some old washed-up samurai," one of the ninjas mocked. "We're not afraid of you."

Sensei Afro placed her hand on the hilt of her katana. She bounced once on the balls of her feet. It all happened so fast my eyes could barely track it.

A trail of fire erupted across the ninjas' open-toed boots. She lunged towards the one who had stumbled on the line of fire, sliding onto her good knee as she sliced the ninja clean in half. Kayla and I immediately closed our hands around each respective twin's eyes. By the time I looked up, another ninja was dead.

Was this what a Captain looked like? I definitely wanted to be her someday.

One of the ninjas reached out a hand, with the kanji for water visibly inked into the center of their palm. I was about to shout for sensei to watch out, but in the span of a second, she rendered the attack useless as she sliced through the ninja's arm and the limb fell, rolling. Blood spurted out, drenching the soil and green leaves.

Sensei Afro swept up that fallen arm, and I stared in shock when she pointed it, and used the ink in the severed limb to send a water dragon gushing against the owner's comrade, throwing him into a tree. She pointed that arm, like her husband had pointed that RPG, and shot another one of the ninjas with water pellets.

The ninja was taken so much by surprise, that she stabbed her katana through his chest in the next breath afterwards.

The last two ninjas decided the job wasn't worth it after all. Together, they formed a water slide and slipped far away down the mountain.

Sistah Afro paused for a moment, at the ready, listening for any more attackers. Forest sounds began to return. The chirp of a bird. The rustle of a brown rabbit darting through the brush.

She finally relaxed, cleaned her katana, and sheathed the blade. Then, she raised the severed arm over her head and water rained down like a shower. She cooled herself off, until the ink of the tattoo flared out, and then she threw the useless limb behind her.

For a moment, Kayla looked at one of the fallen ninjas, considering. Even dead, their skin was nothing but parchment now and the tattoos still had a little bit of ink left in them. Then she shook her head, "Eww. No."

Sensei Afro turned to look at us. The twins took that as permission to run forward and she hesitated for a moment, conscious of the blood streaked across her yukata. But with one look at her daughters' faces, she opened her arms wide. They sobbed and buried their heads into her chest. After they were comforted, she looked up at us, and Kayla sniffed before running forward to join their hug.

"I'm so glad you saw my signal!" she sobbed.

Honestly, after my older brother, my touch gauge was at its limit. So, I ended up standing there, letting their emotion of joy and relief quell some of the tension in my shoulders. I bowed my head. It was nice to feel the heat of the sun on my neck. It had felt so oppressive this summer, something to run away from and avoid, but oh how one moment could change everything, turning a summer of discomfort into gratefulness.

Sensei Afro approached me, leaves crunching beneath her shoes, and I held myself, uncertain. My older brother was a warlord. Our enemy. *My* enemy. But her presence was a balm when she stopped beside me, and her words soothed, "Good job keeping the twins safe. Let's go, girls."

Let's go, girls.

I smiled and felt comforted by her praise. It was something I didn't remember my father ever giving me. Despite knowing that this wouldn't be the last time I saw my older brother, or that my father was out there somewhere. It didn't matter.

This time, I refused to run away.

SISTAH SIMONE

AGE: 36

FAV FOOD:
DANCING SQUID SASHIMI

INTERESTS:
FIGHTING
DANCING
MUSIC

WILLPOWER: ★★★☆☆

VISUALIZATION: ★★★★½

KANJI PROFICIENCY: ★★★★½

WEAPON PROFICIENCY: ★★★★★

CHAPTER 11

TYRONE (LIVE)
SISTAH SIMONE

I followed the tracking talisman as it zipped through the village, running over anyone fool enough to get in my way. I worried that the ink would run out before I caught up with the ninja who stole Lisa. I followed the talisman out of the village gate, and the moment I exited, it was zapped out of the air with a zigzag of lightning. I rolled up from the ground, where I had ducked under the flashy attack, and narrowed my eyes at the man standing across from me, waiting for me in the middle of the road.

"Grand rising, goddess," the warlord greeted. "Aren't you tired of all the demons keeping us down? I have been granted a grand vision by the Almighty Kami to unite the territories of this fractured land. Your vigilance over this village has come to an end, Sistah Samurai. I do not like being in conflict with a beautiful goddess like yourself, but I am compelled by a higher calling and I advise you not to stand in the way of my purpose. Respectfully, I ask that you lay down your arms and move aside."

What the fuck? I admittedly looked around to make sure no one was playing jokes on me. I turned back to the guy with a crooked kente cloth hat on top of his head, wearing all black robes with kente patterned lapels over his shoulders. He held a bamboo staff covered in various talismans in his left hand.

How warlords ruled over their territories were as varied as their personalities. Some were reasonable to work with, while others I would cut their heads off if I ever got the chance. But I had never met a warlord like him before. I bet he was from up north.

"Are you Warlord Scrub? The one who took Lisa?" I demanded.

"Warlord Scrub is a fellow associate faithful to the vision, but unfortunately, he is currently occupied with a different task. Perhaps I may relay the message of your discontent once you agree to step aside and relinquish your guardianship of this village to my hallowed stewardship."

"How about I beat his location out of you, instead?" I spat, even as I mentally went through the talismans I had created before Lisa showed up for lunch. I had only the standard ones: Fire, Trap, and Lightning.

"Then you leave me no choice," he said, after a mighty sigh. "My sincerest apologies, goddess, for what I must do."

He grabbed his staff with both hands and pounded it against the ground. The EARTH ruptured, creating a fissure that raced alarmingly towards the village walls.

The earth crumbled under my foot and I moved aside to thrust my katana toward him like a spear. LIGHTNING crackled from the blade, traveling along the steel in a bright flash and striking against his SHIELD. The defensive sphere glowed around him, lighting up one of the talismans on his staff. And yet, his assault on the earth continued.

But that wasn't possible. No one could visualize two talismans simultaneously.

I leapt towards him, and his staff swept horizontally before me. The earth continued to rumble as WIND barreled out the staff and swatted me out of the sky.

I quickly grabbed for the TRAP talisman and activated it. A cage wrapped around me, creating a barrier as I was flung into a tree. The trunk of the tree audibly vibrated as leaves fluttered off the trap's steel bars. I deactivated the talisman and landed on my hands and knees, with a sharp throb shooting up my index finger. I had broken a nail. *That motherfucker.*

Then, a loud rumble sounded behind me.

The fissure had reached the village gate, and the stone walls rumbled, groaning, before falling like a rockslide in a tumble of dust. *Shit.* Without the wall, the villagers would be hard-pressed to protect themselves from roaming demons. I've seen too many times how people were so willing to accept the rule of tyrants if they thought it would protect them.

I took my hoop earrings off. Okay. Motherfucker. Let's go.

I peeled the lightning talisman from my katana and placed it on my calf. I closed my eyes, careful of how I visualized this next move. Then, I imagined myself as lightning, as fast as a dry summer storm. Sparks crackled at the bottom of my feet, and I shot forward.

The warlord turned, surprised. This time, he failed to get his shield up in time and my katana sliced through the coat sleeve, cleaving through flesh, and biting bone. I landed on the balls of my feet. Got 'em!

I popped my booty in quick celebration and turned a pirouette. My katana clashed with his wooden staff. Behind the tough bamboo, his face lifted in a clear look of disgust and disdain. This close to him, his features oddly looked familiar.

"Samurai don't twerk," he said, disapprovingly.

"I'll twerk on your grave," I hissed.

The warlord held his bleeding arm against his body. His blood stained his black cloak even darker, and I smirked at the sight of it—at the result of my violence.

A talisman glowed on his wooden staff, and I had only a second to read the kanji (爆). EXPLOSION.

I activated the TRAP talisman as heat blasted my face. The eruption sent me flying through the air as my braids spread before me like wings. The trap began to close around me, but I lost hold of the visualization as the concussive force of the explosion knocked me out.

I was brought back to a sudden and painful awareness when I landed hard against one of the fallen bricks of the gate. With a groan, I glanced up to see that punk ass warlord standing there, cloak fluttering, largely unscathed.

I spat out blood and wanted nothing more than to snatch that stupid hat off of his head and stuff it into his mouth until he choked on it. Sometimes, a hot violence took a hold of me, as if a demon of the same name had possessed me at birth. I shook with the need to release it, to break bones, and to fuck him up.

The warlord activated an EARTH and FIRE talisman at the same time, or fast enough for it to look like he had activated them at the same time, but I was beginning to believe the former. I wasn't one to dismiss my own eyes regardless of what years of scholarship might say. This guy could activate two talismans at once, and I only had a fire talisman left.

His two talismans glowed.

Combining two attacks, the warlord launched a fiery meteor towards me and the village. My breath left my lungs at the sight of it. Looking at the attack, at the sheer size of it, reminded me of standing in formation with my fellow Sistah Samurai before the sheer immensity of demons overran the walls of Edolanta. There came a point where something became too large to describe, and scale felt meaningless, and the only point of measurement was your own stupid bravery and foolhardy pride.

"Brotha Monks! Formation!"

I blinked, surprised when the Brotha Monks stormed out over the broken walls and their orange robes formed a forest of maple leaves before me. The meteor descended on us like a second sun, scorching us with an unbearable heat that heralded its arrival.

"Brotha Monks!" The Head Monk slammed his large calligraphy brush against the ground, "Protect!"

Each monk, all of them rocking a different number

of chains and medallions, raised a talisman between their forefingers, written with a single kanji. PROTECT (保).

They closed their eyes, enduring the heat with droplets of sweat beading on their foreheads, creating stains in their white durags. Together, they activated their spell. Individually, a Brotha Monk wasn't all that strong, but through years of honing their minds on a single visualization, together, they created an indestructible defense.

The Brotha Monks' shield was so large it covered me and the entire southern half of the village. The shield was so visibly thick, it was like standing inside of an orb. I hadn't heard of such a strong group visualization since the Grit Wars, but large-scale group visualizations had always been a defining strength of the Sacred Order of Brotha Monks.

The meteor slammed into their shield and for all of the warlord's lone strength, his attack could not overcome their collective power. I worried the monks might faint from heat exhaustion, and even I, born of the fire clan, was beginning to feel faint. I was impressed by how they all managed to stay standing.

The warlord's ink ran out first. The meteor disappeared, blinking out and snatching away the heat as sudden as an eclipse.

Behind the shield, the Head Brotha Monk called out, "You are not welcome here, warlord!"

The warlord studied the monks, and then he glanced at me through their shoulders, where a young apprentice had helped me to my feet and applied a healing talisman to my arm. The warlord reached into his sleeve, and the monks tensed as he tossed out a paper talisman. We all watched anxiously as it drifted to the ground.

"When you are ready to gain what you have lost, call me."

A TELPORTATION talisman glowed on his staff, and he disappeared right before our eyes. I blew out a bitter breath, annoyed that I didn't get a chance to take another shot at him. But I also had to think of Lisa and how I was going to get her back.

The Brotha Monk from the nail salon approached me, looking all contrite and ready for this ass kicking I was about to give him. *What the fuck happened to keeping an eye on the warlords? And where the fuck did this warlord come from?*

"Aye, what the fuck?!" I demanded.

He stopped a good distance away, as well he should. He apologetically explained, "Warlord Scrub was a decoy, fooling us to look at one hand while they had a reverse card in the other."

"*Then who the fuck was that?*" As the question left my mouth, the realization hit me as to why the man looked so familiar. After all, I'd been training his daughter for the past summer. *Oh.* Poor little tink tink.

The Brotha Monk looked grim as he answered, "That was Warlord Tyrone, a friend to fuck niggas everywhere, and the leader of The Alliance of Hotep Warlords."

AGE: 40

FAV FOOD:

SPICY MISO RAMEN

INTERESTS:

MIND YA BUSINESS

WILLPOWER: ★★★★★

VISUALIZATION: ★★★★★

KANJI PROFICIENCY: ★★★★★

WEAPON PROFICIENCY: ★★★★★

CHAPTER 12

FAFO

SISTAH MONIQUE

I spun the comforting weight of the blunt in my hand. I had it stored away for tough days, and despite the pregnancy, I was tempted by its brief promise of escape. Anything to dull the rage quaking through me with nowhere to go and no one to impale it on. The ninjas had fled. The warlords were gone. They had left no leads for me to track them down.

I surveyed the damage—household items toppled over and washed against the sodden walls, the garden flooded, and the embers from an explosion had caught part of the forest aflame. Kayla and Imani were working to put the fire out with factory ink water talismans, but the wind rained black leaves over their heads like ash, while Kayla's teddy bear floated face down in the koi pond as if it had been drowned.

A distant figure approached up the mountain path. Rips and tears scarred Little Sis's clothing. The beads in her hair had been stripped from some of her braids. She had lost a nail on her right hand. She certainly hadn't had an easier time of it.

Before we could assess the other, the twins rushed out of the house and jumped into her arms. Visibly alarmed at their sobs, she looked at me over their heads.

"They took him," I said, in explanation. By the time I had

returned to the house with Kayla, Imani, and the twins, my husband was gone. As I said the words, I crushed the blunt around my hand, my anger forming an unintended fist.

"They took Lisa," Little Sis echoed. Once the girls settled down, hugging my legs, Little Sis joined me on the top step of the stairs. "Give me that if you're just going to play with it."

I handed it over, and she lit it up with a fire talisman. She leaned back, and we sat in silence for a while, taking in all of the destruction like some sort of chaotic artwork with too deep a message for us to understand.

Between her forefingers, she handed over a talisman and I glanced at the kanji, TRANSMIT (伝) written on the paper. I activated the message and felt the innate resistance of using someone else's ink. Vertical sentences appeared on the paper: a time and a location to meet in three days.

Little Sis took a drag of the blunt as I crushed the letter in my hand. The twins cuddled into my side, and I held them, even though the only thing I imagined holding in my hand was a sword hilt. At Little Sis's return, Kayla and Imani trudged over to collapse on the last step of the stairs. Imani dropped her head in her hands, while Kayla leaned her face into Imani's shoulder. Behind them, Little Sis exhaled smoke into the sky, thickening the night air.

In the end, I found little comfort even in the smell of it and doubted the blunt would have done me much good. I knew I would know no rest until my husband was safe and back in my arms. Not until all those who dared to trespass onto my territory, who dared to destroy my home, who dared to try and kidnap my girls, all come to learn the name of my blades.

They done Fucked Around and pissed me all the way off. We in the Find Out phase now.

RETURN OF THE SISTAH SAMURAI

YO GIRL, TRIPPIN?
call Tyrone
話
234-7
Disclaimer: Warlord Tyrone will provide all of the relocation assistance that you require in exchange for your loyalty, your commitment, and your soul as sacrifice to the cause. No returns available.

Signed Books

$Swag

Available

WWW.TATIANAOBEY.COM

夏祭り
SUMMER FESTIVAL
4月1日
19:00-24:00
ENJOY:
FIREWORKS
FOOD STALLS
LIVE MUSIC
DANCING
TAIKO DRUMMING
CARNIVAL GAMES
AND MUCH MORE...
SPONSORED BY:
THE SACRED ORDER OF BROTHA MONKS

experience the
STREET
PROPHET
CONSULTATIONS & READINGS
payment only in old era currency

RETURN OF THE SISTAH SAMURAI

RETURNS TO ITS REGULARLY SCHEDULED PROGRAM.

AGE: 40

FAV FOOD:

SPICY MISO RAMEN

INTERESTS:

MIND YA BUSINESS

WILLPOWER: ★★★★★

VISUALIZATION: ★★★★★

KANJI PROFICIENCY: ★★★★★

WEAPON PROFICIENCY: ★★★★★

CHAPTER 13

BLACKBIIRD

SISTAH MONIQUE

"Don't burn the bodies."

Kayla and Imani had wrapped their hands so they wouldn't touch the dead directly, but they still gagged as they dragged the corpses, and pieces of corpses, into one large pile. At my words, they both glanced at me in confusion.

Kayla asked, "But won't that attract demons?"

Ideally, we would retrieve a Brotha Monk to perform the rites and see that each person received a proper burial, ensuring a safe and speedy transition of their soul. But that was an ideal world. More often than not, after a large battle, the Sistah Samurai collected the corpses and burned them on a large pyre, hoping to eliminate the bodies before the stench of death could attract any demons. Except tonight, when that was exactly what we wanted to do.

Little Sis and I had a long discussion about how we would retaliate against the warlords. To challenge them, not only would we need more ink, but it would be an advantage if we could all use that ink at the same effectiveness.

Whether they were ready or not, we needed Kayla and Imani to become Sistah Samurai.

I pushed against my knees and groaned to my feet, aching

from the heaviness of our decision. Little Sis said from the top stair, "They'll be alright."

Sometimes, you don't get to choose when you are ready. Sometimes, you aren't afforded the years of training, or the time to master your craft. Sometimes, the world cruelly thrusts you into the moment and expects you to perform. And even though you may rise to the occasion, even though you may answer the call to the best of your ability, even though you stepped up when no one else did, despite all of your sacrifices, the world could choose not to protect you. Instead, it could judge you. It could critique you for your flaws and imperfections. It could question why you hadn't done better. It could tear and break you down. Because to the world, our girls don't get to be heroes.

Kayla and Imani would need Little Sis and I's protection more now than ever before. Hopefully, we were enough to affirm them, and to model what heroes could look like.

I announced, "Tonight, you are going to go through the initiation ritual. Tonight, you are becoming Sistah Samurai."

Both of their faces fell. I had assumed they would be excited by the announcement considering that joining the sisterhood was what they had worked towards all summer. But sometimes death had a way of changing what folks wanted. I wouldn't blame them if today had them reevaluating their priorities.

Imani refused to look at me, more distant now than the first time I had met the young woman. Kayla whispered softly, "You're making us Sistah Samurai? But we failed."

Ahh. I stepped down the stairs and placed a hand on Kayla's shoulder. She looked up at me, with cuts and bruises placed haphazardly on her face like children applying stickers. Imani looked at the ground, one hand in the pocket of her breeches and the other rubbing the pads of her fingers over the buttons of her demon egg. When I first saw these two in the ramen shop, they were the furthest from Sistah Samurai I had ever seen—too loud, too quiet, too colorful, too fidgety, too young, and whatever else I could use as an excuse to protect them from themselves. But no matter my judgment, no matter their past, no matter their mistakes—*they were enough.*

"Today, you were outnumbered and out-inked. Despite the odds against you, you still fought for my family. You tried, and that is far more important than anything else. I've been doing this for a long time and one thing you learn early—you don't always win. Sometimes, learning how to pick yourselves up after a loss can be even more important than winning."

I surveyed the ruins of my house, and remembered all of the losses, great and small, that I've experienced throughout my life. People often show you who they are in defeat rather than in victory.

Far easier on these young women than I ever was on myself, I told them, "Lose the battle, learn your lessons, and give your grief space. Give yourself rest when you need it and never let anyone minimize your anger. Then after everything is said and done, you strap on your swords, tighten your headband, and continue the fight. You got my daughters back and got off a signal for me to return home. Perhaps it's small in your eyes, but your actions mattered. You may have lost, but don't forget to celebrate the small wins. They matter too."

I wished for the girls to absorb my words and accept them. I wanted to push the meaning of them against their chest and into their souls for them to carry all of their days. But their doubts and insecurities created a shield as stalwart as any made by a talisman. I've learned the hard way that some words were meant for later, when they were ready for them, and not the now. Before me, Kayla shook her head, unable to accept them just yet.

"I don't deserve it," she insisted. "There's so much I haven't told you. I-I killed the Sistah Samurai!"

The truth came out of her in a gush of tears. "I was so so so stupid, and I should have never snuck Xavier into the Salon. But he had been asking, and I was graduating that year, and I figured it couldn't hurt to show him around at least once and-and I didn't know! I didn't know he would get caught up with the wrong people and blab about the secret entrance and then before I knew it, everyone was dead! Attacked by demons they said! But then Xavier was walking around with all this money, showing it off, and it was soooo suspicious! I confronted him and he cracked and he told me how he sold information about the entrance, how they had left corpses, and attracted demons to the Salon. If I hadn't listened to him, none of it would have ever happened. And-and-and…" she collapsed to her knees and wailed, "IT'S ALL MY FAULT!"

Then she clutched her hands to her eyes and released great body-wracking sobs, different from her usual shallow tears. Over her shoulder, both Little Sis and Imani stepped forward, but I gently held them back with a soft glance. I crouched down and lifted both of her hands. "The reason why I wasn't in Edolanta was because I had gotten pregnant by the son of my Daimyo."

Kayla's glossy face lifted to stare at me in horrified awe.

"I carried my Sistahs' deaths with me for a long time," I told her. "It's easy for people to tell you it's not your fault, but it's harder to believe it. Trust me, I know. No matter the truth, you still feel that guilt. It slithers inside of your being and eats away at your mind. It distorts your reality. But Kayla, you are not at fault for someone else's manipulations and lies. And whatever part you did play—there is no redemption until you forgive yourself. Yes, carry your lessons forward but trust me when I say, I would be proud to call you a Sistah Samurai."

"Really?" she whispered.

I wiped the tears from her dark brown cheeks with my thumbs. "Really. What's that you're always shouting to yourself? Believe it?"

She nodded, watery, and then threw her arms around me with a renewed bout of tears. But the tone of them had changed. They were lighter than before.

"It was worth it," I said softly.

"Huh?" she asked as she sat back on her haunches.

It was just a stray thought, but I followed it as I explained,

"When we first met, I had asked you whether chasing after some boy had been worth it? But I've never asked myself the same."

I looked around the ruined house, the destroyed garden, and the aching emptiness left behind in my husband's absence. I had also broken the rules of the Sistah Samurai for love. And I had no regrets. If given another chance, even knowing what would occur, I would make all the same choices.

"Sometimes, they're worth it."

"But how do you know which one?"

"That's the hard part, isn't it?"

With a sigh, I lifted from the crouch. Kayla followed, and I was thrown at how fast this girl's mood could switch as she immediately began fixing her clothes and hair in preparation for the initiation ritual.

I looked over at Imani. Sometimes, a direct question with her was more effective, or else she would never say anything at all. "Imani, what's wrong? Are you also having doubts? You don't have to do it."

"I want to do it, but are you sure you still want me to be a Sistah Samurai? Even though my older brother… and my father… even though they are our enemies?"

"What is up with your father anyway?" Little Sis asked as she planted her hands on her hips and stretched her leg out into a lunge, incensed ever since her fight with the warlord. "What is his deal?"

Before Little Sis and I discussed our next steps, I had asked everyone to give a report on their individual battles. I wanted to make sure we were all on the same page, and I admit, I wasn't exactly amused by everyone's individual connections to some of our opponents. The last thing I expected was for Warlord Tyrone to be Imani's father. The past always had a way of coming back around, like a damned ex you couldn't get rid of. Quite literally, in Kayla's case.

"He's always been like that," Imani said. She reached down to pick up a small gecko that had crawled onto her foot. She cupped it in her hand as it crawled over her palm. "He's always believed that he was placed on this earth for some higher calling, but he was a terrible father, and I ran away from home to join the Sistah Samurai when I was ten years old. I haven't seen any of my family since then. Honestly, I doubt he missed me." She shrugged. "He's got a hundred kids."

Little Sis settled deep into her lunge, "Like, literally?"

Imani was quiet for a moment as she watched the gecko crawl up her arm. We allowed her the time she needed, before she finally said, "The vision of unifying the land is a new thing, but when I was little, he believed that Kami tasked him with single-handedly repopulating the island in the wake of Edolanta's downfall. He offers women protection in exchange for having as many of his kids as possible. He wants to return society to what it was before the demons appeared, where men were the head of the house and women were property that cared for the children."

Little Sis tilted her head and said slowly, "That actually isn't historically accurate…"

"Yeah. He believes his own history," Imani said, and crouched down to let the gecko trail off into the grass. Still crouched, she said, "On principle, he hates the Sistah Samurai and everything they represent. That's why I ran away to join them. I don't know. I thought they could save me from my father."

She hunched her shoulders, so obviously full of shame and embarrassment, that even my armored samurai heart softened for her. It was obvious she had been through a lot. While I longed to go full 'mama-bear' on her like I did with Kayla, I didn't know if that was what she wanted or needed. While I saw my mistakes in Kayla, I often saw my hyper-independency in Imani. Indeed, she stood straighter against the sky and said, so fierce and determined, "I want to be a Sistah Samurai."

"The Sistah Samurai would be honored to have such a brave young woman as yourself," I told her. "It's not easy, fighting family. Sometimes, they are the ones who hurt you the most. They may lay our foundations, but we are the ones who construct who we are."

"We've all got *those* family members," Little Sis scoffed from behind me.

"I'm an orphan!" Kayla pointed out.

"Uhh…" Little Sis said, uncertainly.

"But that's okay. I've got Imani-chan!" she chirped and grabbed around Imani's forearm. She shook Imani's arm with a little bit more of the excitement I had initially expected from them. "Imani-chan, we're going to become Sistah Samurai! Wait, how do we become Sistah Samurai?"

I smirked, and answered, "We capture a demon."

"What?" she asked, her voice dropping a notch in confidence.

"It's part of the initiation ritual," I explained. Because of our current collection of dead bodies, no doubt a demon will come along sooner or later. "Now, we wait. Take this time to prepare yourselves."

I left them for the house to make sure the twins were still asleep. I had set them up on a futon just inside the main room where I could easily put my eye on them through the busted-down front door. After such a long day, they had curled up next to each other, holding each other. This wasn't what I wanted for them. I never wanted them to know the fear that they experienced today. Why did so many consider the innocence of children such an acceptable sacrifice for their greed and ambition? When it should be the most treasured gift one could bestow.

I rested my knees and sat down on the deck. It was odd, not seeing the glow of the protection talismans in my periphery. The darkness seemed more absolute without them.

Before long, I had to get up and do something. It was hard to relax with my house in the state that it was in. I began picking up items and putting them back in their places. I didn't ask, but the others were soon beside me, helping me clean up the rest. They helped me straighten the walls that had bent out of shape. They helped me pin the clothes that had gotten wet onto the clothesline and helped me gather all of the rice that had fallen from the sacks in the kitchen.

Surprisingly, when I entered the altar room, I found it in perfect condition. As if the room had been an island that the wave of attacks had parted around. The pink plated samurai armor stretched a shadow across the room while I sat on my knees and lit one of the incense sticks. I held it between my hands, hoping the smoke would lift my prayers, despite being weighed down by so many troubles.

How did they know?

How had the warlords known about the location of my house and my family? I didn't wear my wedding ring into the village. I had never spoken of my family to anyone. I was careful not to use the same vendors so my buying habits wouldn't be tracked. It couldn't have been Kayla or Imani, as they haven't been anywhere else since they arrived.

Of course, all of this would happen right when we had finally started to build something. Was this punishment for my hoping? For my wishing for something better? Was I truly the right one to continue the clan's legacy if I couldn't even protect my home?

"Sistah Sensei, a demon is here!" Kayla whispered, urgently.

I picked myself up from the floor and bowed to the altar. Then, I stepped outside of the house to hear a demon snarling through the forest.

"Remember, we need to catch it," I told them.

The demon, a black hooded creature, slithered into the light of the gate post. Imani and Kayla visibly recoiled when the light hit the face underneath the hood—a visage full of gnashing teeth and stretched skin, looking like a blind upright mole rat. I have confronted and defeated this sort of demon many times in the past.

"Do you know which demon this is?" I asked, testing their studies of the bestiary, as the demon warily weaved through the threads of lamp light. When we didn't move, it rolled in a cloud of smoke toward the closest corpse and began sucking out the lingering soul.

"The Despair Demon," Kayla whispered, her voice appropriately hushed for once. "But I didn't understand the note in the bestiary on how to defeat it. It said…" she paused, struggling to remember it verbatim. "We cry—no, we laugh…"

"We laugh to keep from crying," I corrected. I wrote that note myself. It was another one of those sayings that my granny used to say, that I understood better now that I was older. I explained, "It is a demon that feeds off your despair, so we laugh in the face of it."

I reached into my belt for the last TRAP talisman in my possession and handed it over to Little Sis. She knew what to do with it. I walked toward the demon and as I neared it, I didn't draw my katana. I simply crossed my arms as it lifted its ugly head.

I didn't consider myself a humorous person. I was never the class clown, eliciting peals of laughter from my peers. I wasn't Little Sis, with a wise-ass remark always at the ready, or the person you depended on for a joke to lighten the mood.

The demon surged towards me in a cloud of smoke. It raised its hand with two great talons extended.

I said, ready, "Yo momma is sooo ugly, they think *you're* the pretty one in the family."

The demon's blow swept right through me, as if it was an apparition, or just a gust of wind. This demon couldn't hurt you as long as you refused to give the despair power.

"Is that the best you've got?" I mocked. I looked over my shoulder at Kayla and Imani. "Your turn."

Kayla scooted forward and pointed a finger at the demon, as if her joke would land harder if she could clearly identify her target. "Yo momma so… Yo momma so… ahh! I don't want to be *mean* to it. It can't control how it looks."

The demon raised its hand to swipe at Kayla, and I clutched the hilt of my katana, afraid that she had failed. Then, out of nowhere, shy and fierce Imani said, "Yo momma so ugly, but you'd still be my daddy's kid."

There was a moment of silence to process her joke before we all burst with laughter. My sides strained at the force of it. The demon's claws swiped straight through Kayla's giggles. Little Sis, who should have been getting the drop on the demon from behind, couldn't help but to jump in, "You got a brother you don't know about, Imani-chan? I think we found him."

"Maybe if he wasn't too busy telling everybody else what to do, he could keep up with all of his kids," Kayla joined in, gleefully finding the one target that deserved her ire.

Already laughing before the words came out, I snickered, "They asked your daddy how many kids he wanted, and he said over 9000!"

Kayla looked at me, and that's when I remembered my age. She said, "I don't get it."

I laughed some more. The world was cruel, and so often, the only power the powerless had was to crack jokes at it. We laughed and howled, as the demon swiped at us harmlessly, the sharpness of its talons minimized in the face of our humor.

Little Sis activated the TRAP talisman. Bars rose up around the demon, and its talons screeched useless against the metal bars. The talisman wouldn't last long, and there was a lot to prepare quickly. This would be the trickiest part of the night.

"Now," I said, straightening up for this next part. "The demon must try to consume your soul."

The laughter stopped immediately, and the void was filled with the cascading buzz of cicadas. A wave of life even after everything had seemed destroyed.

"What?" Kayla asked.

"I warned you that the initiation ritual would be dangerous when you agreed to train with us. There are many who don't survive this ritual. If you don't want to become Sistah Samurai, we can exorcise this demon right now. I wouldn't blame you. But if this is what you truly want, you've got to let the demon touch your soul."

"I'll do it," Imani said, fiercely, without hesitation.

"Me too," Kayla said, right beside her. They reached out and held each other's hand.

"I'll be the anchor," Little Sis said as she placed a hand on my arm. She glanced down at my belly, the only one other than my husband who knew the secret. She lowered her voice, and spoke between us, "I'll do it. It's too risky in your condition."

I didn't argue with her, and I appreciated her for volunteering. "Thank you."

"Come on, ladies," Little Sis told Kayla and Imani. "I've never been the anchor before, so it'll be a first for all of us. Follow me."

Little Sis chose a patch of soft grass under the moonlight. She laid down and stretched out like a child in awe of the stars. It was right in the spot where I had once considered planting sunflowers, but thought better of it, because they would remind me too much of the past and old griefs. But it also reminded me of the smell of my granny's hugs.

Kayla laid down on Little Sis's right, looking at me like a child waiting for their mother to tuck them in. Imani lay on Little Sis's left, unafraid and full of anticipation. I couldn't remember what I had been feeling lying there beside my peers, as the feelings after had overwhelmed the feelings before. But there had certainly been more ceremony during my initiation ritual. It was bamboo matting instead of a field of daisies and dandelions. It was in a secret room under the shrine on the grounds of the Salon, instead of a wide-open field, the summer night sky, and the glow of fireflies pillowing their heads.

But the stench of fear was the same. I could still remember the clammy hands of the girls who survived the ceremony with me, and the cold hands of the girls who did not.

I reached inside the cage and hissed when the demon cut a claw across my palm, sinking into my skin now that my thoughts had turned to darker things. I ignored that stinging pain. As I tied a rope around the demon's neck, I pushed away all of the thoughts of the ritual going wrong, and clung, desperately and greedily, onto hope.

Hope was like a sunflower, always fighting to reach the sky.

I peeled the talisman off of the demon's cage and attached it around the rope. The bars disappeared, but the rope held fast onto the demon, even when it tried to escape. Like a stubborn horse to water, I led it towards the girls.

"Feed," I commanded.

It opened its mouth and its sharp narrow fangs framed a dark endless void. Their bodies glowed marigold as their souls were pulled from their bodies. Their souls shimmered—bright golden orbs. Yellow stars of their own universes, and yet, small and fleeting.

I held my hand to my womb, and reassured my little one, "I don't know what the future will bring us, but I'll never stop fighting for it. Now, die, Despair, because I've got to get my husband back."

I pushed my thumb against the tsuba of my katana, loosening it out of its sheath. Then, I lunged toward that dark unending hunger. I sliced through Despair and came out the other side of it.

Gold souls fluttered into the air behind me.

The night ached with cicada-songs and owl hoots as I sheathed my blade. I turned to the sight of the three glowing souls hovering outside of their bodies. No one was a Sistah Samurai until they've faced death.

I crouched and carefully cradled Little Sis's soul in my hands. It wasn't just her soul. She carried the souls of all the Sistah Samurai, a mosaic of pieces of all those who came before us. Tears ran down my cheeks as I listened to the voices, envisioned their history, and heard their laughter. But I couldn't linger. The longer the soul was outside of the body, the less likely the soul would want to return.

Little Sis's soul was fierce and loyal. Kayla's soul was bright and cheerful. Imani's soul was kind and warm. I pushed them together, combining them. Then, I split it back into three pieces and placed the combined soul into each of their bodies. I envisioned a Sistah Samurai doing the same during my ritual, tethering my soul to not only my peers, but also to the anchor—the vessel of all the Sistah Samurai, so that we may carry them for the rest of our days.

There was a song the Sistahs would sing while they waited. I hadn't thought about that song in years. I sang it now, while sitting on the slightly uneven swing. The words ballooned to fill the silence.

Sistah Cherry / don't you worry / for all the mighty fall
Sistah Cherry / don't you know / roots will never die
Sistah Cherry / don't you cry / blossoms bloom anew
Sistah Cherry / don't you worry / see you again next springtime!

Little Sis opened her eyes. She picked herself up with a groan and pulled out a leaf clinging to one of her braids. "That certainly doesn't get any easier."

I couldn't help myself. I lunged forward and pulled her into a hug. Only two seasons, and she already felt as dependable and sturdy as the cherry blossom tree in my front yard.

"Was that the Sistah Cherry song?" Little Sis asked amused. "I haven't heard that in years. How does it go again?"

Together, we sang. It was her idea that in the absence she left behind, to lock Kayla and Imani's hands together. Imani's eyes flew open immediately at the touch. Her eyes were glazed over, as if she had been walking between worlds, but she blinked slowly, coming back to herself.

She sat up and looked down at Kayla. "When will she wake up?"

"Soon," I assured her, but time seemed to stretch on without any movement. Every second sliced at my confidence, and I regretted my earlier assurances. Nervousness and anxiety settled into my gut. I picked up Kayla's wrist and pressed my thumb into her fading heartbeat.

"Something's wrong," Little Sis said. When Imani caught on to the fact that something wasn't right, devastation crossed her face and she flung herself over Kayla's still form.

"No. No. No." Imani pressed into Kayla's shoulder. "Come back to me, Kayla-chan. We were supposed to do this together.

I can't do this without you. Please. Please. *Please.*"

Imani looked at us, for some sort of direction and guidance, but neither Little Sis nor I knew what to do other than call to mind the hollow gazes of senseis with students that never returned. But Imani, refusing to accept the circumstances, clutched onto Kayla's hand and spoke to her, hammering each word into her soul.

"You *are* a Sistah Samurai. You *are* a Sistah Samurai."

"Imani-chan, why're you crying?!"

We all jolted back at the sound of Kayla's high-pitched voice. Imani released a hurt and triumphant cry, before pulling her into her arms. They sobbed against each other.

I sat back, all sorts of relieved. I pressed my hand against my racing heartbeat, trying to still the rushing adrenaline. Gratefulness flowed over me like cold water in the summer. Little Sis had tucked her head between her knees, just as shaken up. We almost lost her. I didn't know if I had it in me to do this one more time, and I wondered if that was the same thought that senseis have made in the past, before doing it all over again the next year.

There was no rhyme or reason as to who made it back, and that lack of control was so vicious and humbling that I would rather not face it at all. I lost peers that were better than me. I lost peers that I looked up to and others that I despised. At the time, I hadn't truly understood the gravity of the initiation ritual, despite all of the words and preparation, because youth was fearless. Until you weren't. Until you were a distraught sobbing mess in the wake of your best friend never waking up again.

I raised my head, tears unashamedly streaking down my cheeks, to those golden lights in the sky.

"Thank you," I whispered, hoarsely. *"Thank you."*

"When do we get our swords?" Kayla asked brightly, as if she hadn't just flirted with death. I pulled the girl into my arms and smothered her with a hug. Little Sis did the same, shaking her back and forth. I couldn't imagine us without Kayla's bright optimism, or Imani's keen observations, or Simone's fierce loyalty. Somehow, before I had known it, we had already become a whole.

"It's not official yet," I explained. "Now, we've got to say the oaths."

Kayla sat cross-legged. I sat on my knees. Little Sis leaned an arm against her raised knee and Imani curled her long lanky legs behind her. We positioned ourselves in a circle and held each other's hands. I often wondered whether we should keep the oaths, change them, or dismiss them all together. At times—they were a goal, something to aspire to, and standards to meet. At other times—they felt like chains, multiplying guilt, and exposing mistakes like a raw aching wound.

But I've lived my life with them for so long, I couldn't conceive of a life without them. It wouldn't feel right not to carry on this legacy.

"Never waste ink," I said. They repeated the words. My solo turned into a chorus.

"Never harm innocents."

"Never betray your daimyo."

"Never abandon a Sistah."

Then, Little Sis, unable to take anything seriously, jokingly added, "Never forget your glasses."

I glared at her, and she smirked, shrugging her shoulders innocently. Both Kayla and Imani had shadows of such seriousness on their faces, until the light of Little Sis's humor had chased those shadows away.

"Never go into battle without looking your best," Kayla added, cheerfully, inspired by Little Sis's contribution.

"Never let anyone make you feel less than," Imani added.

Perhaps this was for the best. These oaths shouldn't control us. Nor should they minimize us into fodder to be used for someone else's frontline. They shouldn't chain us to weights or lock us into expectations too heavy to carry. Oaths should always serve the purpose. And if that purpose was no longer serving us? Then oaths were just words written on wind.

I smirked and added, "Never get too old or too tired for this bullshit."

We all laughed, and it felt good to begin our sisterhood this way.

I shared, "My name is Sistah Monique."

"My name is Sistah Simone."

"My name is Sistah Kayla."

"My name is Sistah Imani."

"From this night on," I recited. "We carry each other's names. We carry our oaths. We carry the legacy of the clan. We carry, now and forevermore, the souls of those that have come before, the present of our own making, and a future worth fighting for."

We said together, "Sistahs forever."

SISTAH KAYLA

AGE: 22
FAV FOOD:
BROWN SUGAR MOCHI
INTERESTS:
FASHION DESIGN
CRAFTS
HANGING W/FRIENDS

WILLPOWER: ★★
VISUALIZATION: ★★★⯪
KANJI PROFICIENCY: ★★★
WEAPON PROFICIENCY: ★★

CHAPTER 14

SAILOR MOON – 2.0
SISTAH KAYLA

"What happens next?" I asked, with a yawn I couldn't catch fast enough. We had been up all night burning the bodies and watching out for demons. It had taken *forever* to wash the smell out of my clothes, and I kept yawning up a storm, but despite it all, nothing could take away that I was finally a Sistah Samurai.

After so many years and so many tears, I finally did it! I wanted to rub my new headband into the face of the woman who expelled me, but she was dead, and that was mean, and I did break the rules. I would forever be grateful for this second chance, and maybe one day, that strict old lady would be content to know I will do my best to carry her soul.

"We need ink. Lots of ink," Big Sis Monique answered as we all sat around the table eating breakfast. It felt wrong in many ways for her husband—*the daimyo*—not to be there. "Which means we're going into town. Little Sis said the Brotha Monks would be willing to help in that regard. There's a lot of preparation we need to do before we meet with these warlords in three days."

Big Sis Monique cut into her bacon and egg okonomiyaki, and I watched eagerly, studying her face as she placed my concoction into her mouth. Previously, I've only cooked for

Imani, but she was the type of person who ate anything. Everyone knew Big Sis was the true food critic. I clutched my knees as she chewed so excruciatingly slow, crunching on the cabbage and wiping her thumb across a stray bonito flake.

I held my breath in anticipation. When she nodded and reached for another piece, I inwardly cheered. From the other side of the table, Big Sis Simone gave me a congratulatory wink.

Once I calmed myself down, I asked, "Do the Brotha Monks make their own ink? They don't use an inksmith as well?"

I didn't know much about how their order worked, and the Salon hadn't taught much about them, other than strict orders not to flirt with their apprentices. I may or may not have always followed that rule either.

"No, they do not need an inksmith," Big Sis Monique answered. "Before the fall of Edolanta, most samurai clans sourced their ink from a local craftsperson, a rule established by the former Emperor to maintain a balance of power among the clans and to keep the guilds happy. But, since the Brotha Monks were a religious organization, they've never had such restrictions. They made their ink in house but in doing so, they were not allowed to sell it. They were only allowed to give it away, but..." Big Sis raised her eyebrow. "In my experience, the ink was never free. While the Brotha Monks and Sistah Samurai have often had the same goals, there have been disagreements in going about those goals. It was important for the clan to be self-sufficient and have our own supply of ink but many of those sources and supply lines have been destroyed or disrupted since the Fall."

Big Sis Simone leaned forward to say, "So eat up. You'll be giving a lot of blood today."

Imani and I looked at each other. I've never owned ink made from my own soul before, and I could only imagine how much more powerful my attacks would become. I buzzed with excitement as I imagined the possibilities.

We finished eating breakfast. As we cleaned up the table, Big Sis Monique disappeared inside the altar room and when she returned, called to us, "Sistah Imani. Sistah Kayla."

Sistah Kayla. I didn't know if I would ever get used to the title. When I was expelled from the Salon, I hadn't thought it was something I would ever get the chance to hear. I pressed my hands to my chest as if I could physically clutch those words and keep it against my heart forever. Every time it was spoken, it was a reminder of everything, of all the ups and downs, triumphs and failures, that it took to get here. I smiled, immensely proud of myself.

I squealed when Big Sis Monique presented to each of us our own pair of swords. I accepted the coveted wakizashi and katana that all students of the Salon aspired to own. My eyes traced the sexy cherry blossom curves of the tsuba and the bright gold pommel sheen. I glided my hand across the smooth saya and gripped the rough pink cord wrapped around the hilt.

"The swords of a Sistah Samurai are forged to withstand tamashii magic. They're less likely to break on you, compared to other weapons that degrade faster. If we're to face these warlords, you will need them." Then, she said even softer. "I found this pair in the ruins of the Salon. I don't know who they used to belong to or what their names had been before, but every time a Sistah inherits a pair of swords, you are given the right to name them."

I had already chosen their names in my first year at the Salon.

"I introduce to you," I lifted the wakizashi, "Sugar-Spice," and then the katana, "Everything-Nice."

"What if we don't know their names yet?" Imani asked, uncertainly.

"You'll know. Take your time," Big Sis advised. "Now, get dressed and meet us out in the yard. Once we set off toward the village, we're not returning until our mission is complete. Bring what you think is appropriate."

Big Sis Simone winked at us, at *me* and said, "Wear your best."

I squealed and rushed off to mine and Sistah Imani's room. I threw open the closet to reveal the fit I had been preparing all summer. No more ugly apprentice robes!

I pulled on a pair of stitched shorts that I made myself, because dealing with thigh-burn during a fight was absolutely no fun. Then, I shuffled my cherry blossom embroidered frilly pink skirt past my thighs. I retrieved my high platform shoes that made me feel tall and of a height that demanded people's attention. Imani helped me to string on a loose battle-ready corset. Then, I parted my hair into two afro puffs, taking the time to meticulously shape them into two five-pointed stars. I placed my newly acquired swords into my belt. Then finally, I tied the Sistah Samurai headband around my wrist like a bracelet and tied it off with bow.

I grasped the hilt of my katana, and for the first time, finally felt complete.

Sistah Kayla.

Those warlords, especially my dumb stupid ex, didn't know what was coming for them.

Imani dressed in the pink jumpsuit that I made for her, which was comfortable *and* stylish if I do say so myself. She hung her skates over her shoulders, clipped her Tamagotchi on her hip, and strapped her bamboo scroll of demon cards onto her back. She smiled at me, and I think we were going to break our faces at the way our smiles wouldn't go away. My cheeks hurt, but I didn't care.

Oh wait. I *was* missing something. I couldn't believe I had forgotten!

I went in search of Teddy-san. I had lost track of him during all of the mayhem yesterday, and I was relieved when I found him propped against the frame of the front door.

"You're protecting the house? That's so sweet of you," I said as I picked him up. He didn't respond, but that was understandable, as he's been quiet lately so not distract me from my training. His poor yellow fur had hardened from the wet pool water, all brown now with muck and dirt. With so much going on last night, I feared I might have neglected him.

"Look, Teddy-san! I'm a Sistah Samurai now." With both hands, I carefully held him at arms-length to make sure he didn't get dirt on my clean clothes, but also so he could check out my outfit. "Wonderful, isn't it? Come on, we've got to clean you up too. You certainly can't go into battle looking like that."

Of course, I was bringing Teddy-san to the big fight. I certainly couldn't leave him here all alone. I lowered him, where the sun briefly caught on the black beads of his eyes. Now that I was a Sistah Samurai, perhaps it was finally time to tell the Big Sistahs everything.

"Maybe we should tell them the truth, huh?" I asked him. "Okay. Let's do this together."

I marched through the house with Teddy-san in search of Big Sis Monique and Simone. I heard their voices coming from the altar room. I raised my hand to politely knock and froze when Big Sis Simone clearly said through the crack of the door, "There's something I've got to tell you."

Gasp! *Tea.*

I swiveled my head around to find no one was watching me. *No. Kayla. It would be extremely rude to eavesdrop. You shouldn't do it. You shouldn't!*

I dropped to the floor, set Teddy-san beside me, and pressed my ear to the rice paper.

"It was me," Big Sis Simone said. "I told Lisa about the house. I shouldn't have, and I wasn't really thinking, and I… fuck. I really don't have any excuses. I fucked up."

My mouth dropped open in shock. The ensuing silence was *painful.* It cut holes in my lungs, weakened my knees, and twisted my gut until I was feeling nauseous. My heart raced for reasons I didn't understand, as if I was in that room subjected to Big Sis's judgment and scrutiny.

Finally, she hissed, "*I trusted you.*"

"*I know.*"

"My business wasn't yours to tell."

"*I know.*"

"See? This is why I can't trust nobody but myself. I should have known it was you. You were messy back when we were kids, and you're messy now. You always have to go and open your BIG MOUTH!" Items toppled over and something fell to the floor. A small pewter bowl from the sound of it, that echoed round and round on the floor until it stilled.

"I'll get him back," Big Sis Simone insisted. "I'll fix this."

"Ninjas and warlords attacked my home! How are you going to fix my daughters fearing for their safety? How are you going to fix the fact that ninjas know the location of my house and can sell it to the highest bidder? How are you going to fix the fact we asked those girls to become Sistah Samurai before they were ready? And what if those warlords are just playing us? And my husband is already—" A croak escaped her throat, unable to say the word. "Get out of my face."

"Big Sis, I—"

"GET OUT!"

I scrambled to push myself off of the floor. Big Sis Simone's boobs almost hit me in the face as she stepped out of the room and closed the door behind her. I looked up at her, at her blank expression. Before I could think to stop myself, I slammed into her with a hug. I was scared that she would be angry at me for the eavesdropping, but she accepted the embrace. She wrapped her arms around me and settled her chin atop my head. Before I knew it, it felt as if she was the one giving me comfort.

The entire conversation had brought me back to when I was expelled, back to that moment when all of the senseis who trained me for six years surrounded me with their crushing disappointment and disapproval. I had thought it was so unfair at the time. It was one boy I snuck into the Salon for only a few hours—a boy I had known my entire life and thought I could trust. But sometimes, you don't know the extent of your mistake until much much later. You never consider how a kernel of disobedience could implode everything.

Sometimes, I wished life was a game where you could go back and change your choices. How cruel that you have to live with it, even when others have died.

Big Sis Simone patted me on the back. "Actions have consequences, yeah?" she said before pulling out of the hug. I watched her walk away, through the house, off-beat.

I picked up Teddy-san and looked back at the closed door of the altar room. Big Sis's shadow was hunched over the altar as the smell of incense leaked through the cracks.

"Yeah, maybe now is not the best time. We'll tell her later," I decided. "Come on, Teddy-san. Let's get you cleaned up. Once we save everyone, I know that everything will be alright."

Of course, the moment I returned to the room, I told Imani everything I had overheard.

"It wouldn't have mattered," she said softly. "Lisa or not, my father would have figured out the location of this place. My older brother has a flying demon drop. It would have taken some time, and maybe we would have been more prepared, but he was coming for us anyway."

Once Sistah Imani, Teddy-san, and I were ready to go, we made our way to the front yard. Big Sis Simone was waiting for us, stretching in the middle of the yard in her signature slit hakama, so nonchalant as if the conversation in the altar room had never happened. She wore a loose haori that showed off her cleavage, and she had decorated the ends of her braids with gold beads and clasps.

Then, the twins came out of the house wearing the most adorable kid-sized pink hakama over their kitty-kat yukatas. Before they could step down the stairs, a hand reached out from inside the door and slathered glossy wax over their faces. The twins stepped into the sun, faces shining like diamonds.

But the breath caught in my throat when Big Sis Monique appeared out of the doorway, approaching us like a general walking the battlefield. We hadn't made it to the warlords yet, but you got the sense that the entire world was her battleground. She had donned the pink Sistah Samurai armor that had been on display in the altar room, and it was a vision to behold—from the pauldrons, to the grieves, to the leather linked plates. A golden crescent adorned the helmet, reaching toward the sky like sparrows in flight.

"You look *amazing*," I complimented.

"I'm lucky it can still fit," she grumbled, and slid the mask of the helmet down over her face with a clank. The mask grimaced with an intimidating expression. "If it gets too hot, I'm taking it off. Let's go."

"Wait," Big Sis Simone said.

"Yes, *Sistah Simone?*" Big Sis's face was covered by the mask and the metallic question caused everyone in the yard to flinch. Since I've known them, she has always referred to Big Sis Simone as, "Little Sis," a title of familiarity to refer to younger members within the Sistah Samurai clan. That one question increased the tension so much it was palpable.

"I ain't gonna take long. I just want to say that you all probably know by now it was my fault that the ninjas and warlords attacked this place," she said, looking meaningfully at me, having already anticipated that I had told Imani. "I'm sorry for putting all of you at risk and for all of the harm that you suffered yesterday. That's on me. I fucked up. And I will do everything in my power to make this right. But you are my Sistahs now and you deserve an apology."

"It's okay. I forgive you," I said softly, and Imani nodded beside me. I reminded her, "Sistahs forever."

Big Sis Monique was noticeably quiet in response. She turned her sights toward the road. "Despite any conflict between us, we don't bring that into the mission. Like any family, there will be drama, but we don't let that distract us. The warlords are our enemies, not each other. Nothing matters but the successful execution of this mission. Let's go."

We stepped onto the road alongside one another, with Big Sis Simone and Big Sis Monique at the center. Sistah Imani and I walked on either end. The twins, Ari and Alex, walked in front of us as we started down the mountain path, ready to do battle.

The sun rose behind us, a blaze of yellow to our streak of pink.

No one was ready for us to look this good.

AGE: 23
FAV FOOD:
SOUP CURRY
INTERESTS:
ROLLER SKATING
CARD COLLECTING
NATURE
SISTAH IMANI
WILLPOWER: ★★
VISUALIZATION: ★
KANJI PROFICIENCY: ★★
WEAPON PROFICIENCY: ★★★

CHAPTER 15

WONDER WOMAN

SISTAH IMANI

I hated attention. I hated people's eyes on me and the inexplicable pressure their weighty gazes built up in my chest. But when I entered the village as part of the Sistah Samurai, an important part of a whole, my shoulders straightened in a way they never had before.

Being a part of something lessened the weight of stranger's gazes, which brushed past me with the light flutter of a butterfly's wings. And they looked. They looked the moment we entered through the village's destroyed walls and its hastily erected checkpoint. They looked as we strolled through the streets. They stumbled out of our way, making room, as if we were a parade of geisha. Little girls clamored to climb on top of shoulders and pushed their way through the crowd to see us.

We were a wave of power. We were a wave of strength. We were the ocean with all of its ferocity and grace.

"Look, mommy! IT'S A KITTY!" The image fractured when one of the twins ran towards a tabby cat lying across the feet of an old man playing dominoes. Big Sis Monique's eyes widened in alarm. She reached out to snatch the girl but missed her. I held my arm out like a barricade and caught the twin when she rammed into my forearm. I swung her up and hitched her onto my hip.

"I'm sure we'll explore later," I told Ari.

She turned to look for the cat, but it had run off in fright. Her little fingers clutched the strap of my jumpsuit as she pouted, "*Okay.*"

Big Sis Monique sent me a grateful look. I didn't think anything about today was easy for her. It hadn't been easy when the twins complained about their feet hurting, or how we had to constantly stop to take potty breaks as we made our way down the mountain. Nor did I think it was easy for her to walk into the village showing so much vulnerability in the faces of the two young girls that looked so much like her.

She laid a hand on the other twin's shoulder, keeping her close as Alex rambunctiously waved to everyone that we passed along the streets. A few in the crowd were kind enough to wave back.

Paper littered the ground, and it bothered me that someone would be so disrespectful to the streets. I could accidentally slip if I was wearing my skates. I began picking them up as we walked.

"That's mommy!" Ari pointed.

I looked down at the poster and was surprised to find a stylized sketch of the Sistah Samurai versus The Hotep Warlords with a date and location of where they had asked us to meet. If they'd been distributing these posters all over town, that meant everyone knew of the impending showdown. I handed it over to Big Sis Simone, who only laughed at it.

"They want to humiliate us," Big Sis Monique said after she looked at the poster. "They want everyone to know that if we don't come back, it was they who defeated the Sistah Samurai."

She passed the poster to Kayla, who immediately scrunched her nose. "Of course, Xavier drew this. Ugh."

"At least he got my ass right," Big Sis Simone laughed.

We arrived at the temple where the Brotha Monks were headquartered. A tall, tiered pagoda stood at the center of a courtyard filled with monks buzzing around it like bees in their orange robes. The buildings at the front were open to the public for anyone who wanted to pray at the shrine or access the soup kitchen. But toward the back, beyond the gardens, was the monks' private space.

The apprentices, young men with single silver chains, paused their sweeping to watch us walk by.

We followed Big Sis Monique up the stone steps toward the pagoda. A pair of intricately designed statues of the divine panther crouched at the top of the stairs. We walked into the main floor, and I froze at the overwhelming amount of texture and color. Fresh flowers and strong incense decorated the altar, itching at my nose. Gold effigies and intricate decorations blinded me with their sharpness. It was so much sensory information, that I felt more overwhelmed than at peace. I tucked my head into Ari's shoulder to avoid the impending anxiety attack.

I was relieved when a monk greeted us and ushered us through a side door to the gardens. We stopped underneath a shaded walkway, where we saw monks meditating atop flat stones peppered throughout green pathways. Maple trees created shaded overhangs, and lotuses floated along a winding pond.

I studied the monk who had greeted Big Sis Monique and Simone. He wore a long white durag draped over his forearm, and his chains and medallions rattled against each other like windchimes. I deflected my eyes at how they glittered when catching the sunlight.

Once the introductions were out the way, where Kayla gratefully introduced me along with herself, Big Sis Monique handed over the message my father had left on the talisman paper. The monk studied it with a grave face. "I have also seen the posters their ninjas have left around town. They have taken someone important to you?"

"My husband," she said.

"Ah. *Ahh.*" A dawn of realization broke over the Brotha

Monk's face. He looked at the little girls. In Big Sis's distraction, Alex had wandered over and poked at one of the meditating monks.

"Mommy, is he sleeping?"

The closest, Kayla, quickly grabbed the loose twin. It was a small thing, the embarrassment on Big Sis's face, but she covered it quickly as she crossed her arms, daring the monk to say something. The monk was certainly wise beyond his years as he sagely chose to stay silent. Instead, he motioned for us to follow him down the walkway. We entered an adjoining building at the back of the pavilion, and I fell back to walk with Kayla, each of us carrying a twin.

My eyes widened as we passed a series of rooms. The first was a hot room, where bare-chested monks, both old and young, sat around steamed charcoal. Their sweat gathered in rivulets that drained down gutters. Kayla's breath hitched. She grasped at my arm, face heating, as she craned her neck toward the room for as long as possible, ogling the half-dressed monks. I deflected my eyes, not a fan of any attention whatsoever.

The blood room was next, where medically trained monks drained their fellows of their blood. The natural vibrancy of their skin looked leeched from their faces.

In the room after that, grown men sat and wept. It was one of the strangest things I have ever witnessed, as if the rules of my world were suddenly broken. *Boys don't cry.* My father had beaten those words into my brothers, even though I knew they were not true. I've seen my brothers cry from a broken arm, or while they were being disciplined, or arguing with one another. But I've never seen grown men, like my father, do the same. But here they cried, providing their tears to create talismans of protection.

We exited the building into a courtyard where a hundred apprentices trained with bamboo staffs, all following their teacher in fluid synchronized motions. Their bald heads glistened with sweat underneath the harsh sun.

Big Sis Monique said, "You told my Sistah that you would

offer us your assistance. We need ink, and we need it made from our own souls. How long will this take you?"

If we were to create ink from our souls, that meant that I would be taking a turn in each of those rooms. Sweating, bleeding, and crying.

"If everyone is working on it, we can have the process done overnight," the Brotha Monk said. "With the amount we can extract from the four of you, within the safe parameters, we should be able to produce a shou of ink."

Big Sis Simone whistled. Kayla's jaw dropped. I never imagined anyone could possess that much ink. It had been explained the Brotha Monks contributed the ink for the defense of the village walls, but I still hadn't understood the capacity of what they could produce.

"And how much is this going to cost us?" Big Sis Monique asked.

"The order has never given away such a large amount of ink before nor have we processed souls other than our own. We will be exposing secrets and techniques honed throughout generations, but we are willing to make this concession because all that we have built and all the progress we have made in this region is threatened by the presence of these warlords. Some of my Brothas see this as an exception, but I hope it will be the first step toward a more beneficial relationship. Our orders have had their differences, but it is apparent that if we are going to survive, it will have to be done together. We can't protect the village, rebuild the wall, and fight the warlords at the same time." Then the Brotha Monk said more slowly, "There might also come a day when we'll need your help, Sistah Samurai. I hope you will answer the call, as we have answered yours."

Ink in one hand, and a favor in the other.

Big Sis frowned, disgruntled, but we knew what we would have to give up when we came asking for help. We needed the ink.

"Fine," she agreed. "Let's get started."

SISTAH SIMONE

AGE: 36

FAV FOOD:
DANCING SQUID SASHIMI

INTERESTS:
FIGHTING
DANCING
MUSIC

WILLPOWER: ★★★★

VISUALIZATION: ★★★★★

KANJI PROFICIENCY: ★★★★★

WEAPON PROFICIENCY: ★★★★★

CHAPTER 16

OTAKU HOT GIRL

SISTAH SIMONE

The jug of ink sure was heavy when the Brotha Monk handed it over the next morning. It better be because I couldn't tell you how much blood I had given over. Even though we were all given healing talismans and rested at the temple overnight, there remained a bone deep ache, as if my soul had been twisted and squeezed out like a dirty kitchen rag. But it was worth it. Even as a Sistah Samurai, I have never possessed so much quality soul ink on my person at one time.

"If you need further assistance, some of our apprentices, the young bucks, can also accompany you."

"No. Focus on protecting the village and rebuilding the wall. Leave the warlords to us. Thank you for your assistance," Big Sis said.

She turned to leave, and all of us began making our way down the steps when the Brotha Monk took a tentative step forward. Personally, I thought he had the hots for our Captain, but he was also a monk, supposedly rejecting personal attachments and all that jazz. I put the observation in my pocket to tease Big Sis about it later…well, much later as in after her husband was saved and this whole thing was a distant memory. She's been distant ever since I told her the truth of what I had done, and I understood her anger, but all I could do was own up to my mistake and apologize for it. It was up to her to extend forgiveness.

From the top of the stairs, with the pagoda behind him looking like a pendant decorating the neck of the sun, the Brotha Monk said, "I regret the lack of support we have given to the Sistah Samurai in the past, but we stand with you. I stand with you."

She studied him, that stare of someone inherently distrustful of everyone. I hated that I ended up confirming her distrust. I didn't know what our relationship would look like after this, but I was so damned disappointed in myself. I hated that I let her down.

She nodded up and said, "Stay safe, Brotha."

"Stay safe, Sistahs."

I cradled the jug of ink as we walked away from the temple, as gentle as if I was holding one of the twins. Perhaps harassing the inksmith to get an apprentice had always been the wrong way to go. We should have been forming an alliance with the Brotha Monks from the start, especially now that there was no central government to oversee what they were doing with their ink. Perhaps we could figure out a more formal agreement in the future. With this much ink at our disposal, and a pathway to making more at this quantity, we could truly begin making this place a home.

After leaving the Brotha Monk's temple, Big Sis decided to convene at the ramen shop. Surprise. Surprise. But when I looked up, I found that I had fallen behind.

I didn't regret telling her the truth. Holding onto it and risking the chance for that information to come out at the wrong time in the middle of a battle was amateur shit. I was at least mature enough to be up front about it.

I brought my hand up to wipe at my sudden tears. Girl. What are you crying for? You messed up this relationship, just like you've messed up so many others. You are always too loud, too messy, and too much for other people.

Sometimes, I think way too fast to remember to shut the fuck up. But there was nothing to be done about it now, other than to make sure I saved her husband. That was the least I could do.

I walked through the doors of the ramen shop, and even though I was feeling down, it hit me that this was where we met the two young women who would become our younger Sistahs. Convening here felt oddly fitting. It felt like it was just the other day when Lil' Sis Kayla's squeal was ringing through my ears, searing itself forever into my memory.

She waved over at me, dramatically so as if she was swatting at mosquitoes, as if I could somehow miss that they were sitting at the usual table. But her energy was infectious, and it pulled a smile from me as I joined them.

We spread out all of our supplies: the paper we purchased, the jar of ink, and a calligraphy brush for each of us. But before we could start making the talismans, one of the twins interrupted with a shrill, "Mommy, we're hungry!"

"You just ate," Big Sis said, confused. The monks had been kind enough to fix us a large breakfast before we left, although it was kind of bland. I didn't know divorcing oneself from earthly possessions included seasonings. What a sad life.

"But it's our snack time."

"Daddy always gave us snacks," the other twin, Alex, corroborated.

"I miss daddy," Ari said in turn and suddenly, both twins were on the verge of tears.

Big Sis looked at them, at a loss at what to do.

"Here, Sistah Samurai," the son of the chef said as he came over with a bright helpful smile. He offered his hand to the little girls. "Do you want to help me pound the noodles?"

"Yes! We help our daddy all the time!"

He looked at Big Sis for permission, and she gave him a reluctant nod. He led them toward the bar and set up a station for them, far enough away that they wouldn't be too loud and underfoot, but close enough to where Big Sis could see them.

I reached over and squeezed her arm, forgetting that the touch might not be welcomed. But I wanted to let her know that it was alright, and that it was going to be okay. I had no doubt she was overwhelmed. The twins were generally obedient, especially with her, but what could you do when the children haven't stepped a league from their home for their entire lives? Of course, they were curious and amazed by every little thing. She couldn't hide them forever.

With a resigned sigh, she moved her arm away from me and spread a map of Buredonoshima along the table. "This is the village where the warlords have asked us to meet at." She tapped her finger atop the location. "It's a coastal fishing village."

"Ooo, do you think we can visit the beach once we're done?" Lil' Sis Kayla asked excitedly. The glare Big Sis sent her way immediately tempered her excitement. She sat back with a pout that bloated her cheeks. "Okay. Fine. I just thought it would be nice after we finished kicking all that warlord butt, you know?"

It wasn't a bad idea, honestly. A mini summer vacation to cool down tensions and relax did sound nice. I leaned forward, and Big Sis sent me a glare before I even said anything.

"We'll talk about a beach day *after* we've defeated the warlords," she said. "For right now, let's focus on the problem at hand. No doubt, we'll be walking into a trap, so we'll need to carefully plan what talismans we are going to use. We'll use half of our ink in pre-planning, and we'll leave the other talismans blank, saving them in case you need more flexibility during a fight. I advise everyone to have a good number of healing talismans."

Lil' Sis Imani split up the paper evenly and passed them out. Big Sis did the standard ones—creating three healing talismans for everyone at the table. She was faster than the rest of us, throwing down kanji with such precision and speed, all three of us stared at her with envy before we remembered we should probably start working ourselves.

I thought back to my fight with their leader, Warlord Tyrone. Someone was going to have to take him down. Preferably, it would be me. I needed something that would prevent any of his attacks, no matter what they were or how fast he executed them. It would no doubt be a talisman that would use more ink than I ever have before, but for once, there was plenty of it.

I chuckled as I leaned over and began applying the kanji. There was an art to it. The way the gloss of ink slipped across the paper. The way kanji combined to create a visual. The way white space balanced with the impenetrable black. I looked up when I was finished and found them all looking at me strangely.

"What are you chuckling about?" Lil' Sis Kayla asked curiously, not so subtly trying to lean over and catch a peak.

"Nothing." I waved her off and returned to my masterpiece.

Lil' Sis Imani's calligraphy suddenly veered, distracted when the twins ran past her. The shamisen had arrived for her shift, and she had beckoned the curious twins over. She was now teaching them how to pluck the strings of her instrument. After they grew bored of that, the old man let them hold the white fluffy cat that often lounged atop his bamboo hat. Then, the tour guide came in, waving at the chef's boy amiably, sending the little sistahs a shy smile before entertaining the twins with a spinning top from his pocket. The entire ramen shop had rallied to take care of and entertain them while we worked.

"No," Big Sis said of the kanji Lil' Sis Imani had been working on. "That one is going to misfire." She grabbed the talisman and balled up the paper and gave her another one. "Again."

"Sorry," Lil' Sis said, apologetically.

"It's alright. Do it again," she said patiently. It was nice to have so much ink that for once, making mistakes wasn't so stressful.

Once we finished, Big Sis made sure to check over all the

talismans that Little Sis Kayla and Imani planned on bringing into battle. They were our Little Sistahs now. We had to make sure we protected them and that they were as ready as they could be.

As we began cleaning up, the ramen chef approached us with a tower of bentos. He offered them to us, so that we would have something to eat during our travels.

"This is unnecessary," Big Sis said.

"*It is necessary*," the chef said staunchly. "I don't know the full details of what is going on, but I know it must be serious. Anyone who messes with our samurai messes with us. Go kick those warlord's asses."

"Yeah!" The regulars of the ramen shop exclaimed, echoing the sentiment.

Big Sis looked around the shop, at this small community that stood ten toes down for her. She forced a smile and accepted. "Thank you. Thank you all."

She held the wrapped stack of bentos in her lap. Then she looked at us—at me, Imani, and Kayla.

We've already talked through the plan. We've prepared our talismans. But there was one big stank in the room that had not been discussed yet. I glanced over at the twins who were taking turns petting the old man's cat.

Guess it was up to me to bring it up. It always was.

"What are we finna do about the girls?" I asked.

"Maybe we can ask the Brotha Monks to watch them?" Lil' Sis Kayla suggested. "They seemed really nice."

"No," Big Sis said, decisively. By how quickly she responded, I could tell the problem had already been on her mind. "Judging by the posters all over the city, there are most likely ninjas still in town. The Brotha Monks have their strengths, but they do not have the appropriate security to stop a hood ninja from infiltrating their compound. Most likely, the warlords have planned for the ninjas to snatch up the girls the moment that we leave. No. They are not safe here." She looked at the twins and gave a great deep sigh. "We're going to have to take them with us."

I couldn't think of a better solution, and knowing ninjas the way I do, there was probably one with us right now in this ramen shop. I wouldn't advise leaving the girls behind either. With no reliable babysitters, Big Sis had no choice but to take the twins to work.

"I know it's not ideal, and they might be a distraction but—"

"We got this," Lil' Sis Kayla said, determinedly. "We're not going to let anything happen to your girls."

"They're going to be safe with us," Lil' Sis Imani promised.

"I know promises from me might not seem worth a damn right now, but I won't let anything happen to my nieceys," I said, fiercely. "You can trust me."

She stared at me, her expression saying a hundred different things right now. She dismissed our offers of assistance, "I should be able to handle it."

The lack of trust hurt. But trust was showing up one day at a time, until the day my presence was a given. I promised to never stop showing up.

We gathered up the girls. When we reached the door, everyone in the restaurant—from the chef, to his son, to the shamisen player, to the tour guide, to the regulars who join Sistah Samurai every day during her lunch hour—all stood to their feet and bowed.

"Come back home safely!" they called after us.

I was surprised by how much their support and well-wishes lifted my spirit, despite the current tension between Big Sis and me. It has been a long time since someone has looked forward to my return. I hadn't anticipated how quickly a place could make you feel so welcomed. Maybe I'll stop being so hard on Big Sis about her ramen. This place was more than the food.

It didn't matter if Big Sis never forgave me.

This was my home too.

SISTAH MONIQUE

AGE: 40

FAV FOOD:

SPICY MISO RAMEN

INTERESTS:

MIND YA BUSINESS

WILLPOWER: ★★★★★

VISUALIZATION: ★★★★★

KANJI PROFICIENCY: ★★★★★

WEAPON PROFICIENCY: ★★★★★

CHAPTER 17

FAMILY AFFAIR
SISTAH MONIQUE

I had come through this place a few years ago when it was still a humble fishing village, but it has been completely abandoned since then. Boards peeked through broken windows, weeds crowded the alleys, and deer bounded through the deserted roads. Some of the buildings had collapsed over time, with walls slumped, resigned to the elements. The temperature had dropped, and the entire village seemed braced for an incoming storm.

Through the broken village gate, I could see blurry figures up ahead, but it wasn't until we got closer that I could distinguish the different warlords from one another. Warlord Tyrone, immediately apparent by Sistah Simone's description of him, stood in the middle of the dusty road. His black cloak and kente patterned epaulets fluttered behind him in the wind.

Sistah Imani's brother, Warlord King, hovered over the roof to our right, his demon cloak holding him aloft like a black kite against the sky. On the roof to our left, Warlord X held his demon drop staff over one shoulder in such a lackadaisical manner, I could probably knock it out of his hand without much effort.

Ahead of us, walking out one of the dilapidated homes, an

unknown warlord tauntingly held Lisa by the back of her neck. That must be Warlord Scrub, the one who had been absent thus far but was probably the one who stole my husband. Just like a scrub, always touching what isn't theirs.

Sistah Simone tensed at the sight of them. Her hand twitched, and I knew she longed to place it onto the hilt of her sword, regardless of how our opponents would react. But not everyone was in attendance yet.

I did not see my husband.

"Grand Rising, my beautiful Black Sistahs," Warlord Tyrone greeted. I frowned at the way our title came out of his mouth, with a tone that suggested an unearned familiarity. "You have honored us with your presence here today, humbling yourselves like true Queens to stand before the altar of my knowledge and wisdom on this Kami-given morning. Let me put you on to some knowledge, my Sistahs. Our minds are shackled. Our country is at war. The demon scourge is a trial sent from our ancestors to test us, to force us to mend our broken ways as we have deviated from the one true path. Surrender your arms and let today be the first glorious step into our brightest and blackest future!"

I blinked and blinked some more, as their leader widened his arms, and raised his face to the sun, as if he could absorb power from it or something. It was Warlord X that released the laugh everyone seemed to be holding onto, but I didn't find any of it funny.

"Five years ago, I received the vision, and I knew that this was a holy land, but a land fractured by the disbelievers and the weak of mind—" By this point, he was really getting into the groove of his sermon, modulating his voice to project it to the cobwebs and spiders in every corner. Sistah Imani hunched her shoulders so high in her embarrassment. Not once had her father acknowledged or addressed her.

But I wasn't here for a preachin' to. Tired of his exposition, I interrupted his tirade and demanded, "Where is my husband?"

"Yeah, where's our daddy?!" Ari shouted from behind my

leg, and I waved my hand behind me to remind the twins to shut the fuck up.

A dark frown overcame the warlord's face, and in that expression, I could see the man Sistah Imani was so afraid of. "Don't you know it's rude to interrupt people? The problem with our society today is that we have strayed too far from old social mores, when a woman knew how to respect a man. When we are born, all Kings are entrusted with an essence of the heavenly kingdom, a masculine spirit that—"

"Can we get to the fighting part already?" Sistah Simone interrupted.

I couldn't have said it better myself.

I snatched a talisman out of my belt. Immediately, people jumped into action and grabbed their own talismans in response, everyone but Warlord Tyrone, who was still preaching to himself.

Lisa screamed as Warlord Scrub pulled her back by her hair. The sound sliced through Tyrone's sermon, and he looked at *her* annoyed, as if his fellow warlord wasn't pressing a tanto against her throat.

"Salami, Sausage, and Bacon," Warlord Scrub greeted. Lisa tried to reach back and claw at him with her nails, but the warlord laughed as he twisted her hair and forced her to bend back at an awkward angle. "You know, she told us everything about you. Everything about your little mountain home and your cute little family."

The fight expelled out of Lisa. She broke down crying as she dangled from his grip. It pissed me off, the utter disregard in the way he treated her.

"It's okay," Sistah Simone said, trying to soothe her. "I understand. It's okay."

I wanted nothing more than to get that poor girl away from that man. I didn't blame her for her role in this mess. She was a victim coerced to share information that she should not have known in the first place. She wasn't the one in my confidence. She wasn't the one I trusted. She wasn't the one who I had welcomed as a sister.

I still could not believe how Sistah Simone had so carelessly placed my family in danger. I didn't care how much she cared for the geisha; she had only known the girl for three months and the location of my home wasn't her secret to share. The warlords were going to come. The ninjas were going to come. But it was her fault they knew about my family, and I didn't know how I could ever forgive her for that.

But right now, I knew my anger and discord would only be to the warlord's advantage. I tried to tamp down my urge to stomp on Sistah Simone's music player in retribution.

"I—" Sistah Simone glanced in my direction. "I'm sorry."

An eruption exploded beneath our feet.

I activated a SHIELD talisman. Sistah Imani couldn't visualize hers fast enough and she was thrown to the ground, but Sistah Kayla ran over to place a shield over them both. Sistah Simone and I widened our shields to encompass all of us and we stood before the explosion Warlord Tyrone threw at us.

Then, hired ninjas appeared along the top of the buildings like a flock of hungry crows. No doubt lackeys to throw bodies at us, forcing us to expend our ink.

Sistah Simone and I glanced at each other. We slapped two talismans of the same kanji onto our palms and clasped those hands together. Then, we performed a double visualization. Our formation used to practice this one repeatedly, and we barely needed to think as we called down lightning from the sky. Thunder rumbled as the flash of lightning brightened our vision.

We started from the right. A sequence of lightning strikes that chewed through the ninjas. Some of the roofs went up in flames, further adding to the chaos. Warlord King and Warlord X attacked in an effort to disrupt our spell.

EARTH emerged from the ground. We released our hands, and I slapped an earth kanji onto the wall that had sprouted between us. I took control of the earth, ripping it away from whomever controlled it with greater willpower, and sent an avalanche of bricks spraying at the incoming warlords.

Elements whizzed back and forth, becoming chaotic. Both Sistah Kayla and Imani were frozen, but I didn't blame them. This was their first time in a battle with multiple attackers, and it was easy to feel confused and overwhelmed. Even the twins had tightened their grip on my legs, despite keeping their heads down, like I had told them to.

Sistah Simone followed my earth attack with WIND. The two young warlords were blown back beside their elders. Then, all four warlords held their talismans aloft. I squinted at the kanji, trying to find a shape in the blur.

"Shield!" I commanded, regardless of whatever it was.

Sistah Simone and Kayla activated their defensive talismans, but Sistah Imani was a little bit slow as the words stumbled out of her mouth. Our shield shattered before the force of their combined attacks, a twirling mix of EARTH, WIND, WATER, and FIRE. I used the momentum from the blast to throw my body over the twins. Then strength from somewhere shoved me to my feet with a speed I didn't know I possessed anymore as I countered the downswing of Warlord Tyrone's staff. Dust from the blast wreathed him, flapping up his midnight cloak.

We exchanged a series of counters and parries, and I knew immediately that he had once trained as a samurai. I wondered what clan he belonged to, probably one of the old traditionalist ones from far in the north. He looked past me, over my shoulder, to where the twins huddled. He tsked, judgmentally. "Such an irresponsible mother for putting your children in such danger."

I rolled my eyes. As if it wasn't his fault that I had to bring them out here in the first place.

Out of nowhere, surprising the both of us, Sistah Imani jumped onto Warlord Tyrone's back. She hooked her legs around him and locked her skates together as she tried to grab for his staff. It was one of the tactics we had discussed to use against him—a priority to separate him from his staff. With a simultaneous talisman activation, he coated his skin in ROCK and crackled with ELECTRICITY.

Sistah Imani lost her grip but caught herself on her forearms as she fell. Her father looked down at her, sorrowfully. "I am deeply disappointed in you, my child. I thought I raised you better than this."

Beyond them, Sistah Simone attacked Warlord Scrub, trying to get Lisa back. Warlord King hovered in the sky, seemingly uncertain on how he wanted to engage in the battle. Sistah Kayla was thrown off her feet after a harsh blow to the gut, and her backpack rolled across the ground. Warlord X stood over her, with a smug smile anyone would want to smack off of his face.

"You should have chosen me, Kaybunny. I tried to save you, but now it's too late. I could have given you the world."

"I don't need you, X! I've never needed you."

"Oh yeah? It looks like you need me now. Didn't you want your tailor shop? With the mannequins in the windows and the fabrics folded on the shelves along the wall? What about all the dolls displayed along the counter? Don't you want that?"

"*Wait.* How do you know what my tailor shop looked like?" Sistah Kayla asked, a soft punctuation between all of the magical blows and the sharp keen of clashing katanas.

While Sistah Imani distracted Warlord Tyrone, who had sent him off on another lecture, I swung at his back, but my katana bounced off of his SHIELD spell. I slapped a talisman onto his defense and canceled it out with the same kanji. He turned to me, surprised, as my katana swept down without any resistance.

Blood sprayed my face. He had swung his staff too late, and my katana bit into his collarbone. A talisman on his staff glowed. This time, I was close enough to clearly read what it said. I raised a shield, but found myself blasted back by the force of AIR he sent against me.

"Answer me, X! How do you know what my tailor shop looked like? *Was it you?* Did you attract demons to my village?!"

Sistah Kayla's voice, always loud and high-pitched, rang out across the battlefield.

Movement in the corner of my eye. I leaned out of the way of a sharp and poisonous vine, as Sistah Imani's brother dropped down in front of me. He grabbed his father by the waist, who had activated a healing talisman to knit together his wounded shoulder. They ascended into the sky.

"I didn't like seeing you happy without me."

"YOU ASS!"

I helped Sistah Imani up off of the ground, and together, we looked over to where Sistah Kayla stood with her feet apart and fists clutched to her sides. She was angry, and I don't think I've ever seen that girl angry before. Frustrated, yes. Tired, yes. Sad, yes. Whiny, yes. But never angry.

"Oh no," Sistah Imani whispered. "She's not supposed to get mad."

The backpack moved.

I thought I was imagining it at first, until a yellow furry hand shot out of the bag. Then another. The yellow teddy bear emerged out of the backpack and then picked itself up on two sturdy legs.

What. The. Fuck?!

The teddy bear *ran,* and it stood before Kayla to defend her. Almost everyone on the battlefield stood frozen, in awe and shock of whatever was happening.

"Ya'll trippin.' I ain't afraid of no teddy bear," Warlord X said. He cocked his leg back to kick it.

The teddy bear yelled with a shockingly deep booming voice, and a visible fire surrounded it. I choked on the unmistakable feel of its demonic aura. Only then did the reality of the situation sink into my head. This wasn't one of Sistah Simone's fancy spells, or some sort of demon drop I didn't know about. *Kayla's teddy bear was a demon.*

The kick missed. The teddy bear had jumped over it and landed on the warlord's shoulders. It lifted a paw, small claws extended and catching on the sunlight. Then it clawed at the

Warlord's face. I covered my mouth, shooketh, as the warlord screamed bloody murder. Blood sobbed down his cheeks. His staff clunked to the ground. Warlord X yanked the bear off him by the back of its fur and chucked it into the air.

The teddy bear glowed.

"RUN!" Sistah Kayla screamed.

Sistah Imani skated towards Sistah Kayla's direction, but she disappeared underground with an EARTH talisman. Warlord Tyrone had teleported away with his son. Sistah Simone charged toward Warlord Scrub who raced with Lisa toward the cliffs beyond the village. I ran for the girls. I scooped up the twins and activated a SPEED talisman to get the hell out of there.

The resulting explosion consumed the village, more massive than any individual spell that I have ever witnessed, as if the sun had widened its mouth to take a chunk out of this part of the island.

The force threw me forward and I took refuge inside the closest building. I huddled against my girls at the overwhelming sound. I counted my breaths as I waited until the ringing in my ears faded down to just the drum beats against my chest. Pressed back against a half wall, I looked down into my daughter's faces.

"Are you two alright?"

"The teddy bear exploded!" Ari cheered. "I want one too!"

"I didn't like the loud noises," Alex complained.

I dropped my head back, relieved that the girls were okay. I wouldn't have brought them if I didn't have to, but my gut just knew there was a ninja waiting to scoop them up the moment they left my side. Or maybe I was a paranoid mess, but years of hard experience told me that I was right. This was the best worst option, but that didn't mean I wanted them around all of this destruction and violence. I thought about our peaceful home on the mountain and wished that peace had lasted just a little while longer.

I gathered myself and peeked out of the doorway. Everyone

was gone and scattered amongst the ruins of the village. I hoped the others were alright—for no other reason than when I found Sistah Kayla, I wanted to kill that girl myself.

My kill list was getting annoyingly long.

I pulled a talisman from my pocket and visualized my husband. I was relieved when he was close enough for the TRACKING talisman to activate. Clutching the girls' hands, I followed the talisman, a glowing thread that led away from the village.

I trusted the others to take care of themselves.

SISTAH KAYLA

AGE: 22

FAV FOOD:

BROWN SUGAR MOCHI

INTERESTS:

FASHION DESIGN

CRAFTS

HANGING W/FRIENDS

WILLPOWER: ★★

VISUALIZATION: ★★★⯪

KANJI PROFICIENCY: ★★★

WEAPON PROFICIENCY: ★★

CHAPTER 18

SURVIVOR (REMIX)

SISTAH KAYLA

Oh no. Oh no. Oh no. Oh no.

I ran through the ruined village with the torn head of Teddy-san bobbing from side to side, hanging by a thread and trailing fluff behind me. I caught sight of an old tailor shop, and the old, faded text of the shop sign felt like a beacon of safety. I swung inside and collapsed against the door.

"Oh no, Teddy-san," I said regretfully. The fluff had curdled around the neck wound and the explosion had blackened its yellow fur. Honestly, sometimes I forgot he was a demon. Unlike those demons that haunted the roads, he was my friend. He kept me company, and was sooo huggable, and was also nice enough to defend and protect me. In exchange, all he did was take the souls of my enemies. He was really nice most of the time, I swear.

I took a moment to catch my breath. Then, I reached for the thread and needle in my pocket and began sewing Teddy-san back up. I had only packed pink thread, but I thought it was cute how the pink zigzagged through his yellow fur.

"Thank you for protecting me. I know you fought really hard," I soothed. He usually spoke to me in my head, but he didn't respond this time. No surprise since he had expended a lot of energy, and most likely, he needed some rest.

I finished sewing the wound, and wished I had something to clean him up with. He wouldn't like to be so dirty. Even though I only had a limited number, I placed a HEALING talisman onto his soft tummy. I activated it and carefully stuffed Teddy-san back into my backpack. I hugged my arms around the bag and rested my cheek on the top of his head.

I had no idea that battles would be like this. It was far more chaotic than fighting a single demon on the road. Not only that, but somewhere out there were still all the super strong warlords, and my stupid ex-boyfriend.

My eyes watered, and I cried into Teddy-san's soft fur. How could X have destroyed a whole village just so I would never be happy without him? How could it be possible to give yourself so wholly to another person, and they thought that gave them the right to destroy you so wholly in return? I had given him *everything*—first kiss, first time, first love—and in exchange, he's given me nothing but devastation.

How could someone be so… so… *cruel?*

I wiped my tears on my arms and pulled on the straps of my backpack, knowing that I couldn't stay here. I peered out the back door of the dilapidated shop into a narrow alleyway. The entire village was dirty and neglected, and my poor platform shoes were having a rough time of it with the dusty potholes and uneven roads. At least it wasn't so hot anymore. With the coming storm, the temperature had dropped drastically.

I reached into a side pocket of the backpack and pulled out one of the tracking talismans, hoping to find Sistah Imani or one of the other Sistah Samurai. I closed my eyes and began to visualize her—her locs drawn up in a bun atop her head with two pieces hanging free, framing the front of her face. I visualized the height of her when she shaded the sun out of my eyes, and her grounded energy that absorbed mine like the earth to lightning. The talisman glowed and—

"Crying already, Kaybunny?"

"It's Sistah Kayla to *you*," I corrected, and turned to find my ex-boyfriend leaning a shoulder against the wall. The alley was so narrow that his body completely closed off that pathway. He lounged there, as if he had been waiting for me to notice him, but in the end, had been too impatient.

He conceded, and echoed, "*Sistah* Kayla." Then, a corner of his mouth lifted as he mused, "You know, it does sound good on you."

I shuddered. How did he have the power to make everything sound the opposite of a compliment? I glanced behind me, toward the clear opening of the alley. Our first objective for the mission was to secure the civilians: both Lisa and Uncle. That was our main priority.

I glared at Xavier. Wasting time with him could mean risking someone's life. I raised my chin, grabbed the straps of my backpack, and then swiveled around and walked away.

"Hey! Where're you going? You're just gonna dip in the middle of our conversation?"

I ignored him and continued walking.

"Kayla, I'm sorry."

Beyond my better judgment, beyond all the warnings blaring in my head, my feet skidded to a stop. In all the years I've known Xavier, he has never apologized for anything.

"I know what I did was wrong, but I was tired of struggling. I was tired of the streets. Who wouldn't have made the same choices that I did? I didn't know what the Warlord would do with that information. I didn't know, but the money was good, and I didn't care. And about your shop… I know it was wrong but…I couldn't help it. I missed you, Kaybunny."

Now he wanted to be all contrite and apologetic? My fists clenched at my sides as I shook my head. An apology wasn't enough to fix all of the pain, reverse all of the harm, or bring back all of the lives that he had stolen. His apology was too many years and too many hurts too late.

My head jerked up at the sound of something barreling towards me. I threw myself awkwardly to the side, slamming my shoulder against the nearest building as Xavier's staff extended diagonally, crashing through the opposite wall and barring my way like the rudest game of limbo. Of course, he hadn't meant a word he said. Even his apologies were used as a weapon.

It was obvious I wasn't going anywhere, until I went through him.

I glared at him until he retracted his weapon and swung it over his shoulder. I pushed myself off the wall and faced him in that dark narrow alleyway.

Ironically, Xavier and I had met in an alley. He had been drawing graffiti on the walls. I was awed by how ocean waves magically sprouted from the can, sprayed along the worn wood. I felt transported to the beach, a place I had never been at that point in my life and was amazed at the experience. That one image had been the spark that had propelled an orphan to dream. But some people could make the most beautiful, awe-inspiring things and still be ugly on the inside. It was a hard dichotomy to wrestle with. His art had changed my life. His art had been a comfort. His art had inspired me to create my own.

But there was no amount of talent, impact, or influence that would ever justify all of the evil things that he had done, or the ways in which he weaponized it against me and others. Sometimes, I mourned the loss of his art more than his love.

Thankfully, I've learned to love myself more.

'Kayla, my beautiful goddess, is he bothering you?'

'Teddy-san! Are you feeling better!'

'Enough to kick his ass!'

'Good!' Xavier had his demon drop, but I had my own demons too. *'Let's kick his ass together!'*

'Then I can eat his soul?'

'If he has one!'

Teddy-san hopped out of the backpack. Xavier took an uncertain step back at the sight of him. He raised his hand to his face, even though he had since healed from the wounds that Teddy-san had inflicted.

I placed my hand on the hilt of Sugar-Spice and handed

Teddy-san Everything-Nice. The wakizashi was comically larger than him, but he wielded it effortlessly. He only stood as high as my knee, and in that moment, I envisioned him in miniature pink samurai armor—oh, that would be so cute! I made a mental note to work on it once all of this was over.

"Come on, Kaybunny, you don't want to fight me."

"AHHHH!" I screamed as I charged forward. I didn't care if I was dramatic. I didn't care if I was a crybaby. I didn't care if I was emotional. Maybe I was crying, but I would kick his ass while I was at it!

I was better as a long-range fighter, but to defeat my ex with his demon drop that could extend to any length, I knew I had to make this a close-range fight. I'd been working hard on my sword skills, and it was time to prove that all of my hard work this summer had paid off.

His arrogance was to my advantage as I closed the distance between us. His eyes widened by the time I was only a stride away, and he reached into his sleeve. A SHIELD sprouted into existence between us. The yellow sheen lit up his eyes, a brown warmth that used to feel like home, but I jumped back. I reached into my belt, and threw a talisman towards his barrier, another SHIELD talisman to cancel his out. Once it disappeared, Teddy-san spun over my head with the wakizashi, and cut past X's shoulder to the other side of the alley.

"Fuck!" Xavier spat as he clutched his bleeding arm. I slashed towards his wounded side. He stepped out of the way and raised his staff to block the blow. At the same time, Teddy-san attacked Xavier from behind, cutting through the back of his calf. He dropped to one knee, and I kicked a roundhouse toward the hand holding the staff.

His staff rattled to the ground, a loud punctuation between my heaving breaths.

"Teddy-san, go!"

Teddy-san scooped up the staff and ran. I pushed off from Xavier and stepped back, barring him from following after Teddy-san. He attacked me with a roar, and I blocked the katana he unsheathed from his side. The katana moved too fast for me to get a counter in, but I managed to block one, two, three blows. *Oh shit, Kayla! You're doing it!*

We spilled out onto the larger square of the village. His onslaught of attacks stopped when he stumbled and buckled beneath his wounded leg. He slapped a HEALING talisman onto his calf.

Honestly? I needed the pause. I backed away from him and took that moment to catch my breath. I leaned forward against my knees as my chest heaved from the exertion.

Small, abandoned shops surrounded us. A paper maker next to the tailor shop. An inksmith next to a pottery maker. It reminded me of the street where my old tailor shop had been, and of the artisans that had been my neighbors, who I had respected and cared for. And he took all of that away.

I sheathed my katana and reached into my belt to fan out my talismans in a mimicry of our previous encounter. I looked over the top of them with a grin. Without his staff, I had gained a little bit of the advantage. Neither of us had our demon weapons anymore. It was just us, our swords, and our magic.

"Come on Kayla, we can talk about this."

I laughed, bright and unhinged. "No, dummy. I think not."

I felt weird. An emotion I couldn't identify boiled through me, and then I realized it was my anger. I was usually a happy-go-lucky person, and I did not like being angry. I was more than willing to let Teddy-san feed on it through our bond. But for once, my anger built faster than he could consume. Tears raced down my cheeks. I didn't want Xavier to make me feel this way, but like this fight, perhaps instead of avoiding it, instead of running away, instead of giving it to someone else, it was time for me to fight through it.

'Goddess! Do you need help?!'

'No. Keep his weapon out of his reach. I've got this.'

I looked towards Xavier and told him. "You've made me angry."

"Ooh, I'm scared," he mocked. He encased his katana in stone, a sharp cutting weapon turned into a bludgeon. There was the real possibility he could crush me beneath the power of it, threatening to splat me like a watermelon.

If he could reach me first.

I slapped a WOOD talisman atop a wooden plank at my foot. The discarded debris branched out, blossoming with greenery, bearing yellow peaches, as the branches speared towards Xavier.

He hacked the branches away with his stone katana until the talisman expired and my beautiful, conjured tree disappeared. I slapped the ground with an EARTH talisman, and Xavier dodged around the hole I created. LIGHTNING streaked through the air, and I squeaked in surprise when Xavier jumped over the attack altogether. My heart thudded against my chest in panic the closer and closer he got.

I needed something unique that he wouldn't see coming.

I grabbed one of the talismans that Big Sis Monique had squinted at uncertainly. I thrust out the GLITTER talisman and confetti flew towards him like a kunai. Unintimidated, Xavier charged through the glittery cloud. He landed only a few strides away from me.

I kneeled and pulled out a blank sheet of paper. I heard him getting closer, his footsteps heavy and thudding against the ground. Perhaps it was the anger fueling me, but I slapped that ink with determined and confident strokes onto the paper. I raised the EXPLOSION talisman and for a brief second, I could see Xavier's confusion as he read the kanji. Then, the glitter that had stuck to his skin exploded.

He was thrown backwards, flipping once in the air. He caught his landing by slamming the stone rod of his katana into the road. But it stuck there, and he struggled to get it out of the ground. This was my moment. I unsheathed my katana and ran towards him. I raised my sword and—

I was blown back. I landed against the door frame of the papermaker's shop. My sword was jolted out of my hand and the torn and half-dangling curtain fell on top of me.

What happened?

I thought I had him.

I coughed at the dust and snatched the curtain out of my face to reveal the sight of Xavier stalking towards me with black writhing tentacles surrounding him. The menacing aura that he emanated pressed down against my chest.

"X, what is that?" I asked, uncertain.

"It's power," he said, darkly. His mouth stretched into a wide white smile against the curtain of darkness that cloaked him. "Maybe after the Sistah Samurai are gone, I'll make sure that Chigakure is destroyed too. Until all you have left is me."

With my katana no longer in reach, and Teddy-san gone with my wakizashi, I grabbed the moon crescent wand from my belt—the demon drop that I had picked up from the Gatekeeper Demon. I held it before me like a shield.

I honestly didn't know what I was going to do with it. Perhaps try to whack him over the head with it like the tour guide had suggested? A pre-written talisman around the handle dug into my finger. I had completely forgotten about it until now. I had created the talisman for fun, not entirely serious about it at all, but I figured why not? We had so much ink. While making it, the words of the Street Prophet had stuck with me, "*You are not a moon princess.*"

I glanced down at the braided talisman I had created.

月

姫

MOON PRINCESS.

With magic, anything was possible.

Xavier continued to stalk towards me. His darkness had grown so large that the cloudy day had turned into an impenetrable night. He had the audacity to say, "You know what? You never deserved me anyways. You were always the one holding me back, keeping me from reaching my full potential. I'll show you what power truly looks like."

"You know what, Xavier? FUCK YOU!" I screamed. Anger

exploded in my chest, so much faster than Teddy-san could consume through the bond.

I activated the talisman. The ink glowed a brilliant gold before me. Then, I floated into the air as moonlight surrounded my form.

Then, my veins lit up with light as if I was made from sparkles. Pink accessories decorated my afro puffs and brilliant white wings fluttered from my back. A dainty tiara extended across my forehead. The silver crystal atop the crescent wand glowed and I felt energized by a power thrumming bright and iridescent throughout my entire being.

I landed back on the ground with a pose. Hand on my hip and peace sign against my forehead. I winked and *real* bubble hearts popped in my periphery. His aura of darkness clashed with mine of light.

I raised my chin and declared, "I am Sistah Kayla! I am a Sistah Samurai, and I protect the innocents from the demons of this world and from ain't shit men like you! You have caused the deaths of far too many people—teachers that I loved, students that were my friends, and villagers whose lives you cut short because of your greed and ambition! You hurt me! You lied to me! You betrayed me! But I am stronger than you! Today, I am delivering justice and kicking your selfish good-for-nothing ass!"

"Come at me then, bitch."

I launched myself forward, flying through the air as each flap of my wings blew away all of the surrounding dust. He launched blasts of darkness towards me. I spiraled around one and swatted another out of my way with a shield of glitter that formed on my forearm.

As I drew nearer, the darkness had completely consumed him, all except the white of his eyes and his shiny silver tooth. He sent a wave of darkness towards me and I surrounded myself with light, becoming the core of my own bright star.

I came close enough to touch his face. I extended the wand, thrusting it out at point blank range.

The inlaid crystal of the wand glowed bright. I considered powering the attack with my anger, but somewhere along the way, it had burnt up like fuel to a fire. It was gone, but in its place, on the other side of all that anger…was true joy. Not the endorphin rush of those small little things I did to desperately convince myself that I was happy, but a true bliss that was no longer weighed down by his actions. The past cleansed themselves of his filth like a window wiped clean. The present lightened from constant thoughts of him. The future freed itself of the anxiousness and uncertainty of his return. He no longer held power over my happiness.

I filled that beam with all my joy—all the joy he couldn't take from me, all the joy I clung to in spite of him, and all the wonderful joys I've yet to experience—and blasted my stupid ex-boyfriend in the face with it.

The entire world glowed white around us. It was brilliant and beautiful, and I cried at the transcendent emotions glittering inside of me. I felt so full. No longer the broken pieces he shattered me into. *No.* I was the moon—with all its imperfect craters, and still shining.

The darkness disintegrated.

The white faded and the edges of my surroundings came back into focus. Moonflowers bloomed throughout the town, beautiful bouquets of white sprouting around the shops. At the center of these flowers lay Xavier's body, bloody and broken on the ground. I cautiously approached, uncertain if he was dead or alive.

His chest moved. He opened his eyes with a groan, and then his eyes caught on me with a glare. Absolute anger overcame his face, as if I had stolen something from *him*. He bit out, crying, "How dare you be happy without me!"

He clutched a talisman in his hand. In realization, I raced forward but I wasn't fast enough. The kanji for TELEPORTATION glowed, and in the next second, he was gone.

"I am," I told him in his absence. "I am happy without

you."

It finally sounded like the truth.

Exhausted, I dropped to my knees and looked down at the pink wand in wonder. Maybe I wasn't born a moon princess as the Street Prophet had described, but as long as I could imagine it, the wand's power was mine to wield.

I wiped the tears from my face and picked at my torn skirt. The lace was hanging off and clutching on for dear life. A hole at the hem was growing perilously larger. I created a new talisman, MEND. I placed it on my skirt and watched as the textiles fixed themselves, the threads tightening and weaving back together.

After all, you do your best ass kicking when looking your best.

Believe it!

AGE: 23
FAV FOOD:
SOUP CURRY
INTERESTS:
ROLLER SKATING
CARD COLLECTING
NATURE
SISTAH IMANI
WILLPOWER: ★★
VISUALIZATION: ★
KANJI PROFICIENCY: ★★
WEAPON PROFICIENCY: ★★★

CHAPTER 19

LIKE A GIRL

SISTAH IMANI

In the dust of the explosion, I emerged in a neighborhood of eerily empty houses. Termites and beetles ate away at the wood, moss and mushrooms wreathed the fences, and overgrown grass punctured through random sections of the road. Overhead, dark clouds gathered. I must have missed Kayla somehow and skated right past her. I hoped she was okay.

"Little sister."

I unsheathed my katana as I swiveled around and faced my older brother. He hovered above the ground with his demon cloak and had exchanged his white shoes for blood red ones. It didn't escape my attention how we both enjoyed unique shoe wear. It ached—how similar we were. Growing up, I didn't feel as if anyone in my family understood me. Imagine my surprise to find that the people of the outside world comprehended me even less, and that those angry, loud siblings of mine had more in common with me than I first understood. Apparently, trauma was as thick as blood.

"I don't want to fight you," he said, shrugging his shoulders. "Honestly, it's a waste of my time."

I kicked off a pile of debris for a burst of speed. I slashed at him, but he floated out of reach of my sword. I dipped my knee and followed the attack with a rising strike that he dodged once again.

I anticipated his next move, seeing it clearly in my mind's eye. I spun, bringing my leg up, naturally following the windmill motion, and kicked something solid. I smiled as I landed on my skates, skidding back from the force.

He clutched his shoulder and pulled back, creating some distance between us. He took on that expression of the bully from my childhood and snorted dismissively, "You hit like a girl."

His words were aimed to undercut my triumph, but I refused to let them hurt me anymore. I raised my chin and challenged, "Then come over here, and I'll hit you like a girl again."

"This is honestly beneath me," he said dismissively. "This isn't even really a fight. But if that's what you want, guess your older brother is going to have to teach you a lesson."

For the first time, he unsheathed his katana. With a talisman, the blade sang with a crackle of LIGHTNING. He spun in the air towards me, like an electric tornado. I didn't think I could counter it with a katana, or activate a talisman fast enough, so I turned and skated as fast and as hard as I've ever skated in my life.

I pulled out a talisman and tried to visualize it as I had practiced—forming an image with my words. I stuttered as the hairs on my arms rose in warning. I threw myself forward. My arms scraped against the dirt road as he sailed over my head.

Skin had scraped off my arm during the fall and my knee twinged sharply. I looked up and flinched back at my older brother's sudden proximity, where he floated upside down before my face. He raised an eyebrow, all smug and judgmental like all of the boys who have ever challenged me. It made me sick to look at him.

"Is this the part where you give up now?"

I tightened my fists, and swung at him. He jerked away, as if being pulled away like a puppet on a string.

I shoved to my feet and skated away from him, toward my right, and grabbed the fence to swing into a manor. It must have been the home of the local village lord. I clomped through the rock garden and jumped up the stairs to land on the smooth wooden flooring of the engawa. Perfect for skating. Most of the shoji walls were missing, forming a hollow shell of wooden frames.

Older brother curved through the frames as he chased after me. I ducked behind a still erected shoji wall and when he drew close, I greeted him with the wheels of my skates. His face almost flew right into them, but he jerked back at the last second.

Through the adjacent room, he twined through the frames and hovered above the garden that lay at the center of the house. This house reminded me of the one we grew up in with its endless rooms and rock gardens, meant to be admired but provided no life.

"It feels good, doesn't it?" I asked, understanding something. "The wind on your face? The speed swooping in your gut? The endless possibilities of an empty sky? You love to fly. But you can't keep running away. Sooner or later, you'll have to put your feet on the ground."

The world was heavy, and sometimes it was easier to fly away from it all. But I have learned that eventually…you're gonna carry that weight.

For a brief moment, something dark flickered around him. Did I imagine that? There was always a dark aura around him, ever since we were kids, but then again, our home was always filled with shadows.

"Let me show you what men are truly capable of," he said as he lifted higher into the air. He raised a talisman and lightning snapped like snakes out of the sky, crashing through the roof. I raised my forearms to protect myself from the sudden blast of debris. I raced into another room and the lightning strike followed. I reached into my jumpsuit pocket for the shield talisman, but every time I tried to visualize it, I had to duck and dodge debris flying at me from every direction.

He was too high to reach with a physical attack, and I couldn't visualize a talisman fast enough. I tripped on a loose tatami mat and caught myself on my forearms as I fell. I was tired of chasing him to no avail. I was tired of running away. Most of all, I was tired of his dismissiveness. This felt like an endless unfair game of tag. Perhaps he was right, and I couldn't beat him. But the least I could do was get back up and keep trying.

I glanced over at a part of the house that had caved in, where the roof had slanted. Without hesitation I pushed forward and threw myself at the roof, avoiding another lightning strike. I easily found purchase in the places of the roof where clay tiles were missing and climbed my way up. At the top, I used the front brake to grip, and then I jumped. My older brother looked up at me, surprised, as I leapt towards him, and struck my fist across his face.

Like a girl.

I landed on my back in the gravel of the dry garden. I screamed when my leg flounced off a nearby stone, and a wave of nausea hit me at the pain. Shakily, I sat up and glanced at my right leg to inspect the damage that the rock had wrought. It had cut through layers of skin and muscle, and there was a brief peek of bone. But it didn't seem broken, thankfully.

Older brother hovered above me, sporting a swelling bruise where I had punched him in the eye. So much effort and pain for a brief bit of color on his skin, but it was worth it.

Annoyingly, he floated sideways in the sky as if lounging on a cloud. He looked down at me, almost pitifully.

"It isn't fair for me to be fighting you. Men are naturally stronger than women. You simply cannot defeat me."

I dragged my hands underneath me, and despite all the pain throbbing up my leg, I steadied myself enough to stand. For a brief second, there was a drop of the mask as he glanced at my injured leg, but that mask quickly returned with his condescending words, "Perhaps you need some help. I'll give you the time to activate one talisman. Choose wisely."

My first reaction was anger, then stubbornness and pride. I almost refused his offer, but with some consideration, I realized he was expecting me to choose a healing talisman. He was concerned about me. Did he not want to fight me because I was a girl, or because, despite all these years, he still cared for me?

And I wondered if it mattered. This had never been a fight against my older brother. Not really. It was always a fight against our father and how he had shaped us. I wasn't that scared and helpless little girl that I used to be. Perhaps he had constructed my foundations, but I've been busy building a home of my own.

I pulled a talisman out of my jumpsuit pocket and winced when I accidentally put too much weight on my injured leg. I placed the talisman on the front of my left skate. It was a maneuver Kayla and I have done before, but this time, I would have to keep the talisman powered myself. Over the summer, I've been learning the power of my voice when I've chosen to use it.

"I am a sky walker. I am a cloud. I am a dragonfly. I float like a butterfly, and sting like a bee."

"What are you doing?" he laughed, as his cloak floated behind him, dark as the gathering storm clouds. "Are you 'manifesting' your win?"

"I am stronger than my enemies. I am faster than my doubts. I am higher than those who underestimate me. The sky is my roller rink."

The talisman activated.

FLY.

I soared into the sky, rising from the garden gravel, ascending above the wreckage of the manor to join my older brother in his domain. The clouds became our ground.

"That is the magic you chose?" he scoffed.

"I zoom through the air. I am a hawk after my prey. The

sky is my hunting ground," I said as I unsheathed my katana. I zoomed toward him. He blinked, surprised by how quickly I whizzed toward his face. A beat too late, he activated the lightning around his katana.

"I am the sky!" I proclaimed. "Lightning is *my* weapon! It is my guiding light through dark storms! Like thunder, you are nothing but bluster and sound. You can't hurt me!"

I blurred past his attack.

"I break glass ceilings! I upend tables! I take up space!" I kicked him in the back, and he went spinning forward. I slashed towards him and he stopped spinning, countering my attack upside down. Letting go of my two-handed grip, I reached into my pocket and grabbed a handful of his cloak with a FIRE talisman in my palm. I couldn't activate two talismans at once, so I stopped thinking about flight, and said one word.

"Burn."

His cloak went up in flames.

We both fell out of the sky, and the rush of wind absorbed his curses. I clutched a SHIELD talisman, and as I fell, I repeated, "Shield. Shield. Shield."

I bounced off the ground, encased in the shield talisman, and caught myself on my knees. My older brother landed with a splat, as he had activated a talisman that had turned the ground to sponge. He tossed his fire-eaten cloak aside and glared at me.

"Now, I'm pissed."

Finally, he had decided to take me seriously. He reached down and pulled off his red shoes. When he dropped them, they indented the ground, revealing themselves to be training weights. Then, he unsheathed his katana and stalked towards me.

We had landed on the street in front of the lord's manor, and as he approached, its dark shadowed outline loomed over his head.

I tried to get up, but the shooting pain reminded me of my wounded leg. I had momentarily forgotten the pain while in the sky. I landed back on my knees, and didn't know what else I could do. Then, in the corner of my eye, I spied where my bamboo roll had fallen.

I dragged it towards me and pulled out the first card. Looking at it, I realized I didn't need to try hard to visualize the image when I had a picture right here in my hand. With trepidation, I wrapped a talisman onto the small card; a talisman that had Big Sis Simone winking when she had given it to me.

生

LIFE.

I raised the card up in the air, and shouted determinedly, "BLUE EYES WHITE DRAGON!"

Bone, muscle, and then scales sprouted beneath me. Wings pierced the sky and the shadow of them cloaked the road. The sweep of its tail toppled houses, and its eyes reflected a blue like the depths of oceans where none dared to venture. The color of its scales glowed with a moonlight hue.

I clutched my dragon friend's nape as he reared back and roared. The sound shook the world, and I admit, I was absolutely elated. I often looked at my collection of demon cards and wondered if they were just drawings from someone else's imagination or if they were drawings of actuals creature that existed in these other universes. Now, I knew the truth. They were as real and breathing as I imagined them to be.

My older brother froze in both horror and awe. He stood so small and tiny before the physical manifestation of everything he used to mock me for. I said, triumphantly, "Get him."

He turned to race away. The white dragon snapped forward, crushing the gate of the manor underfoot, then the rest of the house as it lunged past it and crushed my sibling in its jaws. I don't know if the talisman ran out of ink, if I couldn't hold the visualization right, or because of my older brother screaming beneath me, but the spell collapsed. I fell to the ground with him in my arms.

Nothing was left of the manor but crushed debris. I held my sibling in my lap and whispered, "I win."

"You always had a thing for those dumb cards," he coughed up blood. "It was unfair. All I was allowed to do was train. I hated you. I've always hated you, because you could hide, and people could forget that you were there."

"Why?" I asked, needing to know. "Why did you let me escape that night? Why did you let me go?"

"I figured at least one of us should get out for good. I knew it was never going to be me." he said, hollowly, as if he had gone to the ends of the world and tested this fact for himself. His hand shifted toward his belt, and I tensed, wary of him pulling out a blade. Out of his sleeve, he retrieved a card. A demon card.

"I picked this up a few years ago. It reminded me of you," he said.

"Oh." I stared at it in awe. It was not the small little orange dragon that he had torn in two when we were kids. This one was a bigger orange dragon, with the same fire at the end of its tail. There was a similarity I couldn't quite put my finger on, but it felt as if they were related, or evolved from the other. *And it was holographic.*

A mix of emotions swelled in my chest, and I wondered why having a brother had to be so awfully complicated. His arms dropped, leaving the card in my hands. Then, his eyes closed, and I jolted in alarm.

I rushed to place a HEALING talisman onto his chest.

"*Heal,*" I told the talisman. Heal not just the wounds, but all of the scars as well—the ones I could see and the ones I couldn't. As the talisman activated, something dark and ugly writhed around him like a cloud. I gasped.

"*No,*" he said angrily, trying to push me away, even though I was trying to heal him. He clutched at his chest, in great pain, as the darkness leaked out of him. I tried grabbing at it, this thick black sludge, and tried to pull it away from him.

"Get away. *Run.* Don't you see I'm trying to protect you?" he gasped.

"I don't need your protection," I argued. "I need you to

respect me. I need you to listen to me. I need you to let me protect *you*."

I leaned my weight back, fighting the pain in my leg as I pulled and stretched the darkness away from him.

"*No*," he said, fighting me. I slipped on the grip, and it bounced back, tightening around him even more fiercely than before. He looked at me and said simply, "I am the one who protects you. Because I am the big brother."

Before I could stop him, he grabbed a TELEPORTATION talisman from his pocket and disappeared.

In his absence, I sat there in disbelief, trying to process the implications of what I just witnessed. What was that? Had that been inside of him ever since we were kids? If so, was my entire family infected? That revelation felt so overwhelming, but what could I do about it?

How did you save someone who didn't want to be saved?

I jolted at a vibration on my hip and pulled out my Tamagotchi. Poor thing was hungry. I applied a healing talisman to my leg and fed my monster pet while waiting for the wound to heal. Once I felt strong enough to stand, I picked myself up and reached for my swords. I smiled, finally knowing the name of them:

Blue-eyes and White-dragon.

I began the climb over the various sheets of debris. I took my skates off for easier purchase and swung them around my neck. For the last bit, I slid across the roof tiles and landed past the broken gate.

Once I had cleared that mountain, I looked behind me at all the mess I had overcome.

Finally, free of it.

SISTAH SIMONE

AGE: 36

FAV FOOD:
DANCING SQUID SASHIMI

INTERESTS:
FIGHTING

DANCING

MUSIC

WILLPOWER: ★★★★

VISUALIZATION: ★★★★½

KANJI PROFICIENCY: ★★★★½

WEAPON PROFICIENCY: ★★★★★

CHAPTER 20

NO SCRUBS / TWERK

SISTAH SIMONE

A large lone stone protruded from atop the cliff. From a distance, it looked like a stone giant clutching its toes. The sacred rope that circled the boulder had yellowed over time, which dug into my back as I pressed against it. I apologized to the poor spirit for using it as a shield just as a sweeping wave of water splashed against it, spraying droplets of water that splattered my head and arms.

I peeked out from behind the stone barricade and snarled at the sight of the warlord using Lisa as a human shield. Once the ink in his WATER talisman ran out, I raced out from behind the boulder's protective shadow, chopping my hands as I ran, and ate up the distance between us.

I attacked with a slice of WIND. A distortion of air released from the edge of my katana blade. Then, he shoved Lisa in front of the attack. Alarmed, I canceled the visualization. The edged wind lost its form and brushed past their faces with a gentle gust.

The warlord countered with a blast of WATER, which sprouted from the ground like a geyser. It hit me in the chest, throwing water up my nose and knocking me off my feet. I landed hard on my knee and winced as my kneecap glanced off of stone. The terrain was mostly sparse grass and rough rocks every damn where. When I pushed myself up, the warlord leered at my wet clothes like a creep. *Gross.*

"Damn, you fine, girl. How about you put that kitchen knife down and join me for some fun?"

Why couldn't you kick a man's ass without them hitting on you?

I stated flatly, "I'm gay."

"That's okay, I don't mind watching," he said, wagging his tongue. "I bet it'd be a good time."

"Eww," both Lisa and I spoke simultaneously. We shared a look that clearly communicated how we were both so over this fool.

"How about I give you my number? We could connect with a communication talisman," he said.

I lunged forward to cut his head off his shoulders. I feigned right, throwing my katana to my left hand, and attacked his free arm. He blocked, and his tanto shrieked against my steel as I spat at him, "*No.*"

"You ain't gotta be like that. We could meet somewhere after, you know what I mean?"

"No."

"Come on, girl, it ain't got to be anything. We could just hang for a while?"

"*No.*"

Lisa reached out for me but slipped from my fingers. An explosion of WATER burst between us. My shoulder rolled against the giant boulder, and I reached up to grab the straw rope to pull me to my feet. I needed to figure out a way to separate them. I glanced at my katana in frustration and wished I had brought my kusarigama.

Wait. That was an idea.

I pulled out a blank piece of talisman paper and pressed it against the smooth weathered stone face. I dipped my finger into the vial of ink and swiped a vertical line of kanji across the paper—WHIP, THORN, SWORD. I applied the talisman to the flat of my katana and it transformed into a whip of sharp thorns.

"Oh, you a freak, ain't you?"

Men. How anyone could be attracted to them, I really had no idea.

I snapped the whip and again, the warlord threw Lisa in front of me. This time, with a flick of the wrist, I redirected the attack. The sharp thorns of the whip sliced through the warlord's arm, and then in quick succession, sliced again through the back of the warlord's thigh. He swiveled Lisa in the direction of the previous blow, but I was already turning on my heels and snapping the whip towards his forearm. The weighted end curled around his wrist and bit the sharp thorns into his skin.

They dug in even tighter as I yanked, wrenching his arm back as he howled and dropped his tanto.

Then, Lisa popped her elbow right into his face. His grip loosened, and she slipped free from his grasp. The colorful zigzag patterns of her yukata rippled as she flung herself towards me, reaching out with red-painted fingernails.

I grabbed her hand. *Finally.* I pulled her towards me, into my arms, and hugged her against me. I pressed my face into the rosewater scent of her hair as she began to shake. Once the initial relief flushed through my veins, I pulled her behind me and turned to face Warlord Scrub who had slapped a HEALING talisman onto his arm where he was bleeding at the wrist.

Lisa squeezed my hand, and I turned to find a dark and dangerous flint in her eyes. The woman who I've seen enrapture an entire teahouse with delicate and graceful movements, demanded of me, "Fuck him up."

Ah. A woman after my own heart.

"Will do, babe," I said and cracked my neck to either side. I lifted the music player from my hip and offered it to her. Unfortunately, I could only keep one talisman activated at a time, but I always did my best fighting to some theme music.

"Would you do me the honor?"

She knew the songs as I've let her borrow the music player before, and because of her background in dance, she was pretty good at visualizing music. She gripped it to her chest and nodded. She carried it with her as she scurried around the large boulder to take cover. She peeked her head out, waiting for my cue.

I winked at her, and hoped she enjoyed the show.

The warlord thought to take advantage of my distraction. He charged towards me with jets of WATER propelling the bottom of his feet, as music began to blast from the player.

"You're gonna dance for me?" Warlord Scrub laughed.

"Something like that."

Now that I didn't have to worry about hurting Lisa, it was about time I had some fun. I twisted out of the way of his attack, a pirouette on the ball of my left foot, and snapped my whip around the warlord's torso, catching him in mid-air. Then I yanked him towards me and slammed my foot right into his face.

Tightening my hold on the whip, I stomped him down to the ground. His fingers wiggled beneath the binding, attempting to reach for his stash of talismans. But I snatched that TELEPORTATION shit right out of his hand. Not today.

"Aye, look, I was just playing, you know? If you wanted to touch all of this, all you had to do was ask."

"*No*," I said, a tinge maniacally as I dropped my knee to his chest and clamped my hand around his jaw. I unsheathed my wakizashi, my Ghetto bad bitch of a girl, and lifted her into the air. The warlord shook underneath my grip as the sharp point reflected in his eyes. Then, before he could ask another dumbass question, I snatched his tongue and sliced it right off.

No means no, motherfucker.

I released him as he screamed. All of his screaming was only slightly muffled when he clutched his hands to his mouth. Blood leaked between his fingers and bloodied the ground. He looked so pathetic rolling around on the ground that I almost started to feel bad for him—*nah, I'm messin' with you!*

Fuck these niggas.

As the song continued to play from the music player, I snatched the warlord by his faux locs and I molly-whopped his face to the beat. I laughed as my blows landed, again and again, messing up my own knuckles to break open his nose. And you know what? It felt good.

Perhaps it was a trauma response developed after so many years of dealing with other people's bullshit, or maybe I was born with it—this penchant for violence, this addiction to adrenaline, and this preference to solve all of life's problems with bare knuckled fists or a sharp-edged blade. Women are expected to be submissive. They are expected to be gentle. They are expected to care, and be oh so considerate of everyone's feelings, and do their best to mitigate harm. Well, fuck that shit.

This girl liked to fight.

His screams died the same time the song ended. I dropped the warlord, his face a putty mess after I was done with him. His blood stained the bottom of my sandals and darkened the cliffside soil as he laid there. Huh. I kicked him and realized he was dead dead. There was no healing talisman bringing that back.

"Behind you!" Lisa shouted.

I looked up to a bright flash of fire.

The blast blew me off my feet. I went rolling along the rocky ground, almost off the side of the cliff, but I caught myself before I dropped into the white caps that crashed against the cliff below. Somehow, I didn't break a nail. I pulled myself up, smiling at the burning scrapes and my throbbing knee. The pain felt good, letting me know I was still alive.

"Simone!" Lisa raced towards me in concern. Aww. She did like me. I smiled at her sappily, as she reached for me and helped me back onto my feet.

"I'm tougher than that," I scoffed.

"You better be. If anything happens to you, you won't be

able to take me to the summer festival."

"Yeah?" I asked her excitedly. Sometimes, I worried about showing people this side of myself and feared that there were parts of me too dark for someone to love. Violence was a part of me, only one part of the whole, yeah, but it was something I refused to apologize for. After all, it had kept me living this long.

"Yeah," she said, fiercely. The wind whipped at her hair, her scarf long since lost, and I watched her flyways wave at me with fondness. She stood at my side with an arm around my waist, looking like a vision worth ending the world for.

Yeah, I was in love.

With renewed strength, I faced the newcomer that had dropped out of the sky. Warlord Tyrone's black robes rustled in the wind as he leaned against his staff, and I grinned at the sight of him.

It was about damn time for a rematch.

Warlord Tyrone glanced over at his dead associate, courtesy of moi, and it was funny how he didn't seem all that broken up about it. He simply shook his head in perpetual disappointment. He faced me and said, "This is why women like you are a disgrace, an abnormality, an aberrance that will never have a place in our coming utopia. I see that it is up to me to cleanse you from this world."

I was loud, gay, arrogant, and a woman—the antithesis of everything that this man stood for. Of course, his world didn't include me in it. But this world had tried to wipe me away once before, and I was still motherfucking here.

I reached into the top of my shirt where I kept my talisman. It was a little sweaty from the boob sweat, but once a talisman was dry, nothing could smear it. I raised it between my forefingers and displayed the lines of kanji that covered the paper.

Did he really think I hadn't learned anything from our last fight?

"I'm tired of men thinking that they can control the world,

only ever seeing themselves at the center of it. It's time to fucking decenter yourself, before I decenter you."

"Men are a foundational part of this world. The ones imbued with the trust of Kami to determine the order and hierarchy of society. It is apparent you carry a deep prejudice against men, a prejudice so deep that the light of Kami can no longer penetrate it. You are the problem, staining this world with your hate and imagined grievances."

"You men are nothing but warlords."

"Not all men," he dared to correct me.

I raised my brow. Really? This coming from *him*?

We were just talking past each other. We both had two feet on the same ground but we lived our lives in such different universes. And I was so damned tired of warlords like him always daring to conquer mine when their own was not enough.

Warlord Tyrone lifted his staff. Two talismans along the wood glowed. WIND and WATER created a squalling tornado that spiraled towards me. Lisa tightened her grip on my waist, but I grabbed her hand, assuring her that I could handle this.

"Play me something I can bounce to."

"Not the sort of music I usually play," Lisa joked, giving me unexpected banter amid our life and death situation. So hot.

She activated the music player. I nodded my head and tapped my foot as the warlord's attack descended towards us. But the tornado slowed, and slowed, until it looked completely frozen. A whirl of water hung suspended in the air.

The confusion on the warlord's face was priceless. He asked, "Are you utilizing some sort of shield talisman?"

You bet that I was enough of a cocky bitch to brag. Besides, the talisman took twenty kanji and an untold amount of ink to create. I explained, "I call it the INFINITY talisman. It allows me to infinitely slow any attack or projectile to the point of stillness. In other words," I smirked. "You can't touch me."

Lisa and I moved out of the way of the attack. The spiral of water continued past me to decimate the sacred boulder, wiping it off the cliff face as if it had never existed. Rocks flew in the air and tumbled down into the ocean.

The song started playing right at the chorus. I dipped down, hands on my knees, and popped my booty.

"Don't you have any respect for yourself?!" the warlord demanded. But I kept on dancing.

He launched another attack, this time a combination of FIRE and WOOD. Once again, the attack stopped before it could reach me. I continued dancing.

Twerk. Twerk. Twerk. Twerk.

He exhausted most of his talismans trying to stop me. Oh, how angry he was because he couldn't control my actions. The nigga was trying to kill me and yet, shaking my ass in his face was somehow too much. He expected me to fight him in a manner deemed respectable. But why should I give him any respect, when he held no respect for me?

I dropped down in a split and twerked.

Twerk. Twerk. Twerk. Twerk.

He abandoned his large-scale magical attacks and sprinted forward to attack me up-close and personal. I jumped to my feet and met him head on. But even his staff couldn't get through my defensive talisman. Every swing and thrust slowed to a stop.

The beats between each of his attacks lengthened. He might have a seemingly endless number of talismans, but he was human, and his breathing came heavier. I've been a fighter for too long not to know an opening when I saw one. I deactivated the INFINITY talisman and thrust out my hand.

The kanji that I had painstakingly and carefully tattooed into my arm, tracing that old familiar scar on my wrist, glowed blindingly bright. A maelstrom of FIRE burst forth out of my hand. The heat seared my face, but I had spent so much of my younger years conditioning myself to the heat that I barely broke a sweat. Atop that cliff, fire erupted from my hand as if I had become the physical embodiment of Kuroi-san.

When the ink faded, I dropped my arm. The fire winked

out. Black ash scarred the cliff. Stray embers pricked my skin, and the smoke stung my nostrils. I searched for any sign of a body, and cursed when I didn't find any.

Warlord Tyrone got away.

That scaredy-ass motherfucker.

I lifted my arm and traced the scar there, the scar that identified me as a child of the fire clan. I used to hide this mark from the other Sistah Samurai, as many had looked down on ninja. But I was tired of not embracing all the parts of me. I watered myself down for no one. I would always carry this mark, just as I would always carry the soul of a Sistah Samurai. There was nothing wrong with carrying multitudes.

Once a hood ninja, always a hood ninja—and a Sistah Samurai forever.

"Simone!"

I turned and caught Lisa as she jumped into my arms. I spun her around into a hug, and asked her, smirking. "What did you think of my performance? Think I'm ready for the big stage?"

"A little unorthodox for the teahouse, I'd say. But I'd enjoy a private dance any night."

I threw my head back and laughed, softening when she tightened her hug around me.

She whispered, "You came. You saved me. Even though I betrayed you."

"Hey," I said, as I caressed her cheek and felt the tracks of dried tears beneath my palm. "None of that matter. I get it. I understand. You were only doing what you had to do. But I'm here, and I will always protect you."

I reached down and grabbed both of her hands. A field of butterflies danced in my stomach. I didn't have the patience to wait until the summer festival. The wind rushed loud around us and having to shout over the sound of it wasn't exactly what I imagined, but life was short. "You are truly one of the most amazing women I have ever met, inside and out. I know I can be a lot, but I'll make sure you never feel afraid again and that you'll always feel cherished and protected. I love you, Lisa. Will you be my girlfriend?"

None of the scenery mattered when the soft curve of her smile became the most beautiful thing I had ever seen. She said, placing a hand over mine, "Yes. I would be honored to be your girlfriend."

"Yeah?" I asked, excited. "Truly? YES!"

It wasn't what I had envisioned, but who needed fireworks when we had each other? Sure, I might have been covered in blood and there was a storm about to break over us at any moment, but for all of my worrying, the moment had been truly perfect.

I pulled her into a kiss, and she tasted sweet, like summer ice cream.

SISTAH MONIQUE

AGE: 40

FAV FOOD:
SPICY MISO RAMEN

INTERESTS:
MIND YA BUSINESS

WILLPOWER: ★★★★★

VISUALIZATION: ★★★★★

KANJI PROFICIENCY: ★★★★★

WEAPON PROFICIENCY: ★★★★★

CHAPTER 21

INSECURE

SISTAH MONIQUE

I followed the tracking talisman to the sunflower fields. Since the village's abandonment, the sunflowers had begun to grow wild, staking their place all over the northern hills. I held onto each twin's hands as we traveled through the tall stalks, which reached my shoulders but completely engulfed the girls in the shadows of sunny petals. Many of the flowers drooped heavily under the weight of their seeds, ready to be harvested.

Most folks would argue that sunflowers don't have a scent, but most weren't raised in sunflower fields, or spent their summers helping their parents cut down plump stalks with pruning scissors. Sunflowers had a subtle smell—earthy and nutty, vanilla and lightness, honey and pollen. A warm comforting smell that you missed once it was gone.

At the center of the field, a large swathe of sunflowers had been cut down. A circle of devastation. Standing in the middle of that devastation with his back to us, was my husband. I could recognize his profile at any distance. His favorite white cloak, with graphic kanji written down the back and red flames licking at the hem, whipped up in the wind. The neat tight coils of his hair stood up at a height, defying gravity.

"Daddy!" the girls shouted in excitement, able to see him

through the last row of sunflower stalks. I tightened my grip around their hands and pushed them behind me, back into the canopy of large leafy petals.

"No. Stay here. Stay down," I commanded. I made them both hug a sunflower stalk to make certain they obeyed me.

I continued toward my husband alone. As I approached, he turned to look at me over his shoulder, and his eyes met mine without recognition. He looked like my husband, but I knew immediately that something was wrong.

His nostrils flared, and his lips tilted into an unfamiliar snarl, "Woman, what took you so long?"

I started at his tone of voice. *"Excuse me?"*

He turned around, revealing the metal hilt of the demon drop weapon that I had brought home last year. An electric screech ripped through the air as the weapon powered up. The bright blue light I was used to seeing bled red.

He attacked.

I scoffed. Perhaps the warlords thought I wouldn't hurt my husband, but they had sorely underestimated me. I evaded the initial attack and jabbed sharp fingers into his neck. He stumbled, coughing and wheezing from the blow. Then, he took a deep breath and came at me again. The lightning smell of his sword fried my nostrils as it swiped before my face. He had kendo training as the eldest son of a Daimyo, but he was rusty, and it showed. I hooked my foot into his too narrow stance and tripped him off of his feet.

"Daddy, what's wrong? Why are you attacking mommy?" Alex asked from where she was hidden.

I stood over him, one hand on the hilt of my katana and the other on my hip. "What did they do to you?"

"They helped me to see the light," he answered as he scrambled to his feet. "I've been living in sin this entire time, against the hierarchy that Kami ordained for us. You are the one who is supposed to serve me. I am the head of the household, and it should be my job to protect the family. I have been too weak. If I do not take up my position as the head, then the entire family will fall. Our ruin will be all my fault."

I wondered how many times I would have to knock him out before whatever foolishness those warlords put into his head jarred loose.

I shifted out of the way of his next attack, throwing out a foot when he raced past me. His foot hit my ankle, and all of his momentum was thrown to the ground. He landed softly against the broken sunflower stalks. I crouched down and pulled at his clothes, searching for a talisman or anything that might explain this strange behavior. But I didn't find anything.

"Female, unhand me!"

I rolled my eyes and snatched the demon sword out of his hand by its metal hilt. Honestly, it was more of a danger to him than it was to me. I stowed it safely into my belt.

"You will listen to me!" he demanded.

I ignored him. I tapped my fingers against my sword hilt in thought. What did those hoteps do to him? I wanted my husband back—the husband who promised to be my partner, and who committed himself to fight at my side for our family and our future.

Rustling against the stalks, he pushed himself off the ground and threw himself towards me. Sloppy. The center of his weight wasn't planted right. I had told him to keep up with his judo. Tsk.

I dipped underneath him. I jerked him off balance by his arm, sent him falling over my shoulder, and tossed him back to the ground. With my last thread of patience, I twisted his arm until he rolled onto his stomach, and then I sat on him. I activated a talisman that increased my WEIGHT and wiggled my butt into the dip of his back. I was careful not to crush him, but he wasn't getting back up anytime soon.

I plucked a sunflower seed from a loose flowerhead and tossed it into my mouth to suck on the nutty taste of it as I considered what to do. The shell grew soft, and I parted the seed with my tongue. Then, I spat out the shell against the back of my wayward husband's head.

A sudden realization came over me. Against my leg, I created a talisman with the kanji 魔, DEMON. I didn't like creating talismans out on the field, but I was practiced enough to consider the curvature of my thigh.

I applied the talisman to his back, activated it, and the kanji produced an ominous red light. It was as I feared. This was the work of a demon.

How ironic, considering we were in a sunflower field. Because sunflowers had the ability to extract toxic elements from the soil wherever they were planted, demons generally avoided them. The fact I found my husband in a sunflower field, fighting with them, let me know he was still in there somewhere, trying to free himself.

I flipped through my mental pages of the Sistah Samurai bestiary, searching for what sort of demon could possess multiple people at once, for surely the warlords were also infected. I frowned when I realized what we were facing—a demon that had plagued the Sistah Samurai ever since its inception.

The Misogyny Demon.

My husband needed to be cleansed, but there was one problem. The bestiary didn't have a solution for how to exorcise this particular demon. In the history of the clan, the Sistah Samurai have never defeated it in its entirety. I looked down at him sadly, unsure of what to do. But I knew one thing for certain—I damn sure wasn't going to let some demon have my husband.

"Is that how you truly feel?" I asked him, knowing that demons amplified thoughts and feelings that were already there. "You don't feel that you have protected us?"

"I barely feel as if I have done anything at all," he said, hollowed and crushed.

Was love strong enough to defeat misogyny? Honestly, I didn't know if it was. There were plenty of folks who claimed they loved a person, but they still didn't treat them right. Love, in my forty years of life, was never the happily ever after, end all be all, that people made it out to be. Because love was nothing without respect.

"Do you remember when we fled your manor? We didn't have anything. No money. No ink. No clothes. Nothing. You offered to work in the local ink factory so that we had enough for a midwife to help with the birth of the twins. They drained you every night, and I worried how a pampered Daimyo's son was able to endure it. I feared you'd leave me, because everything was so hard. But you stayed, and you cared for us, and we wouldn't be here today without you."

Hubby had always been so dependable that I never considered he doubted himself too in the same ways that I doubted my own role, that he might also crave validation and security. Or perhaps we lived in a world that would always make him doubt his character when it strayed from the norm of most people's expectations.

"You are a good father. You are a good husband. You are a good man," I told him. "But I certainly know that words mean nothing if you don't believe it for yourself."

I lifted my enhanced weight off of him and then pressed my hands against my lower back to stretch out the ache. "I can't fight this battle for you. Although I wish to, it is one that you must face alone. Would you let this demon defeat you? Would you leave me now? When our girls need us? When I need you? When our little baby needs you?"

He shakily pulled up on his arms, a weak push-up as he crawled back to his knees. I sucked in a breath, gathering my steel, before I looked down on him. "A powerful demon has possessed you, but I refuse to stay with anyone who dares to disrespect me. I will take the children, and I will leave," I threatened. "There is no point in me fighting for you if you're not willing to fight for yourself."

I took a step back, and his hand swiped out to grab at my ankles. He missed and landed on his forearm.

"No," he scowled. "You can't leave me!"

"Then expel that demon out of you!" I demanded. I crouched before him and plucked my pair of sunglasses from my hair. I could never seem to keep up with sunglasses before I owned this pair. I softened as I studied the scuff marks on the lens and the years I had worn into them. "This was the beginning, remember? I was a part of your escort when a demon attacked. It was a bright summer's day, and you noticed how I had squinted through the battle. You bought these for me as a thank you. You said…"

"I may not be able to protect you from demons, but would you do me the honor of letting me protect you from the sun," he finished.

His face twisted and he clutched at his chest, and I saw it now—the black slime that oozed around him.

"No one had ever gifted me something so thoughtful before. Don't let that demon lie to you, twisting you into someone you are not. Don't let it feed on your doubts and insecurities. Don't let it turn you into someone I can no longer love." I placed my hands on either side of his face, brushing my thumb through his beard, and commanded, "Fight. Fight its lies. Fight for us. Fight for the girls. Fight for yourself. *Fight*."

He yelled, and a dark writhing smoke rose from his skin. He stumbled to his feet, then tripped over one of the stalks he had destroyed. He fell back into a wall of sunflower arms. They caught him, entangling him, as the demon ripped from his being. Ooze sizzled as if burned, sloughing off now that its current host was no longer an ideal environment. My husband laid limp on the bed of sunflowers, with sweat glossing his dark brown skin.

I rushed over and released a relieved sigh when I pressed my hand to his chest and felt it rising with life underneath my palm. I gently extracted him from the flowers. He rolled forward, heavy with exhaustion, but he looked at me with bright and clear eyes. I had finally found my husband.

"My love," he said softly. "I don't—I'm so so sorry. I didn't mean any of that stuff. It was as if something had taken over me."

"You're forgiven," I said. After all, even I was vulnerable to succumbing to demons. At least he was willing to fight them with me. "As long as it doesn't happen again."

"*Never* again," he promised. Then, he pulled me into a kiss. "You are my world. You are my home. You are my sunflower samurai."

For me, sunflowers had always represented death and endings, but I was ready for life and new beginnings. I looked over my shoulder and nodded to the girls, who were creeping ever forward. My permission broke their restraint, and they rushed towards us, their hair bobbing. They jumped into our father's arms. "We love you, Daddy!"

"My girls," he said, his voice breaking. He wrapped his arms around all of us. Finally, the family was back together.

I frowned at a rustle of movement in the stalks. Of course, the warlords would have a contingency plan if my husband had failed to stop me. It pissed me off, how the warlords thought they could pit us against one another. I straightened and watched as the heads of ninjas popped up over the sunflowers.

I squinted at the talismans they wielded in their hands, trying to discern the kanji. Beside me, my husband reached into the fold of his indigo yukata and retrieved my thin, wired pair of glasses that he was apparently carrying on him. I waved them away stubbornly.

"I don't need them to take care of a few ninjas," I said. Then, another row of heads popped up behind the first one.

"Darling, wear your glasses," he insisted. I looked at him and at the girls, who he had hiked onto each hip, and at the exhaustion on their faces from being dragged so far from home. Like my husband, I had my own fights to wrestle with, and there was too much at stake for stubbornness.

"Fine." I swiped the glasses from his hand. I handed over my sunglasses in exchange.

He looked at them fondly and promised, "I'll take care of them."

I fitted the glasses over my face and the wire fit uncomfortably in the grooves behind my ears. Already, I didn't like them.

When I finally looked through the lens, I said, breathlessly, "Oh."

The world had sharpened. Someone had sketched in the sunflowers with more shading and color. The clouds contained hues and layers. The leaves seemed greener somehow, veined with light green details and bordered by dark green shadows. I could see the sweat clinging onto the ninjas' foreheads and darkening their armpits with stains. The blurry kanji on their talismans came into sharp focus.

I snatched my hand into my obi and activated my talisman, racing to visualize faster than they could. Before their CHAINS could reach me, the sunflowers attacked. They wrapped long stalks around the ninjas' bodies, grappled them with their leaves, and then slammed seeds into their hoods. Concentration broken, the ninjas' chains disappeared before they could reach us.

The girls besides me giggled and cheered, "Go mommy!"

There were a few ninjas who managed to evade my attack. My husband erected a SHIELD talisman around him and the girls, as I leapt into the sky. WIND spiraled around me, deflecting the kunai thrown in my direction. I landed, spotted the brightness of a tanto, and lunged inside my attacker's defense to block his forearm with my own. Then I cut that forearm off and slashed through his chest in the next motion.

I turned and found a ninja lifting a talisman to their lips, marked with the kanji for POISON. I snatched a kunai from the dead ninja, attached a SHIELD talisman to the handle, and threw it. The blast of poison left the ninja's lips as the shield erected around him, poisoning himself.

I dipped underneath a blast of water. I TELEPORTED behind my attacker and swiped my katana across her shoulders. Sweeping away her head and thick jumbo braids along with a harvest of flowers. The fat seed-heavy flowerheads plopped to the ground.

Sunflowers waved in my peripheral vision. I parried the swipe of a ninja's tanto. Her left foot shifted back, and I was already there to meet her next attack. A twitch of muscle and I knew exactly what was coming next. I blocked the swing and cut across the ninja's stomach.

When no one else attacked, I slapped an EARTH talisman to the ground, using it to swallow the bodies of the dead ninjas.

I paused, always giving time to make sure it was over, before I cleaned and sheathed my katana. I rubbed at my throbbing knee, surprised it hadn't slowed me down as much as I thought it would.

Were my slowing reflexes all in my head? And here I was thinking I was getting old.

Turned out, I couldn't see.

My husband grinned with a clear, 'I told you so' look on his face.

"Yeah, whatever," I said.

The twins clambered out of his arms to hug me about the legs. We each took responsibility for a twin, claiming a tiny hand. My arm swung as the twins skipped between us.

"What a nice family outing," Hubby said brightly.

I snorted at his humor. As far as family outings went, I guess it wasn't so bad. After all, it was a nice cool day, and the rain was holding for now. Maybe the glasses weren't all that terrible as the rolling hills of gold were truly a sight to behold, with petals sketched in such intimate detail that I finally remembered my childhood love for their bright unapologetic yellow.

I happily walked with my family through the sunflower fields.

AGE: 22

FAV FOOD:
BROWN SUGAR MOCHI

INTERESTS:
FASHION DESIGN
CRAFTS
HANGING W/FRIENDS

WILLPOWER: ★★
VISUALIZATION: ★★★⯪
KANJI PROFICIENCY: ★★★
WEAPON PROFICIENCY: ★★

WHAT I CHOOSE

SISTAH KAYLA

If the formation got separated, the plan was to meet at the village shrine to regroup. I was terrible with maps and directions, and honestly, the shrine found me. It thankfully sprouted not far from where I reunited with Teddy-san. Around the modest shrine, green ferns burst forth between stacked stones. Moss covered the stone torii gate. The red paint of the shrine had chipped and faded over time, and the paper streamers hung in tatters from the eaves. Aged bird poop speckled the entire area. I carefully spread my backpack on the steps, before sitting down with Teddy-san in my lap. Lightly scattered drops of rain began to fall.

"I hope everyone is okay," I said, worried by the fact that I was the first person here. Generally, I'm never the first person to arrive anywhere.

'I can go look for them, my dear goddess?'

"No, our orders were to meet here," I told Teddy-san and then straightened to see someone limping up the road. "Imani-chan!"

I raced towards her and put an arm around her waist, while Teddy-san lifted her wounded leg over his head. We helped her hop over to where I had spread my backpack across the stairs.

We sat her down and I immediately applied a healing talisman to her leg.

"I used all my healing talismans," Imani explained. "The ink faded before it fully healed."

"No worries," I told her. I settled onto my knees and closed my eyes to visualize the numbness of pain, muscles knitting back together, and smooth unmarred skin. Teddy-san jumped into her lap, and she patted him on the forehead. She couldn't communicate with him in the same way that I could, but Imani never really needed words to make friends with someone.

"You were supposed to stay hidden, Teddy-san," Imani said gently. "People aren't going to understand."

A rising voice approached down the opposite road. Of course, you could hear Big Sis Simone almost five minutes before you could see her. I brightened to see her walking hand-in-hand with a woman I assumed was Lisa. She was breathtakingly pretty, like the sort of graceful beauty of the perfect flower arrangement.

"Good. You're both here." Big Sis Simone plopped both hands on her hips as she looked at the both of us, all serious like as if preparing to give us bad news, until her face broke into a cheeky grin. "Have I introduced you to my *girlfriend*, Lisa?"

"That's wonderful!" I squealed in excitement. "I'm Sistah Kayla and this is Sistah Imani. We've heard so much about you! She talks about you *all* the time. I'm so glad to finally meet you!"

"Why don't y'all talk while I make these tracking talismans. I'm gonna see if I can pinpoint Big Sis' location." Big Sis Simone said. She stomped her foot against the stone wall as she retrieved her calligraphy materials.

"Thank you so much for your help in saving me," Lisa said, with a smile that reminded me of the nice lady who used to feed me sometimes when I was an orphan. There was such an aura of blue around her, you know?

"Anytime!" I said. "Well, I mean, not that you should keep

getting kidnapped but if you do, we're here!"

"I appreciate that." She smiled sweetly. "But I've certainly had enough of being kidnapped for a lifetime. It is good to meet you both." Her gaze lingered on Imani, and she told her softly, "He protected me—your brother. He was in charge of watching me. He made sure nothing happened to me."

"Oh, I—" Imani couldn't find the words to say anything before Big Sis Simone had activated the tracking talismans. They glowed, hovering above both her palms and pointed in the same direction. She said, "Looks like Big Sis and brother-in-law are in the same location. They'll probably be on their way soon. Take a moment to rest, heal up, and eat something. I don't know, lil' sis, maybe also get your funeral rites ready. Better hope she's in a good mood."

I gulped and looked down at Teddy-san nervously. I should have told them about him from the beginning, but I knew they wouldn't have agreed to train me if they had known. Teddy-san and I were bonded together, and I had made a promise to be his friend. I couldn't just abandon him. But I also couldn't let this opportunity to become a Sistah Samurai slip from my fingers either. It was all I've ever wanted.

Imani tugged at the poofy part of my sleeve, alerting me to the four figures coming up from the road. I brightened at the sight of the twins and was happy to see that the Daimyo was safe and well. Perhaps, Big Sis Monique was in a good mood, after all.

She scanned over all of us. Then her gaze landed on me, and my stomach dropped. I snatched Teddy-san into my arms, afraid she was going to harm him, as she stomped towards me. Big Sis Simone moved to get in her way, but she was no match for Big Sis Monique's glare. She raised her hands and backed away.

Her anger had me trembling as she aimed a dangerous pointed finger at me.

"You had a demon in my home, around my family, around my *daughters*, while we fed, housed, and trained you this entire time?! *How dare you!*"

"He's a good demon," I tried to explain. "He wouldn't hurt anyone who didn't deserve it."

"There's no such thing as a good demon!"

"He is!" I argued.

"You are a foolish and naïve child!"

"He got past your protection talismans," I argued. "The protection talismans blocked the ninjas when they attacked, but they didn't block Teddy-san because he never meant anyone any harm. He's safe."

But she refused to listen. "What deal have you made with it? There is always a price, even if you don't know it yet."

"We're friends! He feeds on my anger, yeah, but I don't like being angry. He's also really scared of other demons. Like, *terrified*."

She became a looming shadow that towered over me as she hissed, "If that's the case, if you believe him to be so harmless, then why didn't you say anything?!"

"Because I was scared!" I sobbed. "I knew you wouldn't understand him. I knew you wouldn't want to train me."

"You damn right I wouldn't have!" She unsheathed her wakizashi and everyone surged forward in defense of me, alarmed.

"Hold on, Big Sis—"

She raised her hand, stilling everyone as if she had activated a HALT talisman. She tossed her wakizashi at my feet. I started at it, not understanding until she explained, "When you make mistakes as an apprentice, you get expelled. When you make mistakes as a Sistah Samurai, there is only one way to regain your honor."

My breath hitched. My knees buckled underneath me and the edges of my skirt landed in a muddy puddle. But I couldn't even focus on the horrors of getting them dirty at that moment as her blade stared at me like a wicked mirror. She was asking me to perform hara-kiri.

My hand shook as I reached for the blade.

"Don't you think this is a little extreme?" Big Sis Simone asked. "You didn't demand this of me when I messed up."

"When you messed up, you told me the truth," she spat. "At least I can trust you to do that. But *you*," she glared at me, "are untrustworthy. You have proven that you have learned nothing since your expulsion. When we started this, I told you I had two rules: Not to waste my time and to keep the location of my home a secret. Keeping it a secret includes not inviting your fucking demon teddy bear in without my knowledge! You have no honor, Sistah Kayla."

Her words stabbed me like sewing needles inserted in every part of my skin. I could see the anger, the disappointment, and the betrayal in her expression and it shattered me into a hundred different pieces. I was back to that moment again—surrounded by the Salon senseis, when they told to pack up my bags and never return. Except this time was worse. This time, you'd think I'd know better.

I'd just confronted my ex, finally coming to terms with the consequences of his actions. Now, it was time for me to take accountability for mine. What sort of samurai would I be if I could not keep true to my oaths? Everything began to blur as tears streamed down my face. I knew Teddy-san wouldn't have harmed anyone. But I had lied to her by omission, and she was right, I had broken my promises.

I unsheathed the wakizashi from the pink sheath. Teddy-san jumped towards me, but I sent a look toward Imani, and she grabbed him for me. She stood there frozen. I hated to leave her alone after I promised her that I wouldn't, but I knew that she would be fine by herself. It was always me that truly needed her.

I looked up at Big Sis Monique, yet another teacher whose expectations I failed to meet. Despite how hard I've tried, I've always managed to mess everything up. Why couldn't I ever do anything right? Perhaps this was why it had taken so long for me to come back during the initiation ritual. Perhaps deep down I had known that no matter how much I wanted it, that the pink swords were never meant for me. The swords were meant for a girl who was perfect—who didn't make careless little mistakes and who didn't know what it felt like to be broken by her own reckless hands. It was meant for a girl who didn't feel the need to cover herself in bows and frills just to hold herself together, and to hide herself in cute pretty things because she had seen the ugliest parts of the world. It was meant for a girl who didn't let her own fear destroy her.

"I'm sorry," I told my Big Sis. "The last thing I ever wanted to do was let you down."

"That is enough," Big Sis Simone said, stepping in front of me. "You're taking this too far. Yeah, she fucked up, but the damned teddy bear ain't hurt nobody. If anything, it was my mistake that got people hurt and got us into this mess. If anyone needs to redeem their honor, it's me."

Despite just rescuing her girlfriend and all the things for her to look forward to, Big Sis Simone didn't hesitate to lower herself to her knees beside me and unsheathed her wakizashi.

"Me too," Imani declared, and she knelt down next to my other side. She unsheathed her wakizashi too. "I knew about Teddy-san and I didn't say anything. I'm just as much to blame as Sistah Kayla. Her dishonor is my dishonor."

"Wait. No. Stop," I told them. One of my biggest regrets was how I had gotten Imani expelled right along with me. I certainly didn't want her or anyone else paying for my mistakes anymore. "It's okay. I might not get to live as a samurai, but at least I'll die as one."

I apologized to myself and tightened my grip on the hilt of the wakizashi, ready to self-immolate for her forgiveness and approval. I moved the hilt forward.

"Kayla-chan!"

'My beautiful goddess!'

"No, don't!"

Then, I moved to plunge the blade into my gut. A strong grip caught my wrist, stopping me. I looked up, to a leaf twirling down from a tree overhead. It landed and stuck to the large afro that hovered over me like a shield talisman.

"Enough," Big Sis whispered, tightening her hold around my wrist, enough to force me to dropped the blade. I shook and sobbed as she pulled me forward into her arms. I messed up. But in that moment, I wondered what would have happened if instead of the Salon expelling me, if they had embraced me instead? I sobbed, *"I'm sorry. Truly. I am. I never meant to hurt anyone. Please. Give me another chance. Please. I'm so-so sorry."*

"I'm sorry too," she whispered above me. "I let my anger get the best of me, as you allowed your fear to get the best of you. Perhaps that's something we can work on together."

I looked at her, uncertainly. "Truly?"

She loosened her embrace and turned to the sky where rain tapped tears onto her face. "That depends on you. Only you can define your honor."

I pressed my hand against my belly, in the place where the blade would have sunk into my gut. Honestly, I didn't know if I deserved her forgiveness. I didn't know if I deserved another chance.

"I don't know," I said hoarsely and told her the awful truth. "I don't know if I should be a Sistah Samurai. I also lied about my age to get accepted into the Salon. I even started with a lie."

"Sistah Kayla, you have one of the most natural talents at visualization that I have ever seen. You are a loyal friend, a determined fighter, and display the skills of a good leader. There is so much potential in you. You are truly a special young woman. But you cannot let fear win. You cannot let those doubts and insecurities win. Or else, you're already defeated. Until the time comes that you can truly and wholly believe in yourself, then I see that it is up to your Sistahs to do it for you. All I ask is that you follow my rules and strive to meet what I demand of you."

Complicated emotions swelled in my chest at her words. Sometimes, the grace of those who believed in you could be far more powerful than the demons in your head.

I pushed myself to my feet and felt a swoop of lightheadedness at the motion. Imani caught my hand and Big Sis Simone steadied me.

"I'll do my best to do whatever you ask of me. I'll never lie to you or any of my Sistahs ever again. This is the last time you'll be forced to carry my dishonor."

"It's all of our dishonor," she corrected, gently, as she scanned the faces of the others. "We'll carry it together."

I nodded, grateful, overwhelmed by how she truly wanted the best for me and wanted to see me succeed. "I'll do better. I swear this to all of you, on my honor."

"We'll hold you to that, Sistah Kayla."

I resolved to never let her or my Sistahs down ever again. Because at the end of the day, no matter my flaws or my mistakes, I *am* a Sistah Samurai.

And I finally chose to believe it.

AGE: 23
FAV FOOD:
SOUP CURRY
INTERESTS:
ROLLER SKATING
CARD COLLECTING
NATURE
SISTAH IMANI
WILLPOWER: ★★
VISUALIZATION: ★
KANJI PROFICIENCY: ★★
WEAPON PROFICIENCY: ★★★

CHAPTER 23

OWN YOUR OWN

SISTAH IMANI

Kayla leaned her head on my shoulder as I played with my Tamagotchi while we sat on the stone steps of the shrine. Even though the events of the past fifteen minutes had happened to Kayla, the high emotions shooting from so many people had struck me mute afterwards. Words just wouldn't come and while I wanted to be a better friend and offer some sort of comfort after everything that happened, I had sunk inside myself until the world muffled around me.

A rain drop splashed on the screen of my Tamagotchi, startling me, and all of the sensory information I had been blocking out returned in a sudden whoosh—the smacking from the twins as they ate snacks that Big Sis Monique had brought for them, the press of Kayla's arm on mine as she wove thread through a rip in Teddy-san, and the tap tap tap of rain. The humidity had become so heavy I could taste the clouds in the air.

I looked over at Kayla and asked, "Are you okay?"

"Yeah," she answered. "Of course, I am."

I dropped my head, uncertain by her unwavering trust in me. "I should have asked sooner."

"That's silly, Imani-chan. I don't need you to do anything

but be you." She raised her hand and stuck out her pinky finger, a mimicry of the promise we had made to each other when we exited the gates of the Salon for the last time. Who would have known that together, our paths would lead us here? "Best friends forever."

With a smile, I curled my pinky around her own, and reaffirmed our pinky-promise, "Best friends forever."

"Aww, how cute."

I whirled around to see Big Sis Simone walking out of the trees behind the shrine. I hadn't even realized she had left.

"We're in the clear now," she reported. "I took care of the ninja trying to spy on us. The only ones left out here is us."

"Good," Big Sis Monique said from where she had been sitting atop her husband's cloak she had spread over the damp grass. He and the twins ate lunch beneath a large conifer as if they were out on a picnic. "Now that you've established a perimeter, we need to talk strategy."

She approached us and leaned against the stone torii gate. "It's time to debrief. How many warlords are still in play? Did anyone take any of them out?"

"Almost," Kayla admitted. "But he got away."

I shook my head.

"Well. I got mine." Big Sis Simone smirked. "I also had a go at it with Warlord Tyrone and got him to expend most of his talismans. I wouldn't be surprised if the reason we hadn't heard from them yet is because he's scrambling to make more of them."

"Or they're setting up a trap," Big Sis Monique mused.

"You don't think they've retreated for good?" Kayla asked.

"No. Not after all the effort they went through to advertise to everyone and their mommas that they would defeat us. I doubt they've given up just yet. They're out there, somewhere."

"But," Kayla hesitated and tightened her hands on her knees, but nothing has ever stopped her from speaking her mind. "We saved the hostages. Shouldn't our priority be to get them to safety?"

"Yes, but if we don't stop these warlords here and now, they'll always be coming after us. If we don't end this today, our loved ones will never be safe. We're going to hunt them down, take them out, and be done with them for good. But there's an additional factor we didn't initially take into account before. It seems that all of the warlords are possessed by the same demon—the Misogyny Demon."

"*Oh*," Kayla immediately replied. When Sistah Monique raised her eyebrow, she explained the darkness she encountered when fighting Warlord X.

"It happened with me too," I said, and told them what happened in my fight with my older brother. During the retelling, I pulled the card out that he had given me and rubbed my fingers across the smooth surface.

"How do we defeat it?" Kayla asked.

A grim expression came over Big Sis Monique's face. "The bestiary doesn't have any clear method for exorcism, but there are a few techniques that our Sistahs have found to be effective in harming it."

She described several tactics that we could use against the demon during battle, and then individual tactics for each of the warlords. But honestly, I struggled to focus on what she was saying. I flipped the holographic card back and forth, and watched the colors reflect a rainbow as an uncomfortable niggle wormed through my gut. I tried to ignore it. I didn't want to cause even more conflict, but the longer the silence sat in my stomach, the more it churned up a storm of anxiety.

I leapt to my feet. Everyone turned to me at the interruption, and I wanted to shrink down and disappear from their eyes. I bowed my head, catching my gaze on the shine of the card in my hands—a reminder that everyone had the potential to evolve. Determined, I raised my head and faced Big Sis Monique, even though I couldn't help but to be reminded of her anger only a few moments ago.

"I-I–" I couldn't get the words out. I paused to take a deep breath and to take my time because this was important.

Someone had to be a voice for those who couldn't speak for themselves. I knew Kayla was standing beside me, and that gave me strength, but I tuned her out as I pushed all my focus forward. I looked at Big Sis Monique and asked, "Are we planning to kill them?"

She and Big Sis glanced at each other, confirming what they had already determined to do.

"You've seen it yourself," I rebutted. "They are possessed by a demon. My older brother isn't perfect, and my father might be the worst, but what if he's been possessed by this demon for as long as I've known him? Aren't Sistah Samurai supposed to protect people from demons? No matter how terrible those people might be?"

Big Sis Monique's jaw tightened and that small gesture of anger sent a jolt of fear through me. Before I realized it, I took a step back, leaves crunching beneath my feet. A raindrop landed on my arm as I pushed myself forward and stood my ground.

"They attacked my home, kidnapped my husband, and threatened my daughters," Big Sis hissed. "No, I had not planned to let them live past this day."

"But how can we determine their actions from the actions of the demon's? How do we know? Our objective shouldn't be to defeat the warlords. It should be to save them."

"This isn't a demon that one can be freed of so easily. It takes a great amount of will, awareness, and determination to break from its hold. My husband was lucky. It was a new infection, but to have been infected for years? You have no idea how hard it is to free yourself of it."

"But it can be done?" I asked, fiercely.

Big Sis Monique quieted for some time. I counted the rain that dropped into her afro. One. Two. Three. Four. Finally, she answered, "It can be done, but we should be prepared to do what we must."

"Why?" I argued. "Your husband has been saved, but now it's so easy to give up on them when they're not your brother?

When they're not your father? How am I supposed to abandon them knowing what I know now?"

"It's not on you to save them. Demons amplify our worst impulses, but the seed is already there. Take the demon away and most likely, he'll still be a shit father," she said gently.

"Then he'll be a shit father who can choose to continue to be a shit father. With the demon, he'll have no choice at all," I argued. "A chance to choose—that's all I'm asking for. What my father does once freed of the demon is on him, but it is our duty as Sistah Samurai to fight for every person's humanity. I didn't become a Sistah Samurai for revenge. I became a Sistah Samurai to protect people and to save the world from demons."

Big Sis looked at me, and I looked at her in turn, battling her gaze. Then she sighed. "Perhaps you are the wisest among us, Sistah Imani. You are right that this clan was founded to protect the world from demons. Therefore, our mission objective going into this fight has changed. Yours and Kayla's fight has proven that with enough pressure, we can get the demon to show. We'll kick the Warlord's ass just enough to force the Misogyny Demon out, and then we'll try our best to separate the warlords from the demon and slay it, if possible. Our primary goal is to kill the demon, not the warlords."

"Thank you," I said, relieved.

"Sometimes, you two do more teaching of me than I do of you," Big Sis Monique said. She placed a solid hand on my shoulder. "You did good."

I clutched the card to my chest and smiled. So proud of myself, as a sense of determination solidified in my chest. Somehow, I would save my brother as he once did for me on that fateful night so long ago and I would set him free.

After all, I was a Sistah Samurai.

And I slay demons.

SISTAH SIMONE

AGE: 36

FAV FOOD:
DANCING SQUID SASHIMI

INTERESTS:
FIGHTING
DANCING
MUSIC

WILLPOWER: ★★★★
VISUALIZATION: ★★★★☆
KANJI PROFICIENCY: ★★★★☆
WEAPON PROFICIENCY: ★★★★★

CHAPTER 24

VENOM

SISTAH SIMONE

I casually stopped beside Big Sis where she had her hands on her hips, staring blankly down the road into the distance. She was the sort of person who needed to remove herself from everyone else's demands on her attention in order to think, but she sure has been thinking for some time now. I stretched my arms above my head and casually glanced over at her and asked, "You okay?"

Her lips pursed at the question. "I pushed too hard. I just…I think about my daughters, you know? What if one day they're too scared to tell me something? Or they're scared I won't understand? I'm trying not to let my fears get in the way of being a good mother, or a good mentor, but it's hard sometimes. It's hard not to be hard on them, to prepare them for a world that will do the same."

"Hey. We're just as new to this as they are, and all we can do is do our best. On the bright side, at least no one *died*."

"I'm too old to be making these sorts of mistakes."

"None of us are too old to keep learning," I said, gently. I found that Big Sis was way too hard on herself sometimes. She had been like that too when we were younger with her perfectionism and over-achiever attitude. I tended to avoid her type as they had little patience for my brand of chaos, but getting to know her, I've come to learn that she had patience for everyone but herself. Every now and then, someone needed to remind her that being perfectly flawed was perfectly okay.

"You can say it," I told her cheekily. "That damned teddy bear is weird."

"Fucking weird," she said, releasing those words like a long-held sneeze.

With a distinct curl of disgust to her lips, Big Sis looked over her shoulder, toward the teddy bear that laid across Lil' Sis Kayla's back as she wrote new talismans. "Leave it to Sistah Kayla, of all people, to make friends with a damned demon. There's nothing in the bestiary about benevolent demons. *None.* And I'm just supposed to take the word of a twenty-two-year-old girl who has never had the best discernment in people?"

"Hmm," I hummed, wondering how we both could see two different things. "It seems to me that the twenty-two-year-old who has experienced the worst betrayal anyone could ever imagine would have the best discernment in people, actually. It did get through the protection talismans."

Big Sis crossed her arms, and admitted, "There is that."

"You know me. I've never been one to stick to the rules, but the reality is we live in a different world than our Sistahs did. There are more demons, more demon drops, and less ink. Hell, this younger generation can hardly fight without their demon drops, so who's to say we shouldn't fight alongside demons too? The world is changing, and we've got to change with it."

"All this changing is giving me a headache, quite frankly. Misogynistic warlords I can deal with. That certainly isn't anything new. But befriending a demon? I…" She paused, and glanced down at how our shadows stretched to the other side of the road. "Is it fucked up that I miss the voice in my head? Now, without it, I can't blame my actions on anyone but myself."

She didn't talk about it very often, the demon that she had been possessed by, which she had told me about on a late summer night when it had been so hot, it was hard to get some sleep.

"You don't have to be in your head all the time. If you need someone to talk to, I'm here," I told her. "We're in this together. *And* if you want drop that bear in the village well, I'll help you do it."

A slight smile tugged at the corner of her lips, and I inwardly cheered at the sight of it. She turned around, but then paused to say, "Thanks for checking on me."

Then, she returned to her family where the twins had fallen asleep in brother-in-law's lap.

I returned to where Lisa sat atop the rock wall that curved towards the shrine. I said, jokingly, as I sat beside her, "Welcome to the family."

"It's certainly more drama than the petty tea house squabbles of 'who borrowed my hairpin?'" Lisa said, smiling, but her humor was fleeting. She grabbed my hand and said seriously, "I truly am sorry for my part in all of this. I feel terrible. I put those girls and so many people at risk."

"No, that's not on you. You were coerced, manipulated, and blackmailed. You were a victim, and I don't blame you for what you had to do. I feel terrible that I put you in that position in the first place. I should have never revealed that information to you."

"But I was fishing for it. I betrayed your trust," she admitted. "I should have told you, but I was scared. They made it clear that they were watching me, and I was afraid for my apprentices. I feared for their lives, and you know I would do anything for those girls, like you would do anything for yours. That was admirable how you stood up for Sistah Kayla."

"They're certainly getting stuck on me," I admitted. Like the little sisters I've never had. "Although, Kayla better not try to stab herself again. That almost gave me a heart attack."

"You'd hope, but somehow, they always find new ways to

test our patience," she said. "I've trained five apprentices now and it never gets any easier. But then, you look at them, and see the wonderful young women that they have become. They come to you, so hurt and traumatized by the world, holding onto all the bad habits that kept them alive, thrown away by those who say they have no value, but you see their light. You see how with a little care and love, they flourish. How bright the world would be if we all nurtured the light of little girls."

"As bright as the summer sun," I murmured. I looked over at Lil' Sis Kayla and Imani helping each other with their talismans. Despite their missteps, I was so proud of them, and I was truly excited to see them continue to grow.

Suddenly, a series of fireworks exploded in the sky. Bright against the contrast of dark storm clouds. I looked up and barked out a laugh. Across the way, Big Sis shook her head.

"Was that a firework dick?" Lisa asked.

"I'm so tired of these guys," Big Sis grumbled.

"You know, that gives me an idea for our own firework," I said considering.

"No," Big Sis said, immediately cutting off that thought. *Boo.* A bright pink vulva would be *hilarious.* I was already thinking of what kanji combinations we could use for it, but Big Sis was immediately ready for business. "Everyone, gather your belongings. It's time."

Perhaps later. I hopped from the wall and stretched my arms above my head and turned back toward Lisa. I reached over and gave her a good long kiss, long enough to keep me thinking about her until I saw her again. I didn't want to let go of her, but reluctantly pulled away when Big Sis declared it was time to go.

Lisa and I gathered around the others as Big Sis handed her husband an INVISBILITY talisman.

"This talisman is for hiding. You, Lisa, and the girls are going to stay here, but keep this activated. Once we take care of the warlords, we'll come back to get you."

I leaned forward to give brother-in-law a hug goodbye,

and as he began to pull away, I steeled my grip. "You ever get possessed by a demon again and endanger Big Sis, brother-in-law will become brother-is-a-corpse, got it?"

"Yep," he whispered. "I understand."

"Good," I patted him on the back and let him go with the biggest smile I could give him. Then, I scooped up both of the twins and gave them a big hug.

"Here, Auntie, it's to protect you," Alex said as she gave me a handkerchief made from the extra fabric of her yukata, and tied it around my wrist like a friendship bracelet.

"I'll take good care of it," I promised.

Beside me, Little Sis Imani handed her skates over to Ari to take care of. The firework had come from the direction of the beach, and most likely, they would just weigh her down. After Lil' Sis Imani handed them over, she straightened up, sure-footed.

"So…" Lil' Sis Kayla tugged the strings of her backpack and said to Big Sis tentatively, "Teddy-san says he could stay behind and protect them, if that's okay, you know, with you?"

"No," Big Sis said.

"He did try to save me," brother-in-law said, suddenly. "When the ninjas attacked the house, he helped to fight with me. He got knocked out when Warlord Scrub arrived, but if he hadn't distracted so many of the ninjas, who knows what would have happened."

Big Sis raised a brow, sucking in air under her breath. "We just saw him explode and claw a man's face off. I don't trust it."

"*I* trust it."

She looked at her husband, and an entire conversation was exchanged between that look. He was the one person who could convince her to give in. She crossed her arms, and surrendered, "Fine."

She crouched down and stabbed her finger toward the teddy bear. "If anything happens to my family, I'm ripping out all of your stuffing and will use your head as a noodle bowl."

The demon teddy bear looked at Big Sis with a blank

expression, an ominous stillness before suddenly, it snapped its hands together to form the shape of a heart, before running off to hide behind Lil' Sis Kayla's leg.

Brother-in-law grabbed the twins' hands. Sistah Kayla whispered (not very quietly) some encouraging words to Teddy-san and left him holding her wakizashi. Lisa folded her hands before her yukata and gave me a smile that hooked into my heart like a fishing hook. Brother-in-law said to us all, "Be careful. Stay safe. And kick their asses."

"You bet, Daimyo-sama!" Lil' Sis Kayla exclaimed.

Together, the four of us marched off toward the beach as the storm clouds thickened and the rain began pouring down in sheets. An excited energy buzzed through the air, crackling along my skin. I lifted my sword over my shoulder in giddy elation of what was coming.

Finally.

It was time for the boss fight.

AGE: 40

FAV FOOD:

SPICY MISO RAMEN

INTERESTS:

MIND YA BUSINESS

WILLPOWER: ★★★★★

VISUALIZATION: ★★★★★

KANJI PROFICIENCY: ★★★★★

WEAPON PROFICIENCY: ★★★★★

CHAPTER 25

HISS

SISTAH MONIQUE

We met four warlords on the beach.

Wait. Four? The rain was coming down so hard that the droplets speckled my glasses, making it harder for me to see. The useless things. I pulled them off of my face and counted the number of warlords again. One. Two. Three. Four.

"Who the fuck is that?" Sistah Simone asked, bringing attention to the fact that the alliance's fourth member was a whole different person we hadn't met until now. It really should be against the rules to bring in a new person in the final hour.

Warlord Tyrone shrugged at the newcomer standing over his shoulder. "There are always more Scrubs."

Just great. I wouldn't be surprised if he had a whole army of them at his beck and call. Sistah Simone grinned viciously, unfazed, "Don't matter none to me. I'll cut this one down just like the last one."

The wind began blowing so hard that I had to plant my feet in the sand to not be knocked over. Waves raged and clawed at the shore with watery talons, and yet a red torii gate stood defiant out in the middle of the ocean like a lone samurai. I feared that this storm was turning into a typhoon. Not the kind of weather anyone should be out in but, unfortunately, the time and place of a well-deserved ass-whooping did not discriminate.

Warlord Tyrone stepped forward and announced, voice booming like thunder, "It didn't have to come to this. You've held your own admirably thus far, but the results of today are already fated. Your defeat will be the harbinger of the great unification—"

"Formation Arrow," I commanded. My Sistahs immediately moved into position. I glanced over my shoulder at Sistah Imani, who had lagged in our previous formations, causing our group visualizations to stumble.

"You got this, Imani-chan!" Sistah Kayla encouraged. Sistah Simone patted Sistah Imani on the shoulder. It struck me in that moment how incredibly brave the two young women were that we had at our side. Despite their fear, despite their inexperience, they were still standing here, willing to fight. I gave Sistah Imani an encouraging nod.

No matter what happened, I was proud to stand with these two young women.

We activated our talismans and formed three initial spears of light, but a second later, a fourth joined the beams to combine into one large attack that we aimed in the warlords' direction.

With their individual talismans, the warlords evaded out of the way. The sand trembled when the attack collided against the ground, a vibration I felt in the soles of my feet. Split into two groups, the warlords charged at us with individual attacks.

"Shield formation," I commanded. This time we successfully visualized the shield in time. Our combined shield mimicked steel that didn't waver no matter what magic they threw at us. Even the storm seemed to thrash powerlessly against our transparent defense.

When their long-range attacks failed, the warlords switched to close-range attacks to brute force their way in. Exactly as I had planned. The shield dropped. We separated. I targeted the leader while the others attacked their pre-planned targets. Sistah Kayla and Sistah Imani switched opponents. Sistah Kayla used her ex's own demon weapon to swat at Sistah Imani's older brother from the sky while Sistah Imani went toe to toe with Warlord X. With her katana, she launched an assault so furious, her opponent could barely activate a talisman.

"You know, you should smile more." Sand swallowed Warlord Scrub 2.0 into the ground, as Sistah Simone jumped and slammed her foot into his face. He wailed, "Damn girl, who hurt you?"

I focused my attention on the leader. We stood apart from one another while the storm battered my armor and whipped at his free form locs. Most of the talismans on his staff had already been depleted. The ones he had left spotted the staff with black like someone losing poorly at checkers.

My katana lit up with fire. His staff lit up with water. My katana lit up with lightning. His staff sheathed itself in hard stone. No matter what talisman we chose, the other had a counter.

At an impasse, almost at once, we both gave up the magic and charged one another with bare weapons. I slashed my katana down as he lifted his staff to block. My katana bit into the wood, cutting into one of the talismans, rendering it useless.

Seashells crunched underneath my feet and the salt air slapped against my armored helmet as we exchanged another series of blows, ending in another stalemate. If I could keep his attention while the Sistahs took care of the others, then we could attack him as a group.

"You are an admirable leader," the warlord complimented. "But you cannot plan for everything."

The ocean surged.

"Watch out!" I yelled, just now spotting the talismans glowing gold against the torii gate. They must have planted them there before we came. I activated my SHIELD talisman, and the ocean roared past me. Fish and kelp splattered against my shield. Crustaceans and rocks dinged off it. The force of the storm surge almost sent me rolling in my shield, lifting me, but it retreated just before I tipped all the way over.

When the ocean retreated, I turned to check on the others. Both Sistah Imani and Sistah Kayla had failed to get their shields up in time and had been thrown back. Soaking wet and coughing, and with sand coating their skin, they were slow to pick themselves up.

The warlords had regrouped. They pulled out four talismans and I cursed, quickly trying to fumble for my glasses. But I didn't need them to see that they were planning a joint visualization and that we were too scattered to defend against it.

"Shield formation!" I ordered. Sistah Simone had been near enough to Sistah Imani to pull her up from the ground, but Sistah Kayla slacked behind as she rushed to gather at my position. Then, the warlords began to glow.

I watched, confused, as their bodies melded together into a bright light, which grew bigger and bigger. They grew even larger than the Ego Demon I fought during my first year as a Sistah Samurai. Then, the bright light faded to reveal a black armored giant.

I had never seen such a thing in my entire life, but recognition flickered in Sistah Imani's eyes. She scrambled to open the bamboo scroll she carried on her back. She pulled out a card that depicted a miniature version of what stood before us, except on the card, the color of it was white. She looked at the image, and up at the monstrosity before us. She said in awe, "It's a gundam."

"A what now?"

Sistah Imani studied the distinct differences and amended, "A Hotep Gundam."

Sistah Simone barked out a laugh.

"Can we do something like that?" Sistah Kayla asked.

"It wouldn't be advisable," I said, unable to believe those warlords could pull off a visualization so massive. There were some equally giant visualizations in the Sistah Samurai repertoire, but Sistah Kayla and Sistah Imani were too inexperienced, and it required a lot of practice. Even I was rusty at this point. They all looked at me for some sort of direction. "They are still using talismans, which means there's a time limit to their magic. We just need to survive until their ink runs out."

Which, honestly, was easier said than done.

"Grand-rising Strike!" the hotep gundam yelled with their combined voices. With a hiss, smoke erupted out the back of the giant monster…erm, gundam, and then it shot into the air.

"Shield formation!" I shouted as the gundam descended on top of us. Like before, we formed our shield, erecting it just before it could squish us. But the shield that had endured so many magical attacks before, began to crack and splinter. *Shit.*

"Release!" I yelled. I could see the doubt and fear on their faces, but they placed their trust in me and followed orders. The moment we released the shield, I activated a WIND talisman and summoned a whoosh of air to throw us in different directions, barely avoiding the giant feet.

The earth shook when it stomped the ground. The ocean reverberated at the force of it, summoning a massive wave to shore. I grabbed ahold of a wooden pillar staked to the ground, a part of a broken fence as the wave overtook me and then just as quickly tried to pull me out to sea.

I sucked in a breath and searched for the others. Both Sistah Imani and Sistah Kayla had remarkably grabbed hold of the gundam's foot, having been pushed back and pulled forward by the wave, and Sistah Simone was clawing her way out of the sand like a newly hatched turtle.

I pasted a FIRE talisman onto my katana and cut at the gundam's metal foot, but the heat nor the blade did any damage. Sistah Kayla zapped its arm to no avail. Sistah Imani tried to stab the ankle joints with her katana, but it got caught in the space between, and she was thrown back when it raised its foot into the air.

Then that foot came crashing down on top of me. I used a STRENGTH talisman and cocked back my hand. Then punched as it descended. I heard it first and then felt the bones of my knuckles crack as the blow ripped through me. Despite using all of my willpower, the giant gundam barely budged. I burrowed out of the way with an EARTH talisman and used a HEALING to mend the wailing bones in my hand.

"This isn't working!" Sistah Simone shouted. "None of our magical or physical attacks are doing anything! We need a visualization of our own."

She was right.

"To my position!" I called.

They grabbed onto me as I used a TELEPORTATION spell to transport us away from the shore and the rising storm surge. In the distance, the gundam's head swiveled on its shoulders like an owl, looking for us. It dwarfed the torii gate behind it, and the howling typhoon hit ineffectually against its legs.

We didn't have a lot of time before they found us.

I tried to figure out how we could make this work. We probably couldn't perform a standard visualization—not the giant suit of samurai armor or the pink Sistah Samurai dragon that I had participated in the past. "We need something that all four of us can visualize, that we all have familiarity with, or it won't work."

"Aye. I got an idea. What about this?" Sistah Simone said. She slid off the bracelet Alex had given her and unfolded it for us all to see it. I stared at the image and my lips puckered sourly at that cutesy white cat on the patterned fabric I had bought months ago—the same white cat that had adorned the twins' yukata all summer long as they had refused to wear anything else. I have seen the damned thing so much that I could certainly visualize it without any problems, and it was a clear enough image that the others could too.

Fuck it. Let's do it.

"This is how we're going to visualize it: white fur, pink bow on the left ear, pink dress, and," I looked up at the gundam, "about 30 meters tall."

"And armor. This is a fight," Sistah Simone said. "Let's give it Sistah Samurai armor like yours."

"And weapons," Sistah Imani added. "We need something to fight with. Maybe the standard Sistah Samurai pair? Both the katana and wakizashi?"

"Ooh, what about a cute pink afro?" Sistah Kayla suggested. We all looked at her, and she looked away, muttering petulantly, "They gave their Hotep Gundam a golden headdress."

Ignoring Kayla, I turned to the others.

"You all are adding a lot of stuff. Can you visualize this?" I asked and looked specifically at Sistah Imani. She grabbed the handkerchief out of Sistah Simone's hand and nodded.

"It helps to have an image I can look at, and that we're talking it out. I can do it," she said.

"We can do this," Sistah Kayla said, more confidently.

"We need a kanji that can pull this off, or…" I looked at Sistah Simone. "If we create a braided talisman with specific kanji that fit this exact visualization, it could be stronger than what they've got, but the risks of getting it wrong are greater. Those kanji need to be perfect."

"You think four kanji would be enough?" Sistah Simone asked. "I could use, 'Big,' 'White,' 'Samurai,' and 'Cat.'"

"Sounds good. We would need four identical talismans. You think you can do that?" I asked.

"If you provide the distraction," she replied.

I turned to the girls. "You heard her. We need to distract that big metal demon while she prepares the talismans. It might be big, but it's slow, so augment yourself with a SPEED talisman and keep moving. Let's go."

We activated our talismans and zoomed towards the gundam. We flitted between its legs, doing our best to confuse and trip it up as it stomped after us. At a distance, it probably looked like it was throwing a temper tantrum. Eventually, it got tired of chasing us and a bright light concentrated at the top of its golden helmet.

I zoomed out of the way of its blast radius, but the attack was so explosive that loose sediment and smooth ocean rocks clipped my shoulder. I slid to the ground as my speed talisman expired. When I looked up, the gundam had gone to one knee and had cocked back its arm to punch me into the sand.

A smooth vine wrapped around my chest and jerked me backwards. I landed against Sistah Kayla where her tiny arms wrapped around my waist.

"Thank you," I told her. She gave a beaming smile as if we were back on our mountain training and I had complimented her on one of her stances.

The ground shook as the gundam's fist collided with the ground. I looked up to find Sistah Imani racing towards it. She jumped first onto the joints, then the wrist, and continued to climb up the gundam's arm.

"I've got you, Imani-chan!" Sistah Kayla yelled at her and activated a talisman that turned the blade of Imani's katana into DIAMOND. It was an unorthodox spell, but a smart one as diamonds were hard enough to cut through metal. But since Sistah Kayla was so far away from the effect of the talisman, there was only a thin coating.

"Do you got another one of those?"

"Of course!" Sistah Kayla said

She handed over the talisman and I strengthened her spell. Another layer of diamond coated Imani's katana as she reached the shoulder. Then, she jumped. A loud crack of what I initially mistook as lightning ripped through the air. Sistah Imani cut through the edge of the golden headdress and a large chunk of it fell with her to the ground. Sand exploded into the air. I created a slide out of the sand using an EARTH talisman to catch Sistah Imani and deliver her to my feet.

"Good job," I told her as I reached down to pick her up.

"I've got it!" Sistah Simone yelled from behind us. She sprinted towards our position, and I caught her as she slid to a stop. She handed out the talismans.

I grabbed it without looking at the kanji. Without hesitation, I hoped for the best. I closed my eyes to help me focus, and once I visualized that cute monstrosity clearly in my mind's eye, I activated the spell.

A group visualization of this size always felt weird, as if someone had reached inside of your chest to stretch out your soul like dough. We grew and merged together. We were suddenly the same size as the gundam, but everything else seemed so small. The rocks and trees looked like toys lying about the twins' bedroom. The waves that had threatened to engulf us hit us at our shin guards.

Everyone's individual voices shot through my head.

"This is amazing!" Sistah Kayla said.

"Whoa," Sistah Imani said.

"Hell yeah!" Sistah Simone shouted.

Across from us on the other side of the shore, the Hotep Gundam said, taken aback, "A *white* cat, my Sistahs?! Don't you know that white is the enemy's color? White is the color of rice, and rice is the tool—"

"Listen up, this is what we're going to do."

"Wait, wait, I want to see where this is going," Sistah Simone chuckled.

"—rice is the tool of oppression, a tool that the bureaucrats use to control the lower classes, therefore white is the enemy. We must aim to visualize our true forms, our perfect forms, that the Grand Kami has divined for us. We are *Black* excellence. In our Blackness, we are divine. Release yourself from your shackles, my Sistahs, and free your mind." The Hotep Gundam tapped against his temple, punctuating every word.

"You know, it would be easier to think clearer without you cackling in my head," I reprimanded Sistah Simone. "Focus, everyone. We have to visualize all of our actions together in order to make this work. Follow my directions. Step forward. Right foot first."

We stepped forward.

"Good. Now, unsheathe our katana."

The gundam stopped its tirade when our katana, a gigantic slab of steel, sang beautifully out of its sheath. The gundam shook its head, and a spread of kunai magically appeared in its hands—wait, no. They were not kunai, but—

"Take-this-pamphlet!" The Hotep Gundam shouted out its attack.

I dictated each move. Left. Right. Up. Down. Our katana slashed through the pamphlets.

The gundam ran towards us, the ground shaking with each step. It cocked back its arm, throwing a punch, and we sliced at the fist with our katana. Shouts of triumph erupted through my head when our blade decisively sliced through the metal, severing the hand at the wrist. The warlords howled as they stepped back, but I was keen on not giving them an inch.

"Counter. Left foot forward. Slash to the right."

The tip of our katana scraped against the gundam's chest. We ducked underneath a heavy swing and a broken arm sailed harmlessly past our white fluffy ears. We smashed our sword hilt against the upward thrust of its knee, slamming against the thigh. The leg swung back, and it fell off balance to one knee. The gundam looked up and light collected at the center of its tall golden headpiece.

"Retreat," I said.

"So, I added in another kanji…" Sistah Simone said, with a smug tinge to her words. I rolled my eyes as she told us the plan. Completely ridiculous, but fine.

We sheathed our katana as we gained some distance.

Then, we brought the paws of our large cat manifestation together and light coalesced between our palms. The light grew larger and larger, rivaling the size of our opponent's beam. The gundam released their blast at the same time we shot our hands forward. Our beam exploded towards the gundam full of sparkling stars and glitter.

The two blasts collided, a tug of war, and we put every ounce of our willpower into the attack. The winds howled and the ocean roared. We screamed, united by our anger, our frustration, and our love for one another. Despite our conflicts and our differences, despite our mistakes and misunderstandings, despite or own individual journeys, we were in this together. Sistahs forever.

Our blast consumed theirs.

It struck the Hotep Gundam and swallowed the beach in a large explosion of sound and power. When the light faded, the gundam had been dismantled, leaving behind four bodies, collapsed, and unconscious in the sand.

"Hell yeah!" Kayla shouted as she thrust out a hand in a triumphant peace sign. But she moved without telling the rest of us, and the visualization popped. We landed onto the sand and a burst of stars rained down around us.

One of the warlords began to move. I pushed myself to my feet and watched, eyes narrowed, while the girls celebrated behind me. A faint wisp of black smoke wafted from Warlord Tyrone. He crawled onto his knees as the demon finally manifested itself, growing into this demonic shadow of sharp claws.

I unsheathed my katana and readied it before me.

"At the ready, Sistahs. It's not over yet."

The girls stopped celebrating.

"Seriously?" Kayla complained. "I'm *sooo* tired."

I eyed the Misogyny Demon, waiting on its move. A black oozing limb shot out and I moved to counter its attack, but started in the wrong direction when, to my surprise, the limb stuck to Warlord Scrub 2.0's chest. The demon began consuming him. Warlord Scrub 2.0 screamed until the black sludge covered his face and the warlord's entire being disappeared within the muck. The beach was silent as we all stared in frozen horror. The silence popped when the demonic sludge pooped out white bones. A skull. A femur. A spine. Then too many that I lost track.

Nothing but bones was left.

"Ah, fuck no," Warlord X spat as he scrambled to his feet. The Misogyny demon stretched out a limb to capture him as he sprinted away. I did promise Imani that I would try to save them. But the warlord tripped, sliding face first into the sand.

"*Oh no,*" Sistah Kayla said, none too sadly. "What a shame."

She tucked an active EARTH talisman behind her back, just as the Misogyny Demon wrapped a limb around Warlord X's ankle. And you know what? I'll give her this one.

Warlord X clawed at the sand as he was pulled back into the demon's body. He screamed, "KAYBUNNY, HELP ME! I'LL DO ANYTHING! ANYTHING!"

Sistah Kayla gave a cheerfully disturbing smile that even unsettled me. But perhaps men should stop hurting the women they expect to save them. Sistah Kayla shouted, "You weren't possessed by a demon when you betrayed me. You weren't possessed by a demon when you sold out the Sistah Samurai. You weren't possessed by a demon when you destroyed an entire village just to take my tailor shop away from me. It's about time you got what you deserved. AND—IT'S SISTAH KAYLA TO YOU!"

The Misogyny Demon consumed him.

As the demon digested its newest acquisition, it shot out another limb. It struck Warlord King's chest, who hadn't regained consciousness and still lay in the sand. Until a katana cut through the black vicious limb. Sistah Imani dropped down over him and covered them both with a SHIELD. She curled over him, viciously protecting him. Her shield wasn't going to last as cracks began to yield under the demon's assault.

"Sistahs, cover her," I immediately ordered.

Sistah Simone and Sistah Kayla activated their shield talismans to replenish Imani's. While they did so, I charged toward the demon, knowing the same tactic I used with my husband wasn't going to work here. I wasn't going to be able to talk-no-jutsu the demon this time. Even though the Sistah Samurai had never figured out how to end the demon, they had found ways to weaken it.

I pulled out a talisman written with the kanji, TOXIC, between my forefingers. While it was distracted with attacking

Sistah Imani's shield, I punched the talisman into its slimy gut. It roared and retracted its limbs, leaving Sistah Imani free to escape with her brother.

The black growing mass extended a long arm to attack me, and I leaned back to evade it. I slapped a talisman onto its arm. I slapped another one onto its formless base. And then another into its roaring goopy face. Four talismans in all.

I commanded, "Together."

My Sistahs formed a line behind me. We each focused on activating each of the talismans. Spokes of light pierced the demon from the inside. It bubbled and boiled like a poisonous sludge, and it grew and grew until it bowed under the weight of its own toxicity. It grew so large that it held back the wind and rain, covering the entirety of the beach until it could no longer tolerate its own poisonous nature.

Misogyny only grows so large until it starts eating itself.

The bubble burst and exploded.

Black splatters rained down from the sky. I lifted a FIRE talisman between my forefingers and blew a cloud of fire at the dark rain, burning it up before it fell to the ground.

The demon had left behind a skeletal man, who knelt on the beach.

I approached the thin figure. What had once been Warlord Tyrone bowed his head before me. The man looked nothing like how he looked before, and it was apparent that the demon had been feeding on his soul for a long time. Perhaps too long, for when he opened his eyes, he looked up at me with blank white eyes. The demon had left a scar, the type of scar that couldn't be fixed by a healing talisman.

"Kami," he mourned. "Why have you forsaken me?"

I should kill him. I had fully planned to do so when this day had started, but I knew what it was like to be infected by a demon, and to have it haunting you for years. And I had given Sistah Imani my word.

Still, I could barely comprehend what sort of power a demon must have to lead a person so far astray that they would hurt their own family and community. Now, he was clean and what he did from here was up to him. I straightened and sheathed my katana.

"May we never meet again, you Blind Nigga Samurai."

I walked away.

At two paces, I heard metal slide through skin and the brief inhalation of breath. Beside the others, Sistah Imani's eyes widened. Red water swept past my feet, and then again, and then the waves turned back to blue.

I reached my Sistahs and gathered them in my arms. We hugged Sistah Imani to comfort her. We were all tired as we leaned on each other and walked away.

Together.

"Where is your older brother?" I asked Sistah Imani.

She shrugged. He must have gotten away during our attack against the demon. The demon hadn't finished absorbing all of itself out of his body, which meant he was still infected. Maybe death would cleanse him, like his father, or maybe the boy would find the strength to fight what the demon had left behind and purge it himself. Either way, it was someone else's problem now.

This fight was over.

The warlords had consumed each other. Some had fled. Others had died. Their leader had been rendered weak and pathetic and ultimately destroyed by his own demons.

The sun peeked through the clouds. The storm was dying down and the wind eased. Out the corner of my eye, a sudden movement. A black blob fled into the water and washed out to sea.

None of the Sistah Samurai had ever figured out how to defeat the Misogyny Demon for good. I had no doubt it would be back again, and that there will be more battles in the future. Perhaps one day, we'll figure out how to defeat it for good.

Until then, the Illustrious Clan of Sistah Samurai will continue to grow and thrive, and protect the world from demons.

Thank you for reading

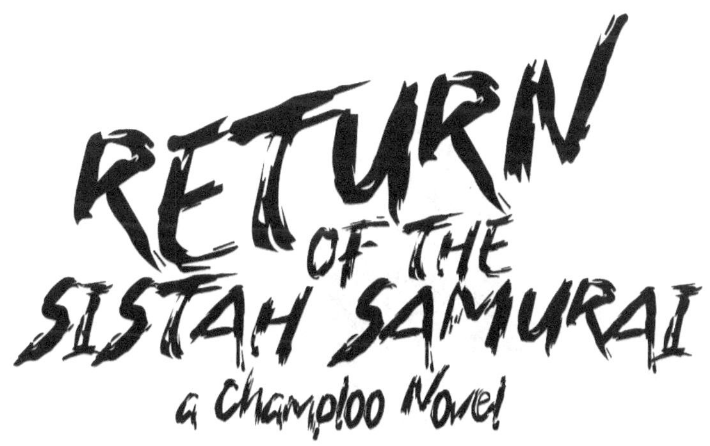

GOT TO BE REAL
SISTAH KAYLA, SISTAH IMANI
SISTAH SIMONE, SISTAH MONIQUE

I kicked my feet under the shade of an umbrella as I sketched an outfit that came to mind while we were fighting the warlords. Something with a lot of frills and lace and ooh, glitter. Yes. Lots and lots of pink glitter. I stuck out my tongue as I drew outfits for the whole team.

"Auntie Kayla! Come help us!"

I only had seconds to cover my sketch pad before Ari and Alex stomped sand all over my beach towel.

"Okay. Okay," I said, as they pulled at my arms. I stood up, and stepped out from under the shade of the umbrella onto the hot sand of a beach near Chigakure. The sand felt sooo good beneath my toes. It was nice to actually have time to appreciate it, instead of, you know, spending all our time battling warlords and fighting for our lives.

I loved the beach. Although it was hot and humid, there was something about being at the beach that made the weather bearable. Waves crashed along the shore and the water sparkled a beautiful blue. I wasn't the swimming-with-the-sea-creatures type of girl, but I loved wearing a swimsuit. I also loved to watch the waves sweep past my legs and spray against my face.

"Over here!" The twins said as they led me to their sad piles of sand that looked like…sad piles of sand. I tilted my head and popped my hands on my hips.

"This will not do," I said. "Teddy-san!"

From where he lounged under the shade of the umbrella beside mine, Teddy-san bounded over.

'Yes! My beautiful goddess! How may I be of service?'

"We need to create the most amazing sand sculpture anyone has ever seen!" I declared.

Together, we helped the twins create a whole city out of sand. I recreated the maze-like alleys of Chigakure, the tall Brotha Monk pagoda, and the sprawling park at the center. Seashells and starfish acted as our residents.

"Look, Auntie Kayla. This one is your shop!"

I crouched over the hill of sand that they had collected. It was just a formless mound of sand right now, but I could visualize the fabrics in the windows, the accessories hanging from the walls, and the counters crowded with all sorts of textures and patterns. Oh. And don't forget my pair of pink swords leaned artfully against the design table, within arm's reach. It would be as I always imagined it: a place full of wonder, magic, and love.

After all, if I could visualize it, I had the power to make anything come true.

I smiled, blinking tears from my eyes.

"It's everything that I've ever dreamed of."

I watched in wonder as a school of brightly colored fish swam past me, and then a stingray glided over my head. It was quieter under the ocean. So peaceful and weightless. Like an entirely different world I could spend my life exploring. I reached out and ventured my hand along the rough coral, and noticed the ink of the two talismans, SEE and BREATHE, wrapped around my arms were running out.

I swam towards the surface of the water and broke my head above the waves. Along the shore, I saw Kayla and Teddy-san helping the twins build a village of sand. Kayla enthusiastically waved and I returned the gesture.

I swam back to shore and the smell of barbecue reached my nose. I listened to laughter as Big Sis Simone covered Lisa's eyes as she tried to whack blindly at a watermelon. Daimyo-sama cooked fish over the grill, while Big Sis Monique lounged underneath a tent that she had erected to shade her from the sun.

Unexpectedly, I was vaulted back to that moment again—when my father had plunged a tanto into his own gut. The red torii framed his emaciated corpse like a headstone, until the waves took him away and the ocean became his grave. He couldn't even see me at the end, but he never did, had he? I don't know what I had been hoping for, but in the end, he had made a choice that was his own.

I gave him that at least.

I wondered about my older brother and wondered where he was now. I hoped that somehow, he would find the help that he needed. I hoped that one day, he would find a good group of people who loved and supported him like I did.

Kayla waved me over to help with the sand village. The clouds of brief melancholy faded, and I smiled. I felt the fullness of my heart as my eyes swept over everyone on this beach, who have made me feel accepted, loved, and given me a place to belong.

I was finally home.

"Want some watermelon?" I asked, bringing over pieces of the watermelon that Lisa had finally cracked open. I leaned underneath Big Sis' tent and placed the pieces atop the wooden table for anyone to come and grab. Not too far away, brother-in-law waved a fan over the grill. Damn that smelled good.

I sat down on a lounge chair next to Big Sis, and after an uncertain pause, I asked, "Are we good?"

I messed up. I hoped she would forgive me, but I understood if she didn't. These past three months had brought us closer together, and she truly felt like the older sister I never had. While I had a lot of friends, I rarely had deep friendships. I was always the crazy one. The one you brought along for a wild time, but not a long time. Not the one you depended on. But I wanted to be that person. I didn't want to lose this relationship. I valued her and our sisterhood so much. In so many ways, she had accepted me for me.

"I'll do better," I promised.

She snorted.

"I'll make it up to you," I said staunchly, determined to be persistent and wear her down if I had to. "I endangered your home and I understand if you no longer want me in it. I'll get my own place in the village with Lisa, and lil' sis will no doubt want to open that tailor shop of hers. We could talk with the Brotha Monks, and figure out a deal, and Lil' Sis Kayla and I can help produce the ink. Let it be my job to deliver the ink to you every day. Let me do that. Give me the chance to earn your trust again."

She was quiet for a moment, and she didn't have to shift her hand to her stomach for me to know what she was thinking about. She still wasn't showing yet, but in a couple of months, she'd have no choice but to put her trust in someone. I had to prove to her it could be me.

"I find that acceptable," she finally said. "You've broken my trust, and you need to regain that. But you do already have my forgiveness."

Her forgiveness hit me like a blow to the solar plexus—shortening my breaths and constricting my throat. It was more than I dared to hope for. I threw my arms around her, relieved that my mistakes weren't irreparable. *"Thank you."*

"We can't be the old clan," she said, softly. "That's not the type of clan I want for my girls. I want people around them who will correct them when they need correcting, who will find them when they go astray, and who will guide them in how they need to grow. I want for them to reach my age and be able to cherish the wisdom of all those who have poured love into them. I never asked for you to stay, and I appreciate you for all the times that you did. But I am doing the asking now. I want you in my girls' lives. I want you in *my* life. As my granny used to say, 'Some friends are for seasons, and some friends are constant through a lifetime of change.'"

"Your granny sounds like a wise woman."

"She truly was. What do you say? You up to watching the seasons change with me?"

Summer was my favorite season. Full of bright laughter, effervescent play, and sunflower hope. I'll miss it, but I couldn't wait to see what the other seasons had in store. "Pssh. You ain't getting rid of me that easy."

"That's all it is then." Big Sis settled back into her chair and reopened the book that she had been reading, a subtle hint that she was done with all of the emotions. I shook my head at her and hoped she never changed. I got to my feet and made to leave, but then she called, "Little Sis."

I paused at the edge of the tent, with one foot in the shade and the other in the sun. I turned back toward her.

"You're the type of person trouble is always following," Big Sis said, "Just make sure it's trouble we can fight our way out of."

I smirked. "You know you like to fight."

She matched my smile and didn't deny my words. Then she definitively returned to her book.

I made my way back toward Lisa, but I made a detour first. Alex looked up, while Ari was still patting her hands against a mound of sand. They squealed as I swept them up in both of my arms and loped into the ocean until a wave swept over us. They laughed, clutching at me and trusting me to protect them. And I knew. This was it. The reason I survived.

To laugh loud, to live well, and to love with the all of me.

"What's wrong?" my husband asked when I joined him. He wrapped an arm around my waist, and no matter how well I tried to hide it, he always picked up on my worry.

"Do you think anyone recognized you?" I asked. "The ninjas or the warlord who got away?"

"I don't know." He shrugged. "But we'll deal with it if it comes. No point in worrying about it now."

He was right, of course. I shouldn't let worry ruin my day.

"Food is ready!" My husband announced, and everyone swarmed him like seagulls on the beach. We sat down at one of the beach tables and ate the grilled fish he had prepared. I smiled at the laughter, noise, and chatter that swept over me. Even the weird demon teddy bear was growing on me.

After we finished eating, I stood up and said, "I have an announcement to make. Or, my husband and I have an announcement to make."

My husband stood up beside me, and I grabbed his hand for support. I waited until everyone hushed, which took a while since Little Sis Simone and Kayla were competing to be the loudest at the table. Once they quieted, I placed a hand on my stomach, and announced, "We're pregnant. We're going to have another baby."

The table erupted in happy cheers. Little Sis Kayla squealed in excitement. Little Sis Imani clapped, and Little Sis Simone smiled smugly, already knowing. The twins jumped from the table and rushed me with hugs and kisses.

Little Sis Simone said, "I think this calls for some party music. It's time to dance!"

"Oh, I don't know," I said uncertainly. I had just eaten, and I was feeling more up to lazing around instead of doing any type of activity. But the twins pulled at my arms as the music started playing, and we moved into the formation of a line dance.

"Don't worry, we'll do an old one," Little Sis Kayla grinned at me.

I rolled my eyes at her teasing. Little Sis Simone hopped beside me, and I did the same as muscle memory took over. I took two steps to the right. We turned, and I lifted my leg, and dropped to the ground. These knees of mine somehow held up.

I've still got it!

I looked around at the laughing faces of my family—at my husband, my daughters, and my sisters. At the start of the year, I never would have imagined this. I never would have imagined a whole day of nothing but love, laughter, good music, and good food. Wouldn't you know it? I was happy.

All in all, it was a damned good summer.

Coming Fall 2026

THE SACRED ORDER OF BROTHA MONKS

a Champloo Novel

CHAMPLOO MIX #3

END CREDITS

AGATHA (AGUEDA) LOPEZ
Alpha reader

AJIRA DARCH (@BOOKSANDBREATH)
Beta reader

ALLMYFRIENDSAREINBOOKS
Beta reader

C.M. LOCKHART
Beta reader

DAMIEN G
Beta reader

ELLE DENNIS
Beta reader

HAERLEE_EXPERIENCE
Beta reader

JACQUELINE JONES
Beta reader

JESSE-JAMES HENDRIX
Beta reader

JOHN NORTH
Beta reader

JONATHAN NEVES MAYERS
Beta reader

LADY AZULINA
Beta reader

MARIA
Beta reader

NATOSHA
Beta reader

SHERIE CARNEGIE, RN
Beta reader

SHERIECE P (@RIECESLIBRARY)
Beta reader

STEPHANIE SUBER
Beta reader

HAERLEE_EXPERIENCE
Beta reader

B² WEIRD BOOK CLUB
Community

THE MELANIN LIBRARY
Community

LA PURVIS
Copyeditor/Proofreader

FÉLIX ORTIZ
Cover Artist

Thank you for helping me grow this garden.

OTHER WORKS

THE CHAMPLOO MIXES
Sistah Samurai: A Champloo Novella
Return of the Sistah Samurai: A Champloo Novel

A FORGING OF AGE DUOLOGY
Bones to the Wind (Book One)
Dragon Your Bones (Book Two)

ADVENT OF WINTER ANTHOLOGY
A Winter Marvel (Short Story)

FIYAH MAGAZINE, ISSUE #32, FALL 2024:
SPACEFARING AUNTIE
Fuck Them Kids (Short Story)

MAGIC IN THE MELANIN: A BLACK FANTASY
ANTHOLOGY
Today, We Are Generals (Short Story)

CONTACT

JOIN MY MAILING LIST FOR NEWS AND UPDATES.

www.tatianaobey.com

SOCIAL MEDIA PLATFORMS

@obeytheauthor